DIGGING UP MOMMA

Novels in the Sam Adams Series by Sarah Shankman

First Kill All the Lawyers
Then Hang All the Liars
Now Let's Talk of Graves
She Walks in Beauty
The King Is Dead
He Was Her Man

Other Novels by Sarah Shankman

I Still Miss My Man But My Aim Is Getting Better
Impersonal Attractions
Keeping Secrets

DIGGING UP MOMMA

A Samantha Adams Mystery

SARAH SHANKMAN

POCKET BOOKS
New York London Toronto Sydney Tokyo Singapore

POCKET BOOKS, a division of Simon & Schuster Inc.
1230 Avenue of the Americas, New York, NY 10020

Library of Congress Cataloging-in-Publication Data

Shankman, Sarah.
Digging up momma : a Samantha Adams mystery / Sarah Shankman.
p. cm.
ISBN: 0-671-89753-5
1. Adams, Samantha (Fictitious character)—Fiction. I. Title.
PS3569.H3327D54 1998
813'.54—dc21 97-32545
CIP

First Pocket Books printing February 1998

10 9 8 7 6 5 4 3 2 1

Printed in the U.S.A.

For my brothers

Al Adams
Joel Bradley
Ben Boswell
Kent Kirkpatrick

Acknowledgments

Many kindnesses . . .

Doug Magnus, proprietor, and Mark Zeigler, invaluable tour guide, of the Millennium Turquoise Mine. Andrea Dewey, for the dish. Rand Lee, for the magic. All my friends in Santa Fe and especially Gloria Donadello, Sarah Barber, Lynda Rodolitz, Judy Graham, Kent Kirkpatrick, Peter Vitale, and Michael McLaughlin, for their many acts of sustaining love. My exemplary editor, Dave Stern, who went the distance and more. And, as always, my agent and home team: Harvey Klinger, Laurie Liss, and Dave Dunton.

DIGGING UP MOMMA

1

THE MORNING HER MOTHER ROSE FROM THE DEAD, SAMANtha Adams stood out in her driveway loading up her car, nothing more on her mind than heading for Atlanta to sing "Happy Seventy-Five" to her uncle George.

Her little blond shih tzu, Harpo, was on her heels, tagging back and forth from the car to the steps of Sam's old wide-hipped house in Covington, thirty-five miles due north of New Orleans across Lake Pontchartrain.

Harpo wore a worried look. To his mind, he'd been abandoned far too much recently. Why, it was only a couple of days earlier that Sam had returned from her latest trip to Manhattan, her publisher getting ready to debut her book, *American Weird*. And here she was headed off again. Was he going?

Sam said, "Yes, sweet pea. Yes."

Harpo did his happy polka.

"Chill, dog," she said. "It's too hot for dancing."

Come August, nowhere in the Deep South is suitable for woman or beast, but south Louisiana is particularly brutal. Walk out of the air-conditioning, it's like hitting a wet electric blanket turned all the way to ten. Even this early in the morning, the air was steaming, filled with the perfume of swamp and rot and finny creatures. Sam found it a struggle merely breathing, much less loading a car with luggage and birthday presents. But finally she slammed down the trunk of her old silvery blue BMW. Ready to hit the road. Crank up Patsy Cline, Janis Joplin, Kenya Walker, and the air-conditioning.

Then Polly, Sam's housekeeper, stepped out on the porch. "For you," she said, handing over the phone.

Sam eyed Polly's grin. Who was this?

"Sam?"

Sam froze, a tall, lean Popsicle in the heat.

It was Harry.

Harry Zack. Her erstwhile lover, a gray-eyed songwriter turned barbecue restaurateur, former bad bad Uptown boy, scion of an ancient Garden District family. Harry, at thirty-two, ten years her junior. Harry, of the broad shoulders, the slow grin, the head of dark curls much like her own.

Harry and Sam had had a parting of the ways this past spring. Sam loved Harry but couldn't give him the commitment he was asking for. When she'd moved over from Atlanta, she'd wanted to be closer to him, but not too close, so she'd set up house in Covington rather than New Orleans, where he lived. She'd tried to explain it to him.

You see, son, she'd said, Loss was her middle name, the loss and death of loved ones major themes. Both her parents had been killed when she was eight. Her first love had abandoned her, had remembered suddenly, after he'd captured her heart, that he was marrying someone else. Her sole marriage had been a disaster, ending in divorce. Mr. Booze, now *he* had been a faithful lover, whose clutches she'd barely managed to escape as he dragged her toward the grave. Then there'd been Sean, the love of her life, killed by a drunk driver in San Francisco only a few years earlier.

Trust me, she'd said to Harry. Death and destruction, they dog my tracks. Let's us be close but not too close; that's the safest thing.

That was nonsense, Harry insisted. No, said Sam. Then, his feelings hurt, Harry had let his glance fall upon a young blonde. *That* wasn't what Sam had intended, not at all. After that, things had become complicated. She'd flown off to Hot Springs, Arkansas, and gotten herself involved with one Jack Graham. Whatever the hell *that* was about. Then, after a bit of to-ing and fro-ing, she'd pulled herself out of the game altogether, told herself she ought not to play at all if she didn't want to play for keeps. Recently Jack had called to say he was heading out to San Francisco to look up an old girl-friend. Sam, who had once lived in that fair city, gave Jack a list of great restaurants and wished him well. But she didn't call Harry.

She'd been fine with her solitude, she'd told herself. She had her garden, her dog, her old house at the edge of a bayou. She didn't have time for anything else, was hard at work on a second volume of *American Weird*, a collection of real-life tales of American strange and peculiar. She'd kept busy. She most certainly had.

Which was not to say that, every once in a while, when she was down in New Orleans, she didn't drive by Harry's cottage in the French Quarter, the one with the tiny square of garden bright with bougainvillea. At night, Dixieland jazz from Preservation Hall next door floated across Harry's garden, leaving blue sharps and flats stuck to his big brass bed. Sam would sit in her idling car, thinking about sweet times and what-ifs. Eventually she'd cruise back home across the causeway, windows open, her curls blowing in the breeze, singing along with Janis's "Mercedes Benz," daring anyone to tell her she wasn't happy to be free.

But right now, Sam—a tall brown-eyed woman in a

red T-shirt, legs for years below white shorts, a grown-up woman who was doing just fine on her own, thank you very much—was standing here on her porch frozen at the sound of her former lover's voice.

"Wha'cha up to?" he began.

"I'm about to head out for Atlanta for a week. George's seventy-fifth birthday is Sunday. Big shindig." Had she kept it breezy? It was tough, with that big bass drum beating in her chest.

"Will you give the old man my best?"

"I will."

"I miss him, you know."

Uh-oh.

"George ever ask about me?"

"Yes. Yes, he does, Harry. You know he's always been very fond of you."

"And what do you tell him?"

She paused. "I tell him you're fine."

"How do you know that?"

Sam stared down at Harpo, who'd planted himself at her feet. He sat with his head cocked to one side, listening intently. Harry was one of Harpo's very favorite people. But then, they'd had some awfully good times, hadn't they, the three of them? Some great adventures. Some of her very best times, actually.

"I hear about you from time to time," she said. "I'm always happy to know that you're doing well."

"Don't suppose there's any way you want to see that for yourself?"

"Oh, Harry," she said.

"Yeah, well." Sam could see his chin jutting. She'd hurt his feelings again. He said, "Just thought I'd give you a jingle. Never any harm in that, is there?"

"No, not at all. I'm always pleased to hear from you."

"Pleased! Hell's bell's, woman. Stop talking to me like I'm the vacuum cleaner repairman."

Sam laughed. At Harry. At herself. "I'm sorry, son." She'd always called him that, a fond reference to the difference in their ages. "Tell me what *you're* up to."

"I thought you'd never ask. I'm about to leave on a little journey myself. Heading out this evening for a rafting trip on the Shuiluo."

"The what?"

"River in China. It's a tributary of the Yangtze, parallels the border of Burma and Tibet. It's never been run before."

See? This was exactly what she was talking about. How could a woman commit herself to a man whose idea of fun was pitting himself against a raging river in To Hell and Gone, where, if his team got into trouble, there'd be no help? He'd drown. He'd die. Sam had attended the funerals of enough people she'd loved, thank you.

"I was real flattered to be asked along," Harry was saying. "Crackerjack bunch of river rats. One of the guys is a descendant of a scout on the Lewis and Clark expedition."

"Can I have your record collection?" Sam asked. "You don't make it back?"

"Now, *there's* a vote of confidence."

"Okay, okay, only the Elvis." Two beats passed. "How long you going to be gone?"

"Run ought to take about a week. Tack on a week traveling over, another one back." Harry's voice had gone happy at her interest. Oh, God. What had she done? Now he was saying, "You want to have a picnic with me, Labor Day?"

Yes, she did. That sounded *wonderful*, in fact. But she didn't hear herself saying that. Sam, Sam, Sam, what are you afraid of? Listen to your heart. Uh-huh. Then listen to it crack.

"Tell you what," Harry said. "You think about it. I'll give you a jingle when I hit town."

Oh, God, no. Don't let me be doing this. I can't open that door again. I'm happy playing my own music, safe. Don't need Harry's blues floating over us, his long low moaning between the sheets. Uh-huh. Then how come you lay awake so many nights, aching for him?

"Sammie? What you thinking about?"

Thinking a woman ought not to be talking to a man who could read her mind that well. At least, this woman shouldn't. This woman who, even after all the years and hard work of sobriety, would not, could not, commit wholeheartedly to love again because she couldn't risk the pain. Who wrote for a living, but couldn't find the words to express her fears. Who found it necessary to curl up around her soft parts like a possum.

She said, "Listen, son, I'd better get moving. I've got six-hundred long, hot miles to drive before I sleep. Let's talk when we both get back, okay?"

He sighed. "Okay, but you be careful."

"This from a man who's putting his life in the hands of river gods who don't even speak English?"

But it was true that Sam had a penchant for vehicular speed. Harry knew that she regularly flirted with death on the freeways and was on a first-name basis with more state troopers across Dixie than most governors. His voice was low and sweet as he said, "You take care of yourself, y'hear? And I'll talk to you Labor Day, if not before." Then he was gone.

Five seconds later, Polly appeared back through the screen door, a pitcher of iced coffee in her hand. "How's he doing?"

"I hate you, Polly. You're not to be trusted. I *told* you to say I was out if Harry ever called."

"Uh-huh." Polly started poking at a Boston fern perched on a white wicker stand.

Sam's protest picked up heat. "I don't want to be involved with anyone. Do you understand?"

Polly brushed away some dead ends, snapped off little wiry runners. She started whistling "Trouble in Mind" under her breath.

"That's it. I'm out of here." With that Sam grabbed up Harpo, the last of her things, and jumped into her car. Throwing it into reverse, she said to herself, Here I come, Slidell. I'll be out of Louisiana in less than an hour, away from these irritating people, folks poking all the time in my business. And she would have been gone, except there was Felix, the FedEx man, in her rearview mirror, blocking her in.

Felix Dupree was a long, lean light-skinned man who played the blues when night fell. Now, tipping his navy baseball cap, he climbed out of his truck. "How y'all pretty ladies feeling today?"

"Fair-to-middling," said Polly, her mouth tightening. Felix's flirtatiousness always made her impatient. Polly didn't have time for nonsense. She was busy studying photography. There were oodles of folks around here whose pictures she intended to take.

Felix said, "Here you go, Sam. Two packages today. Hope there's something good."

Sam reached out, took the large flat envelopes, and ran a finger beneath the flap of the first. "If I won the Publishers Clearing House," she said to Felix, "you and me are headed for Paris."

"Lord have mercy!" he shouted.

Polly gave him a look.

But there was no check in the first envelope, only the tentative schedule for her book tour with *American Weird*. The shipping label attached to the second said it had been sent by someone named J. Hilton, La Fonda Hotel, Santa Fe, New Mexico.

Sam tapped the envelope on her steering wheel and

stared out toward the big lake. Now, who do I know in Santa Fe?

She'd been through the town once, nearly twenty years earlier. She and Jimmy, her one-and-only husband, had stopped for a night. She still had a few snapshots of the place in her head: adobe houses, a grassy plaza in the center of town, on one side of it a café where a bowl of *posole* had fixed her hangover right up. Other than that she remembered only margaritas and marijuana, fighting with Jimmy, making up.

Had they skipped on the hotel bill? Was this it, finally catching up with her?

Then suddenly, like a blue norther blowing across from the Texas panhandle, a shudder of premonition ran up her spine. This phenomenon had happened with some frequency back in the days when she'd been a crime reporter, had saved her life more than once. It still made her sit up.

She ripped into the FedEx package. Inside was an envelope of cream-colored vellum with her name written across it. The handwriting was familiar, but she couldn't place it. Inside the envelope was a single sheet of notepaper. Sam slipped it loose and held it out from her at some distance.

Later she'd remember, it seemed as though Polly and Felix and Harpo and all the other living creatures in her yard had joined her in holding their breath.

Sam unfolded the note and read the greeting: *"My dearest Sugar."*

Sam's stomach lurched. Her face flamed. The world wobbled on its axis, then darkened and narrowed to that single sheet of paper. No one had ever called Samantha Adams *Sugar* except her mother.

But how could *this* letter be from Johanna Adams?

Not *this* letter, handwritten in, she suddenly realized, what looked to be her mother's careful looping script.

Not *this* letter, dated only one day earlier.

This had to be some kind of joke, for Johanna Adams had been dead, her ashes buried in the cold, cold ground, for thirty-four years.

An hour later, Sam sat motionless on her front porch steps. She had read and reread the letter dozens of times, tracing her fingers across the words. . . .

My dearest Sugar,

I must see you. Do not try to write or phone. Please come to Santa Fe, now. You will find me at the La Fonda Hotel, registered under the name J. Hilton. Please come. It's urgent. I need your help.

Your mother,
Johanna Hewlett Adams

P.S. This is no hoax. You see above my nickname for you. The Tooth Fairy gave you exactly ninety-nine cents, all in bright new pennies, for each lost tooth. Your secret name for your teddy bear was Bogalusa. I still have the birthmark high on my right thigh that you said looked like a Santa Claus face. Please call me the moment you arrive, my daughter, my dearest Sugar.

Sam lifted her gaze to a weeping willow that grew where the bayou skirted the corner of her property. But in her mind, she was not on this porch, nor in the state of Louisiana, nor in this year of our Lord. . . .

An early June morning, Sam was back home in Atlanta. She was eight years old, and she was perched on a chair in the breakfast room of her uncle George's rambling old split-timber Tudor house on Fairview Road. She and George, her father's brother, whom she adored, were enjoying scrambled eggs and bacon and a basket of biscuits that Peaches had just pulled from the oven. They were anticipating her parents' return that very day from a grand tour of Europe with the Atlanta Art Association.

"Momma's bringing me a green-and-white tea set from Assisi," Sam said. "That's what she told me when I talked to her last."

"I'm sure she will," said George. "And I'm sure it will be lovely. Assisi, you know, Sammie, is the hometown of Saint Francis, the saint who protects all the animals."

"Like Frank!" Sam leaned over and petted George's black cocker spaniel, waiting, ever-hopeful for crumbs, under the table. "Oh, I can't *wait* to see them again. Momma and Daddy have been gone *forever*."

"I know, sweetheart," George said. "And you've had a horrible time here. All three of us beating you with a stick." He gave her a wink.

Sam giggled. Uncle George had long been a widower, and Peaches and Horace, who'd been with him forever, had no children. The trio of doting adults treated Sam like a fairy princess, and their house was her castle. Staying with them was ever so much more fun than being at home. Not that she didn't miss Momma and Daddy dreadfully.

"Momma says you spoil me rotten. She says that I'll be *incorrigible* when they come back. Which will be in . . ." Sam checked her Cinderella watch with the blue grosgrain band.

Sam would always remember that moment, looking down at the watch, asking Uncle George for the millionth time, if it was eight A.M. in Atlanta and six hours later in Paris, which made it two P.M. there, and the plane had left at noon and the flight took nine hours, what time was it *really* when they'd arrive?

Just then the telephone rang. George, a lawyer with a houseful of phones, reached for the one at his elbow.

Sam couldn't take her eyes off him. Her prescience had kicked in. She could smell something in the air. Something ominous. The ozone before the lightning crash.

"Good morning!" George boomed. "George Adams here." And then someone on the other end, a secretary at the Atlanta Art Association it turned out, talked for a long time while George listened.

Just once George said, "No!" and shoved back in his chair as if a great hand had pushed him. Then he slumped and listened.

After George hung up the phone, he sat there for what seemed an eternity, sinking into himself, growing smaller and smaller, until Sam thought he would disappear. Under the table, Frank licked his master's ankles and whined.

Then George scooped Sam up from her chair and wrapped her in a mighty hug. She could feel his chest heaving.

She didn't say a word. She knew that there was a monster loose in her world. But if I'm very quiet, she told herself, and very still, the creature can't find me. I've proved that, haven't I, night after night, keeping at bay the horrible thing that lives beneath my bed?

But she couldn't fool this monster.

Finally George pulled back from her, wiped his tears, and said, "Sammie, darling, I have something very, very sad to tell you. I wish I didn't. Oh, Lord, how I wish I didn't."

Sam clapped her hands over her ears. If I don't let the bad words in, she thought, they won't be true. But eventually she had to hear George tell her of the crash of the chartered Boeing 707 upon takeoff at Orly. For years to come, she would close her eyes and see, as if she'd been there, every detail of the fiery scene. She could hear the plane exploding into the tarmac, the long silence, and then the screams. She could see the smoke, white at first, then growing blacker and blacker as the greedy flames claimed one hundred and thirty victims. The crash had been the worst disaster in American aviation history up until that time.

For months, Sam relived the crash nightly. But in her dreams there was salvation. There came a moment in her scenario when her parents would rise from the flames and stroll toward her, hand in hand, smiling. They had survived. See?

It wasn't true, of course. Her mother and father were lost. Forever lost.

Her father, Rob Adams, the tallest, most handsome man in the world, would never again come bounding through the back door. Never sweep her up. Never toss Sam in the air as if she were a bright ball, then catch her at the very last moment. She would never again feel that thrill. He would never again hold his hands out, a surprise tucked in one. *Which one, Sammie?* Never snuggle her with his rough chin, his kisses tickling her neck, kisses fragrant with aftershave and smoke and whiskey.

Her daddy was gone, lost forever, as was her beautiful momma, Johanna, whose laughter was like music floating down the stairs. Johanna, who painted the walls of Sam's room with her favorite fairy tales. Johanna, who whispered that Sam was an only child because she was so special there'd been no need for more. Johanna, who'd given Sam her brown eyes and dark curls and sun-lit complexion. Johanna, who was the center of her universe. Sam was the spit and image of Johanna, her momma, everyone said that.

Neither of them was *ever* coming home. Finally Sam understood what George had meant when he'd said that.

But he had said other things, too. George held her so

tightly to his chest she could feel his pulse, and he promised he would love her and care for her forever. She would be safe. He knew that he and Peaches and Horace were no replacement, but their home on Fairview Road would be hers, and she would be theirs, and they would be family.

He had been as good as his word. George and Peaches and Horace had never, for one instant, forsaken her. They had nurtured her and raised her and let her go when the time came, always with love. They had stood by her through the hardest times—her first broken heart, her drinking, her divorce, the death of her lover Sean. No one had ever had better friends and parents than George and Peaches and Horace.

And now, there was no one she'd rather talk with. Sam stood up from the front steps of her house closeby the dark Louisiana bayou and stumbled inside for a phone.

"Hello? Hello?" George said. "Sammie, is that you? Are you all right? You are coming aren't you?"

"Yes, of course I am," she finally managed.

"Great. So what's your news, darling? Are you delayed?"

"A letter came," she announced bluntly.

When she was done reading it to him, there was a long silence on the other end of the line. Then George asked, in a voice that was suddenly old and uncertain, "What do *you* think, Sammie?"

Sam stepped back. What *had* she thought? That George was going to kiss her boo-boo and make it well? That George would have all the answers?

Well, yes, he would have, in the old days. Both he and Sam's father had been white-shoe Atlanta lawyers, New South wheelers and dealers. There had been nothing they couldn't fix. But that was long ago. Her daddy was long dead *(Wasn't he?)*, and George, old and blind, had retired from the center court of life.

"I don't know what to think, George. I mean, what the hell kind of sick prank is this? Which weirdo on the loose?"

"Well, we know plenty of those guys, don't we?"

That was for sure. During Sam's long tenure as a reporter on newspapers in San Francisco and Atlanta, she had had a special interest in the big crime stories, and some of those felons had taken her interest personally. More than one had bellowed threats at her while being dragged away in cuffs. She'd received her share of threatening letters, scrawled in pencil on cheap lined paper. Then there'd come the day one Skeeter Bosarge had escaped a south Georgia jail, popped up from Sam's backseat, and roped her to a tree for target practice.

That kind of vengeance she understood. But this? This was much too subtle for the bad guys she knew.

"It's sick," said George. "And very cruel. Of course, it would be even more cruel, well, unthinkable, actually . . ." His voice idled to a stop; then he croaked, ". . . if the letter really were from Johanna."

Sam let his words float through the air. She could almost see them. Words, she thought, are so strong; it's a wonder that we don't pay them more respect. Worship in the First Church of the Word. Then she said, "Do you really think that that's a possibility, George? That Momma's alive?"

"Well, it's certainly never crossed my mind before. But, as a lawyer . . ." She could see George's shrug as clearly as if she were standing next to him. "Like I always said, 'Endless and unpredictable are the permutations of human behavior.' "

Indignation swamped her. "Human behavior? Jesus H. Christ, George, this is my mother, my father, your brother, we're talking about. This is not some abstraction. Some idea. Some philosophy."

George heard the hope, and the fear, in her voice. "The letter doesn't say a word about Rob, does it, Sam? Not a syllable about your daddy."

No. The letter laid claim solely to her mother's resurrection. But it's a joke, she told herself. Fraudulent. There are millions of people who can rattle off details of my childhood or fake my momma's handwriting. People do that sort of thing every day.

George was silent.

Okay, maybe not millions. But scores. Plenty. Enough. Family, for instance.

"Donna or Darla?" said George. Her mother's cousins? "Do you really think they'd remember details like Bogalusa, what the Tooth Fairy brought you, Johanna's birthmark, even if they'd paid that much attention years ago? Sammie, Sammie, stop and think. Do you really suspect someone in the family of writing you this letter?"

No, of course not. But what if . . . She trolled the thought past George. "Let's just say, for the sake of argument, that this letter really *is* from Johanna."

Johanna, yes, there, that was better, calling Momma by her given name. Remove the subject from the nursery, from the sticky fingers of childhood. Examine it with a cool, adult eye. That's the way to solve the problem, yes, with your intellect. You let your emotions carry you away, cloud your judgment. *Get in touch with your feelings.* They had to be kidding. And wallow in all that pain?

"Okay. Suppose," she said to George, "that Johanna's been alive and well lo these many years. Now what would that mean? That she didn't board the plane? That those aren't her ashes we buried next to Daddy's? Yes, we always knew that they might not be, not exactly them, I mean. Not precisely. What with the fire . . ."

Then Sam's voice broke, her composure evaporating. She was in rough shape here. Inside her, flood waters raced over dams. She was drowning.

"Sammie, Sammie, baby," George crooned. She could almost feel his arms around her.

She shrugged them off, for something else was rising in her now. Anger, the scalding kind, born of hurt. "If this letter *is* from Johanna, where has she *been* all this time? Why didn't she come home? What could be so important that she'd abandon us?"

Us. You and me, George. Family. Friends. It's too hard to say *me.* I can't manage it. It hurts too much to think that Johanna, alive and well, had made the choice not to see me, her only child. Never ever again.

Until now.

George whispered. "I don't know, dear. I truly don't." Then his voice quickened as he hit upon a plan. Mr. Fix-it was back in action. "Bring the letter with you to Atlanta. Bring it along with a sample of Johanna's handwriting. You still have those boxes of old scrapbooks and Johanna's letters, don't you? You can take some of them along with this letter to a graphologist. Why, you could take it out to the crime lab. You still have friends there. An expert can tell you in no time at all if Johanna wrote the letter. And approximately when."

"Yes, I could do that."

"Ah," said George, hearing her hesitation. "But you don't want to. Well, I would understand if you just wanted the whole thing to go away. We get older, and certainly at *my* age, some things simply seem like too much effort. Passions fade. I just don't care as much I used to . . ."

"No, George." She stopped his flood of words. "The handwriting is a great idea. But I don't think I can bear to wait around for it."

"I'm afraid you're going to have to, dear. We all know patience has never been your long suit, but . . ."

Then the words came flying from her mouth before she could stop them. Flying from her heart, bypassing the doors labeled Kindness Toward Others, Thoughtfulness, Tact. "George, I have to go to Santa Fe. Now."

He chose the high road then, pretending he hadn't understood. "Yes, certainly. You can leave from here, right after the party."

"No, old darling. I have to leave now. As soon as I hang up, I'm heading straight for the airport."

"But, Sammie . . ."

"This is rotten. I know it is. I'm hurting your feelings, and I'm so very sorry. I know your seventy-fifth is important to you. It's important to *me*. And I'll be there, I promise, as soon as I can, but . . ."

But what? *My very skin is screaming.* My *skin. Me, me, me. I'm eight years old again. My mother has crashed and burned. She's dead. That's what you told me. That's what the papers said. You held up the tiny caskets and showed me. That's all that's left, Sammie. Your momma's ashes and your daddy's. I didn't want to believe you, didn't want to believe any of it. Didn't, wouldn't, couldn't, not for years. And wonderful as you were to me, you and Peaches and Horace, you weren't Daddy. You weren't Momma.*

Sam said, "I want to be in New Mexico before sundown. I'm sure it's a hoax and I'll be telling you all about it over a cup of coffee in your study tomorrow night, but I have to find that out for myself. Now."

George said, Sure. No problem. He understood. But she knew that he didn't. Or, rather, that understanding wasn't enough. Nevertheless, she couldn't help herself. I *have* to go. I'm already on the plane. I'm knocking at Johanna's door. *Momma?* I can hear myself calling, *Momma, is that you?*

2

THE FIRST SEAT SAM COULD BOOK WAS IN THE FIRST-CLASS cabin of a flight departing New Orleans at one P.M. It cost the earth, but once she was buckled in, she was glad for the extravagance.

This is a time to be kind to yourself, she thought. To be gentle. She tucked the snoozing Harpo beneath the seat in front of her in his little carrying case. She'd promised him he could go, somewhere, and he was going. He just wanted to be with his mom. Me, too, thought Sam as she stretched her legs and closed her eyes, willing herself to relax into the leather cocoon. But she was as wired as a racehorse before the starting bell. *Johanna, Johanna, Johanna,* kept repeating in her head.

Was Johanna alive? If she was, then whose ashes had they buried? Where had she been all this time? Why had she reappeared *now*?

Suddenly, someone bumped Sam's arm, and she opened her eyes to see a little brunette straining on tiptoe to stuff her bag into the overhead compartment. Then the woman plopped down in the seat next to Sam. She pulled a handkerchief from her bag and wiped her brow. "I can't wait to get out of here and back to dry land," she said to Sam. "I grew up here in New Orleans, but, boy, I can't take the summers anymore. One more day and my toes would have rotted off." The woman was close to Sam's age, wearing a simple black linen shift, expensive sandals, a single silver bangle on a tan wrist. She'd tried and failed to tame her wild mane of dark wavy hair with a silver clip. Now she stuck out her hand. "I'm Deborah Wonder. Headed for Santa Fe. What about you?"

Usually Sam didn't mind talking with people on planes. She'd found many a story that way. But today she was hardly in the mood. She introduced herself, allowed as how Santa Fe was her destination also, then reached for a magazine. But Deborah Wonder wasn't that easily put off. "Do you spend much time in New Orleans?"

"I live in Covington."

"Really? My family has a house over there. Where's yours?"

Why didn't you pretend that you don't speak English? Sam asked herself. Or just tell the woman, Please, I don't want to talk. I've had a death in my family. Make that a rebirth. A resurrection.

Next, a stupid scenario clicked in. She was at a party introducing Johanna.

And this is Johanna Adams, my mother.

Oh, I thought your mother was dead.

Well, she was. But she's not anymore.

"Are you married?" That was Deborah. She'd pulled a sheaf of papers from a leather case and was frowning at them.

Sam shook her head no.

"Well, that's good. I wish I weren't." Deborah tapped the papers with a forefinger. "My husband. He's going to have us in bankruptcy court."

Sam definitely didn't want to hear about this. She buried her nose in her magazine. She flipped the pages, snapping them loudly, hoping that Deborah would take the hint. She stared at the parade of designer rags. Nothing like what she had stuffed into her bag: jeans, a denim skirt, T-shirts, a sweater, shorts, running shoes.

She read a photo caption: "The little black dress. Still perfect for every occasion."

Oh, yeah? Should I have packed one for meeting my dead mother?

She shook her head. Flipped the page. And there, staring out at her, was a model—one hand on her hip, legs akimbo—who was a dead ringer for the young Johanna.

Oh, yes. Johanna Hewlett had been a knockout all right. "I hate to take her out in public; she stops traffic," Sam's father used to tease. Dark-haired, dark-eyed, Johanna was beautiful, Audrey Hepburn crossed with Scarlett O'Hara, though just a tad over five feet tall.

Lovely to look at, and then, there was Johanna's unforgettable voice—husky, soft, musical. Sam had always been able to call it back. Even now, if she closed her eyes, she could hear Johanna telling her a story. The ones Sam loved most were the stories of Johanna's own childhood . . .

"My daddy was a judge. He was almost fifty when I was born, and he wore long black robes and had snow white hair and a long beard, all of which made me think he was God!" Johanna's laughter then, sliding up and down the scale like quicksilver. "My momma, you know, Sammie, was much younger than Daddy. She had a weak heart, and she died of that, and pneumonia, when I was three months old. I never knew her. So sad. That's her picture. And this is a photograph of your grandmother at her wedding. See those dark eyes? She was one-quarter Cherokee. That makes me one-eighth. You, Sugar, one-sixteenth.

"I grew up in Daddy's courtroom in Asheville, North

Carolina. I was the apple of his eye, spoiled rotten. I'd hold tea parties under his bench for my dolls while, up above me, tales unfolded of robberies and murders and all manner of black deeds. But I never seemed to pay them much mind.

"I loved Asheville. Do you remember, we took you there once? Such a pretty little town, tucked in the foothills of the Smokies. Cool in the summer. Snowy in the winters. Thomas Wolfe, the writer, was raised there. We went to visit his grave one frosty afternoon. You wanted to climb up on the angel.

"And I, of course"—Johanna always dimpled when she said this—"was the *toast* of the town. I was the *belle* of Asheville. I hated to leave, to go off to school in Virginia. I adored Sweet Briar and all the girls, once I got there, but I was always afraid that I was missing something back home. I went home every chance I got. And it was a good thing, because—"

It had been Johanna's nineteenth spring. The dogwoods were in bloom when Rob Adams, a young Atlanta lawyer, had come calling on Judge Hewlett for advice on a delicate legal matter involving two prominent families, one of Asheville, one of Atlanta. Rob had been talking with the judge in his study when Johanna, having just arrived home for spring break, burst in.

Johanna and Rob were married the following fall. Rob took his young bride back to Atlanta, where Johanna set herself to the not-small task of captivating the city. Sam could track her progress in the old newsclips Johanna had pasted in her scrapbooks. Johanna smiling out of a tea with the Junior League. Johanna in a smart suit, lunching at the Piedmont Driving Club. Johanna in a full-skirted dress at a show of her paintings at a small gallery on Peachtree. Johanna modeling at a charity function, smiling out at the camera in a pretty hat.

"I'm going to kill him." Deborah's voice jerked Sam

back into the present. She turned to her seatmate, whose lap was filled with spreadsheets. "I beg your pardon?" she said, and then Deborah burst into tears. She made a lot of noise for a little woman. Sam reached into her bag and handed Deborah a tissue. "I'm so sorry," Deborah sobbed. "I feel like an idiot. I always cry when I'm mad. And right now I'm *furious*."

"It's okay," Sam soothed.

"No, it's not. It's awful, just awful. I'm going to *kill* my husband." She wiped her eyes and blew her nose with a tiny fluting sound. "You must think I'm a nut. *I've* always thought that people who cried in public were crazy or brought up badly, at the very least."

Sam managed a smile. "Don't worry about it."

"My father—I was just visiting him—he *told* me not to marry Stuart. But I was young, so what did I do? Married Stuart the first chance I got. Stuart Wonder, the wise man from Great Neck, Long Island. Stuart Wonder, the shuck-and-jive artist." Deborah stopped. "You don't know who I'm talking about, do you?"

No, Sam didn't.

"New Age holy man? Books, TV, the guru lecture circuit?"

Nope, though if this Stuart Wonder had been a fundamentalist Southern religioso, he'd have been right up Sam's alley. Snake handlers, footwashing Baptists, Bikers for Jesus, a woman evangelist who gave recipes for her pies on her TV show, Sam had written about them all in *American Weird*.

"And I guess you've never heard of Rancho Maravilloso?"

Sam shook her head, and Deborah began to describe her husband's retreat, a sort of Canyon Ranch for the spirit. Rancho Maravilloso, on several hundred acres just south of Santa Fe, had been built as a movie set for Westerns. When Stuart had bought it, he'd added guest rooms and meeting facilities behind some of the storefronts. Movies and mysticism, Stuart had them both covered. "In fact," said Deborah, "they're supposed to be shooting a TV movie there soon, a kind of docudrama, about Stuart's work. He's pretty famous, my Stuart, but now he's gotten us into some deep financial doo-doo." Deborah talked on, and Sam tried to listen—she really did—but Deborah's words were a lullaby. Sweet surcease at thirty-five thousand feet. And somewhere in her dreams . . .

Johanna, looking exactly as she had when Sam was eight, was lying on a funeral bier dressed in full Western regalia: boots, fringed jacket, cowgirl hat, reams of silver jewelry. Behind her stood a short Jewish man with snow white hair and a silver beard wearing a long black robe. He was murmuring something Sam couldn't make out, waving his hands over Johanna, who appeared to be sleeping. Or perhaps she was dead. Then, ever so slowly, Johanna began to levitate. Before long, Johanna was floating, like a magician's assistant, in thin air. A little girl raced into the room, crying, Momma! Momma!

There was a bump. Three bumps more and a long shuddering.

They had landed in Albuquerque.

3

Deborah had offered to give Sam a ride into Santa Fe, but Sam had said no thanks. She needed her own car to get around, to do whatever it was she had to do about Johanna or *whoever* was waiting for her at La Fonda. This Johanna impostor. This con artist. This fraud. This fake.

Shut up, she told herself. Get in the car and drive.

It was nearing four when Sam pulled the white Ford Taurus onto I-25. Fifty-six miles northeast to Santa Fe, about forty-five minutes, if she observed the seventy-five-mph speed limit. This was not the day to get pulled over. There was no telling what she might say to the man in the Smokey hat.

Holding the rental car in the middle lane, she told herself, Focus on the road. Roll down the window. Breathe in the desert air. Look at the great scenery of the Southwest. People drive thousands of miles to see it.

Once she'd left the strip-mall sprawl of Albuquerque behind, the brown of the high desert was relieved only by grayish green smudges of cottonwood, piñon, and chamiso. To the east, the slate-colored Sandia Mountains jutted two thousand feet. Above the amazing landscape, the blue sky was bigger and clearer than any sky she'd ever seen. The thermometer on a roadside billboard read ninety, but it didn't feel that hot. With Texas separating the two states, the miles and miles and miles of Texas, New Mexico was as dry as Louisiana was damp.

It was a completely different world, this New Mexico. An alien planet inhabited by Johanna.

Momma.

Aw, come on, Sam told herself. Do you really think Johanna's here? Even if she was alive, she couldn't make a home in this place. Johanna, born and bred in North Carolina's green hills, had loved trees and flowers and rolling brooks. How could she survive here?

Besides which, Johanna had been dead the past third-of-a-century, and this was a joke, a wild-goose chase, a colossal waste of time.

How *could* Johanna be alive? It wasn't possible.

Impossible, possible, possible, her tires sang.

Sam hunkered down and gripped the wheel.

God, grant me the serenity to accept the things I can't change. The strength to change the things I can. And the wisdom to know the difference.

Slowly, the trembling in her gut stilled. Hadn't she long ago accepted her parents' death? Filled the hole they'd left in her soul with boys, booze, compulsive work? Yes, she had. Why, she hadn't dreamed about her momma and daddy walking out of that plane in at least a year.

But, *but;* her mind leapt once more to the current specifics. The handwriting of the note *did* look like Johanna's. And who else knew Bogalusa, her teddy bear, her deal with the Tooth Fairy, Johanna's birthmark?

"Stop it!" she said aloud, and Harpo bolted from sleep. "Sorry, sweetie," she apologized, and within seconds the little dog was out again.

Give it a rest, she told herself. You'll know soon enough. Go back to the scenery. Look out the window.

Buttes and flat-topped mesas rose in the west as she passed through Indian lands. Sandia, San Felipe, Santo Domingo Pueblos, there were the road signs, but the reservations were too far off the road for her to see. The unfriendly dark blue Ortiz Mountains threw themselves at the hot sky over to the east.

The landscape was alien. Hostile. Spooky. No balm here for a troubled soul. No comfort. The rent-a-car whined as the road climbed. Sam glanced at the car's gauges, then back out at the baking barren land. If she broke down or lost her way, she'd fry in no time at all. This was no-kidding-around country. She imagined she could smell Mr. Death waiting out there, Mr. D. with his carrion breath.

And who, she asked herself, is waiting for you in Santa Fe? Then she pressed harder on the accelerator, keeping one eye out for flashing blue lights.

Finally, in a slow, punishing haul, she crested La Bajada, the long slope up the mesa. And there, spread out in the distance before her, was Santa Fe. It was larger than she remembered from her long-ago visit with Jimmy, her ex, but even so, merely a town. Behind it rose the green backdrop of the Sangre de Cristo Mountains. They looked bosomy, maternal compared to the jutting Sandias an hour south.

Ah, Sam, she thought then, you can't escape it. You've got mothering on your mind. Can't stop thinking about Johanna. Johanna's everywhere: in the sky, in the earth, in the air.

So, okay, what if, when Sam and Jimmy had driven drunk through here, twenty years earlier, what if Johanna had been in the neighborhood back then?

While she and Jimmy scarfed down *posole* at that little café on the plaza, what was Johanna doing? Was she just around the corner? At the next table? What if they'd spotted her, waved her over, would she have joined them for a cup of coffee? What would they have said?

Though, on the other hand, the fact that Johanna, if it *was* Johanna, had sent the note from Santa Fe, had asked her to come there, didn't necessarily mean that she lived in the town. Probably didn't, or why would she be staying in a hotel? So she was only visiting. Passing through. On her way from where? To where?

Shut up, Sam told herself. Please. You're making me nuts.

She looked down at Harpo. "What do you think, little dog? Do you ever think about your real mom? Your doggie mom? The one Sean took you from when he gave you to me? Do you ever miss her and your brothers and sisters?"

Harpo gave her his crooked-mouth look. Sam was glad she had brought him along. On this journey into the unknown, she was happy for his warm little company.

Too bad Harry was off on his own adventure.

Whoa. Where did *that* come from?

Ixnay. Delete. Forget it.

But what if she'd picked up the phone and called Harry back before she'd left the airport? He'd have wanted to hear all about it, to hear the letter, to know what George said. He'd have offered to cancel his trip, to come along, to hold her hand. Or maybe not. Maybe they'd been estranged too long. Maybe he had someone else he was worrying about. Then why'd he call?

Samantha—she gritted her teeth—you cannot have it both ways. And you don't want Harry here. You're just scared. Now buck up.

She sat up straighter, stared out at the suburban sprawl of south Santa Fe. Here was her exit. Then she turned off I-25 onto St. Francis Drive and drove past strip malls,

Taco Bells, and tire dealerships into the wall-to-wall adobe heart of the ancient city.

The City Different was how Santa Fe billed itself these days. Just another tourist commission come-on, the locals complained, for the swarms of day-trippers and, even worse, the Californians who rode in with satchels full of money, built on the ridgetops, and inflated the real estate values so the locals' children didn't have a prayer of ever living here.

But the town, and it was a town, barely sixty thousand souls even today, had always been honey to invaders. Nestled at seven thousand feet in the deep blue foothills of the Sangre de Cristo Mountains, Santa Fe enjoyed great natural beauty: pine forests, rust-orange-lavender mesas, the nearby Chama River and Rio Grande, heart-stopping sunsets. The high desert climate boasted low humidity, warm days, cool evenings, huge blue skies, three hundred and ten days a year.

The Pueblo Indians had come here looking for water. In 1610 Santa Fe had been dubbed the capital of "The Kingdom of New Mexico," and the conquistadors set about enslaving the Indians and stealing their land. In 1821, the territory won its independence from Spain, and within a year the Americans were hauling fancy goods along the Santa Fe Trail, setting the stage for the Great Southwestern Boutique the town had become today.

One of the more interesting things about Santa Fe was that for many years, due to its location, it enjoyed a kind of isolation in which it not only tolerated but celebrated its unique blend of cultures. Like New Orleans, it was physically part of the United States, but in many other respects not. And, like the Big Easy, Santa Fe's reputation for diversity attracted the offbeat. Artists, writers, hippies, gays, motorcyclists, New Age devotees, crystal gazers, counterculturists, the crazy, the weird, and the alternative had long flocked to Santa Fe's adobe mud huts. Even in the Wild West days, Governor Lew Wallace, in between his day job and negotiating for the capture of Billy the Kid, wrote the novel *Ben Hur* while living in the Palace of the Governors on Sante Fe's picturesque plaza.

The town had always been considered a spiritual mecca. From the earliest days, the ancient wisdom of the Pueblo Indians had sat cheek by jowl with Roman Catholicism, mysticism, and superstition. Locals still painted their doors and windows blue to keep the witches away. The throngs of holy men, seers, shamans, and other practitioners of what was known locally as woo-woo were fairly recent, but no less dear to the heart of Santa Feans who recorded the names and numbers of their psychics, astrologers, channelers, and polarity therapists in their Rolodexes alongside those of their hairdressers.

Today, Santa Fe was home to about a fifty-fifty split of Hispanics and Anglos, with the Indians barely making a dent. But long gone were the good old days of easy to-ing and fro-ing among the disparate elements. The wild parties, barbecues, fiestas, that once mixed members of regal old Hispanic families, artists, dogs, rich Texans, the Native American mailman, gay couples, and the trying-to-make-ends-meet Anglo shopowner were history. Oh, everyone turned out for the Fourth of July pancake feed, Indian Market, Spanish Market, and Fiesta, but money, tourists, and real estate values had changed the town. It was still a good place to be, sweeter than most, but ask anyone who'd been here more than five years. They'd tell you how much it'd changed. How there used to be more tolerance, more ease among people, before the money, before the Californians.

Another thing to be noted about Santa Fe was that, in many ways, it was a woman's town. The most recent mayor was an Hispanic woman. There were scores of powerful females here—wives, mothers, divorcées, widows, and singles, of both straight and lesbian persuasions. But, there was also a machismo that couldn't be ignored. Santa Fe had a history of crimes against women—abuse, assaults, rapes, even some murders—that had not been pursued as stringently as one would have hoped. Santa Fe, despite the appearance of safety, was not a place where women should go hiking alone, nor walking alone, either, after dark.

La Fonda, Sam's destination as specified in the letter, turned out to be the same hotel where she and Jimmy had stayed almost twenty years earlier. An old brown adobe hulk off one corner of the plaza, it was cool and dark and cavernous inside, a welcome respite from the dazzle of the afternoon sun.

"Ms. Adams?" said a handsome young Hispanic woman behind the tall counter where she registered. "Yes, we've been expecting you."

"Thanks, do you have any messages for me?"

"You are to contact your hostess as soon as you are settled into your room. Call back to the desk and we can assist you in that matter."

"My hostess?"

The young woman's smile froze as she leaned across the counter toward Sam. She lowered her voice. "Please do not question this, Ms. Adams. Don't make a scene. If you will go to your room and call the desk for further instructions, we will be able to help you. Ask for me. My name is Estela. Do you think you can do that, please?"

Sam was not in the mood for this young woman, nor her attitude. It had been a long and rocky day. She jerked up her bag, grabbed Harpo, and stomped off for the elevator. Just wait until she got this Estela—the likes of whom she'd eaten for breakfast in her reporting days—on the phone. She could hardly wait.

But once in her room, the door shut, her bag thrown across her bed, Sam fell to pieces. Her knees went weak. What the *hell* was she doing here? Why had she come on this wild-goose chase? Did she really think she was going to find Johanna, alive and well in Santa Fe?

Maybe. Maybe that was the scariest part, that this *wasn't* a joke. Maybe the snippy Miss Estela downstairs *was* going to put her through to Johanna.

Sam filled a saucer with water from the tap for Harpo. She unzipped her garment bag, jerked out a fresh white T-shirt. She brushed her teeth, slapped on another coat of makeup, then marched smartly over to the phone. She jerked it up and listened to the dial tone, drumming her fingers while waiting for the operator.

Then, she slammed the phone down. Which was just as well. Her heart was pounding so loudly she couldn't hear a thing.

She was one call away—well, two, if you counted Estela—from speaking with Johanna.

Maybe.

Perhaps.

If Johanna had indeed risen from the dead.

Sam threw herself across the room and into a chair. She stared at Harpo, who stared back. "Why the hell are we here, little dog? We ought to be in Atlanta, blowing up balloons for George's birthday party. Have we gone mad?"

Harpo cocked his head to one side.

Call her, that's what Johanna's letter said. Just call her, the moment she arrived in town. Ask for J. Hilton.

Sam tilted forward in her chair. She could do that. She would. She'd ask Johanna, when she answered, Hey, Ma, why the hocus-pocus about the name?

Then she'd holler, And where the hell have you been all these years?

Sam stared at the black receiver on her bedside table. It glowered back it her, a tarantula of a telephone.

Admit it, Sam said to herself, you're scared shitless.

She was, and wasn't that pathetic? She'd stabbed George in the heart, the one person in the world who had always loved her, never let her down, in order to jump on a plane, at great expense, to come to this hamlet in the middle of a desert, to make a call—and now she couldn't pick up the phone.

Sam jumped up. She stalked back and forth across the brown saltillo tiles. She stared out the window down into the plaza, a green square gridded with walkways, pocked with benches. A young couple walked a path toward her, hand in hand. The young man was smoking. Sam could taste that cigarette.

I'd give my right arm for one right now, she thought. Even more than a drink, that's what she craved this very minute, for she'd loved smoking. She adored the ritual: pulling the little tab that opened the staticky cellophane wrapper, tapping the first one from a full pack, the strike of the match, the smell of the sulfur. Then that first hit.

Sam turned away from the window. She ran her eyes around the room, taking in the rough-hewn Mexican dressing table and wardrobe, the beams above, the kachina doll in a niche. This was another world, a world where she didn't belong. She should be past Birmingham by now, digesting the sliced pork sandwich she'd have had for lunch at that place outside Bessemer. Barbecued pork almost as good as Harry's.

Harry. He'd say, Go ahead and make the call, babe. No point in torturing yourself any longer. Get it over with. Get the show on the road. Then come on home.

Pretty much the same advice she'd give herself.

Sam glanced at her watch. Allowing for the time difference, it was only ten hours since she'd opened the letter that had put her life on hold.

It seemed like a lifetime ago.

And longer with each moment of stalling.

Any second now she'd pick up the phone, speak with that impossible young wretch at the desk, get the number of Johanna's room, her "hostess's" room. She'd dial the number. A woman would answer. The voice would be familiar. Or maybe it wouldn't be. In any case, she'd say, *Momma?* And then . . .

Back up. She couldn't call someone she hadn't spoken with in thirty-four years *Momma,* for pete's sakes.

Johanna?

Yes. She'd ask for Johanna.

And Johanna would say, "Oh, hi, Sugar, I'm so glad to hear from you again. You know, it's the damnedest thing. I got hung up in Paris, and then one thing lead to another; you know how it is."

Yep. Sam herself frequently found herself hung up for thirty-four years.

Or, maybe the old dame—how old would Johanna be now, anyway? Thirty at the crash, plus thirty-four, that made her sixty-four, not so old, not elderly, certainly. Maybe this Johanna of a certain age had fallen on hard times. She'd beg, "Could you see your way clear to help me out a bit, dear? After all, I did leave you quite comfortably off."

Try this one. Johanna's sick. She's at death's door, and she has the urge to see her only child before she passes. Unless, and now *there's* a thought, what if you *aren't* an only child, Ms. Sam? What makes you think that Johanna, if she has been alive all these years, has given birth to no more spawn? Maybe you're only one of many names on her invitation list for this family reunion.

Hi, Sam! Come on in and meet Myrtle, Mabel, Malcolm, Mergatroid.

Jesus. She had to stop this.

Just pick up the phone, Sam. Get it over with.

She took a deep breath, marched over to the telephone, and reached for it. But her hand wouldn't close. She couldn't make her fingers grip.

She simply could not make the call. Not yet. Sam turned to Harpo. "Wanta go for a walk, little dog?"

Harpo did his best two-step.

The plaza was surrounded by shops, their windows filled with Indian pottery, colorful blankets, fringed leather jackets, tightly pleated broomsticks skirts. On the north side of the plaza stood the long, white adobe Palace of the Governors, for more than three centuries the seat of government in this part of the world. Beneath the palace's wide portal, Indians squatted behind cloths spread with their turquoise jewelry. But Sam took in little of it. Her mind was back at the hotel, dialing Johanna's number, waiting to hear her voice.

Around and around the square she walked. By the third time, she began to feel faint. There was an empty bench in the center of the plaza, where the web of walkways converged. She headed for it, beating out a trio with cameras slung around their necks. She sprawled. Rising before her was a stone obelisk, a monument to the town's dead from the Indian Wars and the War Between the States.

Wait a minute. The Civil War in the high desert? No way. Her War Between the States was the burning of Atlanta, Sherman's march to the sea, Scarlett O'Hara. The Yankees were coming! She knew old ladies who still reminisced about their grannies burying the family silver in the back garden. You wanted to talk cowboys-and-Indians; now, that made more sense here in "High Noon" country. If anything made sense.

This very minute, nothing much did. Sam was feeling

confused, light-headed, a touch nauseous. Harpo, beside her, panted hard. "We need water," she said to him. "We need oxygen. It's well over a mile high here. The air's too thin for us swamp creatures." Harpo wagged his tail.

At one corner of the plaza an ice cream store and a café stood catercorner to one another. "I bet that's the same restaurant that saved my life twenty years ago," Sam said to Harpo. "Now it could save the both of us. Food and water. Nothing on the plane but a cup of coffee, and you didn't even have that. Momma's gonna go rustle us up some chow."

Sam stood, only to find herself nose to nose with an Indian.

The woman was about Sam's height, five-eight, but a good thirty pounds heavier. She was wearing jeans and a white blouse and a garland of necklaces made of tiny beads of clamshell, melon shell, red coral, and turquoise. In one hand she carried a lemonade, in the other a cardboard boat of something that smelled awfully good. You're hallucinating, Sam told herself. Starvation brought on visions. Not to mention the seven-thousand-foot altitude. Climbing from sea level to this height obviously did strange things to the brain.

Then the hallucination spoke. "Mind if I sit here?"

Harpo sniffed the woman's shoes. Sam said, "You're welcome, if you'll save our seats. I'm going on a provisions search. Where'd you get that?"

"Woolworth's, over there." She waved toward the south side of the plaza. "Frito pie. Chili and beans and cheese, jalapeños and corn chips. Here, take it."

"No, thanks, but I can't."

"Sure you can." The woman shoved the cardboard container at Sam, then headed off with a rolling gait. "I'll get the dog some water," she called. "Be back in a minute. You eat."

The Frito pie was gooey and delicious. It reminded

Sam of the chili dogs at The Varsity back in Atlanta. Harpo glared up at her from beneath his bangs.

"Your water's coming," Sam said. "You wouldn't like this, honest. Hold on for your Mighty Dog."

Liar, his look said. Liar, liar, pants on fire.

Then the Indian woman was back. She set a paper cup down on the concrete, and Harpo greedily set to. "Good, huh?" she said to Sam.

Her voice had a funny flat singsong quality that would grow familiar to Sam in the days to come. Both the Indians and the Hispanics of Santa Fe spoke English with an accent that echoed medieval Spain. The villages and pueblos of northern New Mexico had been tucked away from the mainstream for a very very long time.

"Delicious," said Sam. "But I feel bad, taking your food. Let me go get you another one."

"No, thanks."

"Then at least let me pay you for this one."

"Nope. Glad to do it." The woman stuck out her hand. "My name is Rosey Bird."

"Sam Adams. I'm from near New Orleans."

Rosey nodded. "Santo Domingo Pueblo, south of here. You came to Santa Fe on a quest?"

Sam stepped back. Whoa. Then she heard herself saying, "I guess so. I came to see my mother, or someone who says she's my mother." She was babbling. "I haven't seen my mother in a very long time. Actually, I thought she was dead."

"But you'll see her soon?" Rosey asked. Or was that *said?*—more of a question than a statement.

"I'm not sure. I don't know."

Rosey nodded solemnly. "You will."

Wait a minute. Was Rosey saying that her mother was alive? "Do you *know* my mother? Johanna Adams? Johanna Hewlett. Johanna Hilton, J. Hilton, she might be calling herself?"

Rosey deadpanned, "She's your mother. Try to be patient with her, even if you don't understand." And with that, she stood. "I've got to go. My mom is waiting." She nodded in the direction of the Palace of the Governors. "I have to give her a ride back home."

"But wait," Sam cried. What was Rosey saying she should be patient about? What did she mean?

Rosey was already twenty feet away. "Sorry, I have to go."

Sam suddenly felt bereft, painfully aware of how completely alone she was here in Santa Fe.

Rosey smiled at her. "It'll be okay. Don't worry."

"Who *are* you, anyway?"

"Rosey Bird," the Indian woman said, as if she hadn't said it before. "I'll catch up with you again. Now go and see your mom off on her journey."

What journey? Where was Johanna going? She herself had barely arrived.

And Rosey was gone. Sam watched as she made her way across the plaza with her peculiar gait. You're fresh out of excuses, girl, she told herself. You've been fed and watered and cheered on by a mysterious Indian woman. It's time now. Wipe your mouth. Feed your dog. Go see about your momma.

She's your mother. Try to be patient with her, even if you don't understand.

Sure, sure. Easy enough for Rosey Bird—Native American wise woman, princess of the Frito pie, water bearer to a small shih tzu—to say. But then, it wasn't Rosey's mom who'd risen from the dead.

Sam, back in her room, examined her face once more and brushed her teeth. There was nothing left to do. It was now or never.

Sam sat before the dressing table and stared herself down. What are you afraid of? You've covered the knife-and-gun club, witnessed autopsies, stood at crime scenes ankle-deep in blood. What we're talking about here is just a little old lady come back to life. Where's your courage, girl?

Then, before she had time for another misgiving, she grabbed up the phone and dialed O.

"Estela, please."

"Yes?"

"Sam Adams here. I'd like to speak to J. Hilton."

"Just a minute, please."

Then there was a long silence on the other end of the

line, broken only by the shuffling of papers. Finally Estela came back on the line. "Could you tell me, please, your mother's maiden name?"

"I beg your pardon?"

"Your mother's maiden name?"

It wasn't as if she'd lost her VISA card, for god's sakes. But when in Rome . . . "Johanna Hewlett," she said.

"The date and place of her birth?"

"September twenty-seventh, 1934. Asheville, North Carolina."

"And *her* mother's maiden name."

"Samantha Hewlett. No, I mean Samantha Rogers."

"The room number is four-oh-nine. I will ring Ms. Hilton and tell her that you're on your way."

Making her way down the million-mile-long hall, Sam recalled a story that Johanna had once told her.

"I guess I was about six," Johanna had said, "and we'd gone up to Asheville to visit one of my mother's cousins, Millie. I loved Millie, who was blonde and round and so much fun. And she was a wonderful baker. You know that black walnut cake I make sometimes, Sugar? That was Millie's cake.

"Anyway, Millie had twin daughters who were about three years older than I. Donna and Darla, and they were as full of the devil as anybody I've ever seen.

"This particular visit, they waited until after supper, way after Millie had tucked us in, and they told me to come, we were going on an adventure.

" 'Oh, I can't,' I said. 'My momma won't let me go out after dark. Can you? Won't Millie be mad?' "

" 'She won't know if you don't tell her. Besides, if you come, there's a present for you.'

" 'A present?' My ears perked up. I *adored* presents.

"So they took me by the hand, and, in our nightgowns, we crept down the back stairs and out the door and around the house. They walked me down broken side-walks through streets that were completely black, past bushes that grabbed for me like ghosts, and more than once my heart nearly stopped. It seemed to me that we had walked for hours, had gone a million miles, though later I found out that they'd been walking me in circles. Finally we stopped at a dilapidated back porch.

"Donna and Darla pushed me up to the crumbling steps of the old house. 'Go knock on the door. The old woman who answers will give you a present.'

" 'Who is she?' I asked. 'And what's the present?' But they wouldn't tell me. They poked me with their fingers. They called me a chicken. They giggled behind my back.

"The rear of that poor house was terribly bleak. An old wringer washing machine listed to one side in the yard. The screen door was ripped, the paint peeling.

"All the while, Donna and Darla were saying, 'Go on, Jo. Are you afraid, Jo? Don't you want your surprise, Jo? Chick, chick, chicken, Jo.'

"So I gathered my nerve. I put one foot on that first step, and it creaked like a coffin opening.

"I screamed. Donna and Darla screamed. And then we all ran like the wind.

"We hadn't quite cleared the yard, when the screen door cracked a bit, and this pitiful old woman stood there at the door, her night scarf wrapped around her head.

" 'Who's that?' she cried. 'Who's there?'

"I never forgot the sound of that poor old woman's voice, Sugar, all alone and frightened of the night. Fear-ful of the sounds of mischievous little girls. And I felt awful that I'd been party to that because I'd been a greedy gut. Because I'd wanted a present."

And what do *you* want? Sam asked herself now as she approached room 409.

I want my momma. My momma.

How many times had she cried those words to George, to Peaches, to Horace, when she was small, awaking from a night fright?

And, now, more than ever, she wanted her momma.

Sam stood before room 409, watching her right hand rising. Her knuckles rapping on the dark wood.

"Who is it?" a voice called.

"It's Sam. It's Sugar, Momma."

The door swung wide.

One look, no doubt about it, this was Johanna. She was even yet a beautiful woman, but tiny, oh so tiny. Sam knew Johanna was small, but she herself had been only eight, a little girl, the last time she'd seen her, and Johanna had been her whole world . . .

The years had had their way, silvered the dark curls, drawn lines and furrows, but the catlike chin, the brown eyes—yes, oh yes, this woman in the long purple caftan, ropes of silver at neck and wrists, this was Johanna.

Johanna lived.

Her mother's dark eyes were wide now, focused hungrily on Sam's face. I can feel her sucking me in, Sam thought. Then Johanna threw her arms open, and Sam raced into her embrace.

Home. She was home.

Hot tears poured down Sam's cheeks as she grasped her mother's warm flesh, felt her breath, as she inhaled her scent, the old familiar fragrance of Shalimar that would always be Johanna. How many times in the intervening years had she smelled her perfume on a stranger, in a theater, at a party, and had had to turn away as her heart broke?

"Oh, Momma," Sam cried into Johanna's curls. "Momma, Momma."

"Baby. Sugar. Sammie. I was so afraid you wouldn't come."

Sam pulled back and gazed into Johanna's eyes, and it was like looking into her own. She saw fear there. Love. Longing. Worlds whirling. An ocean of need.

"I *had* to come." Sam heard her own voice, ragged.

"I prayed you would. But I didn't have any right to hope. Not after all this time."

Then, somehow, they were on the sofa, their knees touching, their hands entwined.

"If you only knew," Johanna began, "how many times I've dreamed of this moment. How many times I wanted to call you." She stopped. "I did, actually," she whispered. "I called you hundreds of times."

"I don't know what you mean, Momma. When?"

"I never spoke to you, though. I called and hung up."

"When? Where?"

"In Atlanta, before you went off to school. Then when you were at Stanford. And in San Francisco. After you went back home to George's. In Covington."

Sam was stunned. "You always knew where I was? But why didn't you . . . ?"

Johanna raised a thin hand. "I couldn't, baby. I couldn't. It wasn't even safe to call."

"What do you mean, not 'safe'?"

Johanna shook her head and rushed on. "I had to hear your voice, just once in a while. I'd try not to, but then, sometimes my need was like an addiction; I couldn't stand it anymore. I'd listen to your hello. I'd listen to your breathing. And then I'd hang up."

How many times, Sam wondered, over the years, had she picked up a phone to silence? Hung up, thinking it was a child, a prankster, a pervert? Had she ever once thought that the caller might be Johanna?

Never.

She'd dreamed of Johanna and her father a million times, constantly at first, then less often. But she had never really thought they might still be alive, that her mother might be reaching out, listening to her breath on a telephone receiver as she'd once leaned over her, tucked in her little girl at night.

"Momma?" Sam reached forward and brushed a silvered curl from Johanna's forehead. "Why did you say, not safe to call? What happened to you? Where have you been? Why was it not safe?"

Johanna's face crumpled. "Oh, Sugar," she began, then stopped. "I can't tell you how I've dreamed of this meeting. How many nights I lay awake thinking how I'd tell you everything, if we were ever lucky enough to arrive at this moment." Johanna stroked Sam's hand. "I've been so proud of you, baby. You've come so far. You've done so much."

Sam drew a long breath. *Easy does it.* The AA slogan wasn't just a bumper sticker. It was way of living your life. And Johanna seemed so fragile. She might shatter if pushed.

"*Are* you proud of me, Momma?" Sam asked. "Well, you always said that I could be anything I wanted to be."

"Oh, yes!" Johanna's dark eyes lit up. "I knew that you could. You were so bright, so full of life."

"Remember when I wanted to be a train engineer? And you said, 'Fine, okay, Sammie, if that's what you want, I'm sure you'll make a wonderful engineer.' "

Johanna laughed. "I thought then, My God, what have I done? But your daddy said . . ." Johanna stopped and took a deep breath. "He said that there was no harm in it. That *he'd* wanted to be a lion tamer in the circus when he was a little boy."

Now it was Sam's turn to laugh. "And he almost was, wasn't he? Isn't that what being a partner in Simmons and Lee was like?"

"Absolutely. I can't tell you how many nights he came home, bloodied to the hip. Not really, but you know what I mean."

Then they were both quiet.

Finally, Sam said, "Did Daddy . . . ?"

"Yes, Sugar. Your daddy died in the crash."

A stone rolled from Sam's chest. "And you . . . ?"

"I was never on the plane. I didn't make the flight."

Another silence followed. It stretched and stretched until Sam thought it might snap back and slap her in the face. She wanted to know *everything*, to let all her questions pour out. But she cautioned herself once more: Take baby steps. Don't push. Let Johanna come to it in her own time. So she stayed on safe ground, saying, "Do you remember, Momma, when I was going through my train phase, and you took me on the Crescent City to New Orleans?"

Johanna clapped her hands, and the showers of silver bracelets on both her wrists danced. "Oh, my," she said, "wasn't that the loveliest time?"

"I had a little red traveling coat and a matching hat with cherries on it."

"I can't believe you remember that. You were only—"

"Seven. It was Easter and I was in the second grade. We went to visit—what was her name, your girlhood friend from Asheville?"

"Anita. She married a man named LaRose."

"You know, when I moved to Louisiana, a couple of years ago, those same places we visited on that trip—Jackson Square and that wonderful statue of Old Hickory on his horse, Canal Street, ever so much wider than Peachtree, the Cabildo with Napoleon's death mask—well, it was exactly as I had remembered."

"Sammie, Sammie." Johanna's face was flushed. She looked ever-so happy.

"And we had dinner at Galatoire's, do you remember? And oysters at the Acme."

"I do. I do. Everyone thought it was so odd to see such a small girl slurping down raw oysters." Johanna laughed, having the time of her life. She asked, "Are *you* happy there, Sam, in Covington, in your house? And what about your Harry?"

"How do you *know* all these things?" Then a cold finger poked at Sam's insides. Had George been in touch with Johanna over the years? How *could* he? Or Peaches? Or Horace?

Johanna read her thoughts. "No one you know, Sammie. Don't ever think that. Strangers. Private investigators I hired to let me know about you."

"But . . ."

"Please. I know you want to know everything. I want to *tell* you. That's why I called you here." Johanna faltered then. "*Mostly* why I called you here. But, please—" She stood. She was so tiny. She looked like a child as her hands flew to her mouth. "Please, try to be patient with me."

"I'm trying, but I have so many questions, Momma." Then Sam's own voice broke.

"Don't cry. I can't stand it if you do." Johanna's mouth trembled. She grew more agitated with each moment.

Sam stood from the sofa. "I won't. I promise. Now, don't be upset."

"I'm *not* upset." But Johanna's voice spiraled higher and higher, almost out of control. "I'm—oh, Christ, what *am* I? I'm . . . dear God. I'm nothing. I'm lower than . . . Why did I think I could do this?"

"Momma." Sam reached for her.

"No! Don't!" Johanna shied away. Her eyes were wild. "Don't, don't pity me. I'll burn in hell for what I've done, I know that. But I can't stand pity. Not from you. I've injured you beyond repair. I can't stand that, because I loved you more than the world. You . . ."

Sam would never hear the end of that sentence, as the phone rang and Johanna jumped to answer it. "Yes?" she said, her dark eyes wide. They grew even wider, the irises completely encircled in white, as she listened. One hand flew to her throat. Finally, still not having said a word, she hung up the phone, then wheeled toward the bathroom.

"Momma?" Sam said, but Johanna just shook her head and fended off Sam's words with a hand. She closed the door behind her. Sam could hear the medicine cabinet opening, then closing, the sound of scrabbling, then water running. "Are you all right?" she called. There was no answer. Maybe Johanna couldn't hear her. She tried again. "Do you need me?"

When Johanna reappeared in the bathroom door, her eyes were dull holes. Sam thought she had never seen a sadder face. It broke her heart. "Momma," she said, "what can I do for you? You said in your letter that you needed help."

Johanna shook her head. "I can't do this now. That was . . . a business matter. Something I . . . I'm sorry, Sammie." She faltered. "I'm not doing this very well. I . . . this has been harder than I thought it would be. I'm so ashamed." She dropped her gaze.

"Momma, Momma." Sam reached out for Johanna's hands. Sticks beneath flesh. "Would you like to take a little break? Rest for a bit?"

Johanna nodded.

"Why don't you do that? I'll come back later. Maybe we could have dinner?"

Johanna raised her eyes, and they gobbled at Sam's face. "Yes, yes," she said eagerly. "A late dinner. We'll do that. Then I'll answer all your questions. I'll tell you everything."

Sam gently folded the tiny woman into her arms and held her to her breast. "Oh, Momma. There's so much I want to know. We'll talk and talk and talk. We'll stay up all night."

"Yes," Johanna whispered. "Yes, we will. All night,

just like girlfriends." She clung to Sam for a very long time, the two of them breathing together, mother and daughter, even their hearts once more in sync. Then, suddenly, Johanna let go. She took three steps back and gazed once more into Sam's face with her terrible ruined eyes, eyes so much like Sam's, eyes that had seen God knows what. "Now, you go, Sugar," she whispered, pointing toward the door. "My precious baby."

"I'll call you later, Momma. You get some rest."

5

Out of here was Sam's first thought, back in her room. She needed fresh air, space to think. So it was on with her shorts, a T-shirt, and running shoes. She gave Harpo a snuzzle and said, "Guard the room, sweet pea. I'm going for a walk. Answer the phone if your grandmomma calls."

"Up that way," the man behind the desk said. The mysterious Estela was nowhere in sight. "Then cross Paseo de Peralta. You'll see the sign at Canyon. Head up it. And, if you're feeling like a *real* walk, make the dogleg at the top onto Upper Canyon. It's about three, maybe four miles altogether to the nature preserve at the end of the road. Grand view of the sunset."

Canyon Road proved to be a good workout, all uphill, much of it without sidewalks. The lower part of the narrow street was Tourist Land: a plethora of galleries brimming with Southwestern art, coyote-filled boutiques, a sprinkling of chic restaurants. Then the commercial area petered out, giving way to old adobe residences. Sam stopped to peek through a wisteria-draped wooden door, so small one would have to stoop to enter. Inside she spied a burbling fountain and a lovely garden bounded on the far side by the acequia, the ancient irrigation ditch. Planted on either side of the grassy lawn were an old adobe house and a two-story guest cottage. A yellow-eyed cat stared at her from a derelict wicker recliner and said, *"Murph."*

"Murph, yourself," Sam answered, walking on.

The picturesque neighborhood provided a momentary distraction, but her thoughts didn't stray long from Johanna. With every step she thought, Johanna is alive! She lives! Sam had actually put her hands on Johanna's living flesh, heard her voice, felt her tears.

But how naive you were, she thought, to believe that if you saw your momma, if she really was alive, suddenly you would know everything.

Now she had even more questions.

What did Johanna mean, it wasn't safe to call? Why had Johanna refused her help? Patience. It was the hardest lesson of all for her, but she'd have to try. She pumped on up the hill, dodging a red Ford Explorer. Then, suddenly, she remembered, she hadn't called George. Oh, shit. Poor George. He ought to disown her.

She'd dial him the moment she got back to the hotel. Yep, right after she'd gained the top of the hill, the end of the road, the nature preserve, tra-la. For Sam was so energized, the knowledge that her mother lived singing like a lark in her heart, that she felt she could go forever. Except for the fact that she was having a little trouble breathing. This altitude was a killer, all right. At seven thousand feet, the air got mighty thin.

Nevertheless Sam bounded uphill past the very last of the antique shops. Up ahead she could see the top of Canyon where it intersected with another road. This must be the dogleg the desk clerk had mentioned.

Then, picking up the pace, she almost went ass-over-teakettle, a loose shoelace the culprit. Squatting before the playground of an elementary school to retie her shoes, she found herself facing a sky alight with pink, gold, and scarlet. If this sunset had been wired for sound, she'd have been listening to a chorus of trumpets. It was really something.

She stepped up onto a low wall to get a better view of the rays bouncing off the low adobes. This was pretty sensational, all right. The only sunsets she'd seen that came close were those out behind the Golden Gate.

Had Johanna ever been to San Francisco? she wondered, her thoughts looping back to her mother again. I was there for fifteen years, and she knew that. Plenty of time for her to come and take a look. I could have passed her in the street, sat across from her in a café.

Hit the road, girl, she told herself. Up and at 'em. She found an easy pace, then just a way beyond the school, came upon Cristo Rey Church. Set back from the road, it was an odd structure, adobe, as was almost everything in Santa Fe, but lumpy and strangely stolid. Even its twin towers couldn't change the church's resemblance to a huge brown elephant mired in a bog of blacktop.

Sam crossed the street, the church behind her now, and began the march up Upper Canyon. This was a less-populated lane, more steep and narrow than the lower road, its margins crowded with small trees, tall grasses, and pale white-green chamiso. There was no sidewalk, and in many places, no shoulder. She would have to be careful.

Then, as if the driver had heard her thoughts, a car hurtled down the hill toward her, spraying gravel. Sam jumped and glued herself to a mailbox. How many pedestrians had been squashed on this road? There was no room to hide, no place to run. Maybe I ought to stop right here, she thought, turn around and head back for the hotel. Give George a call before I go see Momma again.

But there was that part of Sam that, once having set

a goal, couldn't rest until it was met. So she leaned into her pace as the grade grew steeper, her feet eating up the dust. Then, to her right, a beauty of a long, low log house appeared as if a reward for her efforts.

A quarter mile more and an Italianate villa sat close-by the road's left verge, complete with an arching colonnade, trellises, an arcaded gallery. Perhaps up here, above the town, there was a little slack in the all-adobe building code. Half a mile further, she came upon a Victorian extravaganza trimmed in rococo carpenter Gothic. Then the road turned, and a sign warned that the passage to the nature center was not a thoroughfare. The nature center itself was a simple white frame house. It was locked and empty. But the surroundings were, as the desk clerk had promised, worth the trip. This was a lovely retreat, tranquil and still, perched high on the hills and surrounded by tall trees. Only three miles from the plaza, Sam felt deep in the country. Hawks circled. Huge black crows fussed on power lines. Probably, if she stood long enough, rabbits, raccoons, deer, coyotes, maybe a mountain lion, would cross her path.

But she didn't have time to wait for them. You did it, she said to herself. You reached the top. Now, put it in gear. Head back down. Call George. And then, then, you get to see your momma again.

Sam began to sprint. So what if her knees were feeling their forty-two years? What was a little pain? She was going to see Johanna. They'd go to dinner, out of the hotel. She'd order Johanna a nice wine, and then they'd talk. We'll laugh and talk and talk and laugh, she thought, until the sleepy waiters throw us out on our ears. Then we'll sit in the plaza and talk some more while the moon rises, the stars shine and then begin to fade. We'll stay up till dawn, trading tales like Kitty and I used to do at Stanford, sitting in the swings in a kids' playground. We'll talk until we're hoarse. We'll talk until we can't anymore, not because we've run out of words, but rather out of breath. Then, finally, we'll tumble into bed, and tomorrow we'll rise, after happy dreams, for more talk over coffee and croissants.

Were there ever in the world two women who had so much talk to talk?

Her attention back to the road, Sam realized that her walk had taken longer than she'd planned. Night was gathering fast, and the darkness here in the high desert was quite profound. Her white T-shirt and the small strip of reflector on her running shoes weren't going to provide her much protection.

Dodging bushes, she scooted down the graveled pavement. She didn't want to step in a hole, twist an ankle, bang her already fluky knees.

She was making fairly good time, when a car came whizzing downhill behind her. She turned just in time to see that the driver was cutting it much too close on the narrow road. She jumped to the shoulder to avoid being smashed, and down she went.

She was sliding, gliding. She'd leapt over the verge of the road and was slipping down a gravel drive. Then she lost her balance and grabbed for anything, anything at all to stop her fall, but nothing came to hand. She was going, going, going, gone, scraping skin from knees, palms, her right cheek.

Finally she rolled to a halt. She froze for a moment, stunned, then registered the pain. *Damn!* she hurt. Damnit to hell! She rocked back and forth. She flailed. She howled, but even that didn't help.

The good news was nothing seemed to be broken.

Can I walk? Now, there was the question. She had to get back to town. Okay, give it a try, she said to herself, and managed to make it to her feet. Then her knees folded up on her, and she plopped back down again.

Okay. She'd just sit here until the hurting let up a bit. It couldn't last forever. Could it?

Whooo boy. She felt like a fool. *Everybody* knew it was stupid to walk alone in a semideserted area after nightfall. It was exactly the sort of thing that your mother would warn you against.

Okay. Chalk it up to one more thing she and Johanna could laugh about when she got back to the hotel.

Then, from way down the dark driveway, Sam heard a door slam.

"Hey!" she yelled. "Hello? Hello?" Someone was home down there, though from where she sat in the darkness, she couldn't see a house. There had to be one. Maybe she could use their phone, call for a taxi to pick her up and take her back to La Fonda.

An engine cranked.

And the reality of her situation dawned. Oh, God. She was lying in the middle of the driveway, and whoever that was inside the vehicle, it was certain they were headed up this way. She'd better move, and be quick about it, or she was going to be roadkill.

Sam scuttled, half-scooted, half-clawed her way to the side of the drive, but not quickly enough to escape. Headlights sped like a shot toward her up the graveled lane. The vehicle was headed right for her. There was no escape.

I'm going to die, she thought, throwing her arms over her head. The engine raced closer. Gravel sprayed. Dear God, she prayed, I don't want to hurt. Let me go quickly. Run over my head.

Then brakes screeched and gravel spun, and, three inches from her face, the shiny bumper of a pickup truck shuddered to a halt.

Praise the Lord and thank you, Jesus, Sam breathed.

The truck's door opened, then slammed. Sam heard a

crunch of gravel, and someone said, *"Madre de Dios,"* over and over again.

"Oh, my God," Sam breathed.

"I can't believe it's you," came the answer

"*I* can't believe I'm alive."

And, maybe she wasn't, for what Sam saw through the glare of the headlights seemed to be the face of an angel. Beautiful and slight, dark, young, maybe twenty years of age, the angel hovered over her. Yes, Sam said to herself, she was dead for sure. This was Saint Peter come to carry her home.

"Give me your hand," said the angel.

Sam tried, but the going was tough. Her synapses weren't connecting very well.

"No problem," he said. "I'll carry you."

"I don't think that's such a good idea," she managed. She was a lot of woman at five foot eight, a hundred and thirty-nine pounds, even for someone with superhuman strength. Angels were superhuman, weren't they?

Then the beautiful young man took her into his arms and wafted her into the cab of his ancient truck.

She registered the truck's interior in a daze. It was like being in a chapel festooned with religious bric-a-brac. A black-and-silver rosary dangled from the rearview mirror. Our Lady of Guadalupe stood on the dash.

"My name is Jesus." *Hey-soos*. He stuck out his hand.

"I'm Sam, and God bless your brakes."

Jesus's smile was a knockout. Then he crossed himself and looked heavenward. "Thank you, Blessed Mother, for sending me this Sam." This kid wasn't kidding. The dome light lit his dark head like a halo. He said, "I've dreamed of you every night for many years, Miss Sam. Every single night."

"Jesus," she answered, "I really appreciate your not running me down, and I'd love a lift into town, but I'm not the woman of your dreams. For starters, I'm way too old."

He laughed. "No, no, you don't understand. This is not a dream about love. It's about finding me and my art and shining a spotlight on us. You, Miss Sam, were sent by Our Lady to make me famous."

Great. This was just great. While Johanna waited for her back at the hotel, she was sitting in a pickup in the middle of nowhere with a religious fanatic.

But she could handle it. As a reporter, she'd known all flavors of crazy. "Jesus," she said, "you drive me to La Fonda, I'll be happy to make you famous."

His lovely face grew sad. "You think I joke, don't you? I'm not joking, Miss Sam."

"Absolutely. I can see that you're not. But could we talk about this another time? I really need to do something about these cuts and scrapes. Plus, I'm late for an appointment."

"Certainly, Miss Sam." Jesus cranked the truck's ignition, and they rolled up the lane. "I'm sorry. I wasn't thinking."

"No, no, and I don't mean to be rude. I'd love to see your art, some other time."

"You are sitting in my art! This Chevy—it's a cherry 1948—it is one of my canvases!" Jesus stepped on the brake. "You want to get out for a minute and have a look?"

Sam said thanks, but she'd take a rain check.

Sure, sure. Jesus understood. It was too dark now anyway. But how about tomorrow? Was she busy tomorrow?

6

In her room once more, Sam bathed and dressed her wounds. They weren't nearly as bad as they'd seemed when she was alone, in the dark. Then she dialed Johanna's room. The line was busy. A few minutes later, she tried again. Still busy. Whom was Johanna talking with? she wondered.

Over the next half hour, Sam tried a half-dozen times. Busy, busy, busy.

Patience, she cautioned herself.

Harpo stared up at her, a look of urgency on his pug face. Right, she said. Walkies. So she ran Harpo down for a quick turn around the plaza. Now, she said, as she returned to her room and dialed Johanna's number once more. Now the line will be clear.

But it wasn't. Maybe something was wrong with Johanna's phone. That was it. She dialed O. "Is it possible that four-oh-nine is out of order?"

The snippy Estela was back. "Ms. Hilton has requested that she not be disturbed. So we've switched her phone off. That's why you're getting the busy signal."

"But I'm her daughter."

"Sorry, Ms. Adams. She explicitly said, 'No one.' No

calls to be put through. She did, however, leave a message for you."

"Oh, good." Sam waited.

"Do you want to pick this up, or do you want me to read it to you?"

Read it, sweetheart. This Estela was really getting on her nerves.

"Okay. 'Dearest Sugar. I'm so terribly sorry, darling, but I can't do this now. I want you to leave, to go back home. Please do this for me, now. Right now, immediately. It's important that you leave Santa Fe this very night. I'll be in touch very soon. All my love for now and always. Johanna.' "

What? Sam's ears rang with disbelief. This had to be some kind of joke. "Excuse me," she finally managed to say to Estela, "*who* left that message?"

"Your mother. Didn't you hear what I just read?"

"Yes, but, she wouldn't have done that."

"She did, Ms. Adams. I took the message myself. It was definitely from Ms. Hilton. Now, if there's nothing else I can do for you, I have another call." With that, Estela broke the connection.

Sam stood for a long moment staring at the receiver in her hand. This was crazy. This was nuts. Johanna'd risen from the dead, spent half an hour with her, then brushed her off? Sent her packing? Go home. Go away. Don't bother me anymore. No way. Sam refused to believe it. Refused to stand for it, furthermore.

"I'll be right back," she said to Harpo, who sighed and gave her his poor-pitiful-Pearl look.

Two minutes later Sam was pounding on Johanna's door, but to no avail. There was nothing but silence from 409. Still, Sam didn't give up. She knocked and called Johanna's name until the man in the room next door poked his head out. "Do you mind?"

"I'm sorry. I was supposed to meet my mother, and she's not answering."

The man shrugged. "Maybe you want to leave her a note?"

Clearly, she couldn't continue pounding on the door. Sam took his offered pen and paper and scrawled, *"Johanna, please call. Sam. Room 202."* She slipped it under the door.

Back in her room, she tried the number again.

It was still busy.

Sam paced back and forth across the room, Harpo eyeing her solemnly. This is insane, she thought. What is *wrong* with Johanna?

Something, clearly. A lot. But, then, what did she expect from a woman who had dropped off the face of the earth for thirty-four years? Sam was getting pissed.

How could she have let herself be so bamboozled? She cringed at the thought of her walk, Mommy stars in her eyes. Okay, so the woman she'd talked with was Johanna, but who the hell was that? Surely not the same woman who'd been her mom when she was eight. Who *knew* what this Johanna was up to? What she was all about?

Well, she couldn't sit here and stew all alone. She had to talk with someone. *George.* Of course, who else? George, her old sweetie, her numero uno, her port in every storm.

Wasn't it a shame she couldn't call him and give him the great news, Johanna lives, without adding the P.S.: *But she's gone into hiding again. Has insisted that I leave. She's a major jerk. Or nut.*

George said, "It really *is* Johanna? Isn't that something! My dear, I am *so* glad you went. Don't give a thought to her pulling away for a bit. I'm sure, whatever her story, the circumstances—well, sweetie, she's probably just overcome. She needs a little time to gather herself, to regroup, to be her very best for you. And, do remember, sweetheart, however much she wanted to see you, this thing has got to take time. Now, you just get yourself a good night's sleep and don't worry about a thing."

"But, George . . ."

"Nope. No 'ifs,' 'ands,' or 'buts.' No worrying about me either, I can hear *that* in your voice. The party's not until Sunday, Sammie, and besides which, even if you don't make it, I'll still be here. I'm *way* too old to give a second thought to any of this birthday nonsense."

Dear George. Dear old sweetheart.

"Have you talked to Harry?" he asked, just as she was signing off.

"Harry?"

"He called last night from San Francisco, said he wanted to see if you'd arrived here safely. I told him about Johanna, that you'd headed for Santa Fe. I hope you don't mind."

"Oh, George."

"I know. I know. I shouldn't have. But, damnit, Sam, I like the man. I thought you were great together. Now, enough, I know it's none of my beeswax. This crazy-ass adventure he's off on, river-rafting in China. Can you beat that?"

"George, George."

"*And* I gave him your number in Santa Fe, for which I'm not apologizing. So there. He said he'd give you a call when he arrives in Hong Kong."

She had to admit, talking with Harry right now wouldn't be the worst thing in the world. She'd lean on *any* broad shoulder about now. It had been an awfully long day, and just thinking about its ups and downs was exhausting. "Fine, George," she said. Then thanked him for listening, for always being there.

"Where else would I be?"

She hung up and decided to call it a night. It was only eight o'clock, nine in New Orleans, but she was absolutely poleaxed by fatigue. She ordered a bite from room service and ran herself a hot bath. She hadn't heard a word from Johanna when she drifted off to sleep. . . .

In Sam's dreams, Johanna was thirty again, the same age she'd been when the plane had crashed and burned in Paris. Sam was eight. Wearing sandals and a yellow sundress, she was watching Johanna paint in the sunroom of their ivy-covered red brick house on Atlanta's Lullwater Road. Johanna's canvas was the roof of Uncle George's ancient black Lincoln, which had somehow been transported up the stairs. Sam could never quite see the painting, but Johanna, waving her paintbrush, described it to her. She was painting her autobiography, she said, and the big car was the perfect canvas for her action-adventure tale.

"It was *so* romantic, Sugar, living abroad. I lived everywhere during those years. Paris, St. Petersburg, Venice, Palermo, Barcelona, Ibiza, Marrakesh. The colors, the textures, the architecture, the smells! I saw everything and met everyone worth meeting, even though I was a little old to be on the hippie trail."

"But why didn't you take me with you?"

"Oh, Sugar, I thought about it. I thought about you every day, I promise, but it was no life for a child."

"Didn't you miss me?"

"Of course I did. Desperately. And I kept tabs on you all the while. You don't know that, but I did." Johanna ran a hand through Sam's thick curls, smearing them with scarlet paint. "It's so hard to explain. Once you're *out* there, well, you're just out there. An adventure like that comes along only once in a lifetime. I'm so sorry if that hurt your feelings, but, your being on your own, it built character, don't you think?"

Hell, no, Sam was about to say, but just then, her father, wearing full evening dress, came twirling into the room. In his arms he held a tall dark woman wearing the most luscious taffeta ball gown the color of candlelight. A wide ruff encircled her bronze shoulders, and from her waist flared acres of rustling fabric. Daddy whirled her around, and Sam saw that his partner was Rosey Bird, the Indian woman from the plaza. The Frito pie queen. Rosey and her dad laughed into one another's eyes.

"Daddy, what are you doing?" Sam asked.

"Shhhhhhh," her mother warned. "Don't disturb him. He's having such a good time. And he can't hear you anyway. He's too drunk."

"Alcohol doesn't make you deaf," Sam protested. But she knew very well it did. It blunted your perceptions of the world. Blurred the things you'd just as soon miss.

"Oh, Sugar," Johanna said, "the things that you don't know."

"Then tell me."

"All right. I'll start with the last time I saw your father in Paris. We were staying at the Ritz . . ."

Sam could see that hotel room. High ceilings. Empire furnishings. Lots of gilt. Paris was outside the windows, tender with the pale blue light of late spring. But what was that terrible noise? Banging, banging, banging?

"Shhh," Sam said. "I can't hear what Momma is saying."

"Miss Adams. Open the door, please."

"You remember, don't you, Sammie, how Daddy was when he was drinking?" Johanna asked.

"Miss Adams. Are you there?"

Harpo was nuzzling her. He wanted to go downstairs to the Ritz's dining room. The waiters, who loved him, served him liver and chicken. Harpo was crazy about the Ritz.

But what was *with* this pounding? It was *shocking* in a hotel this grand. Even Harpo thought so. He, who rarely spoke, barked. Once. Twice. A third time.

Suddenly, then, Sam jerked into consciousness. It took her a moment to realize where she was. Not in Paris. Not in the Ritz. She was in La Fonda Hotel in Santa Fe, New Mexico. She grabbed the bedside clock. Nine-thirty—A.M. or P.M.? She leapt from her bed. *Ow!* She'd forgotten about her knees. She limped over to the window and threw open the blackout curtains. The sunlight was blinding. It was morning. The banging was at her door.

"Just a minute." She reached for her robe. "Who is it?"

"Detective Victor Vigil." *Vee-hill.* "Santa Fe Police."

THROUGH THE DOOR, AROUND THE SAFETY CHAIN, POKED A hand holding a badge.

"You're with the police?" Sam was still half asleep.

"Yes, Miss Adams. Miss Samantha Adams?"

"That's right."

"Here's my ID." The plastic card showed a round-faced Hispanic man sporting a handlebar mustache. Late thirties, early forties. "Could you open the door, please?

What the heck was this? Sam rubbed her eyes, pulled her robe more tightly about her body, and let the man in.

"Sorry to disturb you." Victor Vigil looked around the room as he entered. Harpo stared at him, showing his underbite. "The dog friendly?"

"Usually."

At that, Harpo turned his head, feigning fascination with the wall.

"How can I help you?" Sam asked.

"Do you mind if I sit?"

"Of course not. I'm sorry. Please, take a chair."

Detective Vigil settled himself spread-legged. The man's gut bulged over his belt. His navy sport jacket and beige polyester slacks were tired and strained, purchased a couple dozen pounds earlier, Sam would guess.

"So, what's on your mind this morning, Detective Vigil?" Sam, carefully pulling her robe over her legs as she sat, took the other chair. The man's eyes made her aware that she was naked beneath the robe except for her T-shirt.

"You can tell me, do you know a Johanna Hall? Registered in this hotel as—" He pulled a greasy notebook from his pocket. "Johanna Hilton?"

The moment he'd said the first syllable of Johanna's name, Sam's heart had begun to pound. Something was wrong. Something had happened to Johanna. "Yes, I do. Is she all right?"

"So you *do* know her?"

"Yes. Of course I do. She's my mother. You must know that. Why else would you be here?"

"Do you know why she's using the name Hilton?"

"Detective Vigil." Sam could hear her voice rising. "Please tell me, has something happened to my mother? Is she ill?"

"So you can't explain the alias."

Sam wasn't liking this man one bit, but then she'd never liked bullies. "I don't know why she was using Hilton. Or Hall. Her name, actually, is Johanna Hewlett Adams." Or maybe it wasn't, Sam realized, as she said the words. Johanna could have remarried. She could have legally adopted another name. "Now, tell me, Detective, what's your concern about my mother? Is she in trouble? Has something happened to her?"

"You're saying her name's not Hall? Well, isn't that something?" Vigil's eyebrows rose. "We don't get much of that around here. Now, your lowlifes, your ex-cons, they might have a whole string of aliases, but not your nice Anglo ladies. Except for the nut jobs, of course. The psychics—fancy fortune-tellers is all they are—they call themselves Moonmaiden Morningstar, like that." Vigil fingered his mustache and stared at Sam's bandaged knees, peeking out from her robe. "You hurt yourself, Miss Adams?"

Sam rose to her feet. "I slipped and fell, Detective Vigil. I'm fine. Thank you for your concern. Except that my blood pressure's going right off the chart. Won't you please get to the point?" She knew in her heart that something terrible had happened to Johanna. Johanna had become ill. *That's* why she hadn't answered the door, and Sam hadn't persisted. She'd failed Johanna, and now . . .

"That's a shame," said Vigil. "Hate to see a pretty woman like yourself get so upset."

Sam blinked. What the hell was *with* this jerk? Was he *flirting* with her? Or was he trying to frighten her? She'd met more than her share of bent cops in her crime-writing days, including one Georgia sheriff who'd tried to feed her to his pit bulls. Well, whatever this one's game, she wasn't playing. "Detective Vigil, could we cut to the chase? Please? I'm afraid you're trying my patience, which I'm in short supply of on my best days."

Vigil let his pudgy fingers ramble across her Filofax, which was sitting on a table beside him. He looked as if he wanted to flip it open, read it cover to cover. And if he did, what would he be looking for? He glanced back to Sam. "Can you tell me what time you last saw her? Mrs. Hall, I mean? Mrs. Adams, I guess you'd call her."

That was it. Sam shotgunned her words: "Six o'clock last night."

"I see. You have any idea why she's staying in this hotel?"

"No."

"So you don't know why she wasn't staying in her own house?" Vigil consulted his dingy notebook once more. "On Upper Canyon Road. You did know that, didn't you? That that's where she lives?"

"No, I did not."

"Why's that?"

"I hadn't seen her for years. She didn't tell me her address. She asked me to meet her here in this hotel. I did and—"

Vigil interrupted. "Yesterday, at six, that's what you said?"

"Yes, we met for twenty minutes. Half an hour." She heard her answers growing longer. She was trying to explain what had happened, not to him, but to herself.

"And did you see her, your mama, again after that? After six?"

"No, I didn't. I *tried* to. After our visit, I went for a long walk up Canyon Road. I fell down. I skinned my knees. A nice man gave me a ride back here, whereupon I called my mother, but she didn't answer. In fact, I rang the desk, and they said she didn't want to be disturbed. I knocked on her door, but she didn't answer. Then I went to sleep."

"Didn't want to be disturbed? Huh. That's strange, don't you think? Not even by her daughter?"

"That's what the desk clerk said."

"Did you have an argument with your mother, Samantha?"

Ms. Adams, she thought, Ms. Adams to you, jerk. "No, I did not."

"But you hadn't seen her in a very long time, yet you only visited together for twenty, thirty minutes at the most?"

"It was an emotional meeting which my mother found exhausting. So we cut it short, agreeing to meet again later in the evening."

"But then you didn't."

"No. That's what I said."

"Because she wouldn't take your phone call. Or answer her door."

"That's right."

"So what did you do then?"

"I told you. I walked my dog. I had a bath, ordered dinner from room service, and went to sleep."

"You weren't worried about your mother?"

"I was puzzled. And, yes, I was concerned."

"But not enough to call the manager? Not enough to insist that someone open her door?"

"Detective Vigil, *why* are you here? Would you please tell me?"

His answering grin made her feel dirty—and a little frightened. This man was more than irritating; he was malevolent.

"You didn't have a fight?" Vigil let his gaze rest once more on Sam's knees. The scrape on her cheek.

"Are you asking if I hit my mother? Beat her up? Smashed her over the head with a lamp? No, I didn't do any of those things."

"That's very interesting, your answer. Are you often violent with your mother, Samantha?"

"I told you that I hadn't seen my mother in a long time. Since I was eight years old, to be exact. So I would have to say, no, I'm not often *anything* with her."

"Well, that's something, isn't it? Not since you were eight years old, how about that? Why *was* that?"

She stared at him, thinking, Fuck you, Jack. I'm not answering that question. And I'm not dealing with you, asshole, another single solitary moment. "Tell you what, Detective. I'm going to go upstairs and see about my mother. And then I'm going to call police headquarters and register a complaint."

"About me?" He laughed.

"Yes, about you. Your rudeness. Your bullying. Now, if you'll excuse me, please." She clucked to Harpo, who trotted toward her gladly. He clearly didn't like Vigil either.

"Just one more thing. Did you leave your mother a note?"

"Yes, I'm sure you know I did. Slipped it under her door. The man in the room next door to her can attest to that."

Vigil grinned. He had a gold cap on one of his two front teeth. "I see. Well, there you are."

"Where am I, Detective Vigil? Exactly where am I?"

Victor Vigil rose from his chair and sidled toward her until he was very close. Far too close. She stood her ground.

He said, "Where *are* you? Maybe in a little bit of trouble, maybe not."

Sam opened the door. She was up to *here* with this bastard.

"You might want to hold up a minute," he said.

"I don't think so."

"You go up there now, you're just gonna run into the crime-scene guys. They won't let you in."

Sam's heart skipped three beats.

"She's dead."

A great howling wind roared through Sam's head. I misheard him, she told herself. He didn't say what I thought he did.

"Upstairs." He pointed. "Chambermaid found the body this morning when she went to clean the room."

Sam's knees packed right up on her, and she stumbled back from the door and onto a chair. This was some kind of sick joke, right? Even somebody as slimy as this character wouldn't jerk her around while her mother lay cooling upstairs. The man was crazy; that's what it was. He'd escaped from a loony bin. He was impersonating a police officer. Any minute, someone, a *real* cop, was going to come and take him away.

He said, "I don't guess you know anything about this?"

"How did she die?" Sam choked the words out.

"I was hoping you'd be able to help us with that." Vigil licked his thumb and paged through his notebook as if he were looking for a clean page to write down her suggestions.

"Are you implying she didn't die of natural causes?"

"Woman dies in a hotel, cops are gonna be called. You ought to know that, Samantha. Smart reporter like yourself."

Sam didn't even register that last. "But does it *look* like foul play? Is that what you're saying?" And was *she* a suspect? Jesus, was *that* why the man was being such a horse's ass?

"Hard to tell. These suicide-looking things"—he waggled a hand—"you can't ever tell. Have to wait and see what the autopsy says."

Suicide? *Suicide?* Was it possible that her mother had risen from the dead and called her to Santa Fe to witness her suicide? No way! Forget it. The man *was* crazy. But, for all her refusal, a kaleidoscope of images filled her mind: Johanna hanging from the shower rod. Shot through the head. Sitting in a tub of scarlet water.

"Tell me," she demanded. "Tell me how she died."

Vigil didn't answer.

"Fuck you," Sam said. "Fuck you, Detective."

Victor Vigil smiled.

Sam sat on the sofa of her hotel room, her head in her hands. Tears gullied down her face.

Johanna was dead.

Dead again.

For thirty-four years, Johanna had lain in her grave. Then for about twelve hours, Sam's heart had sung. Johanna had risen from the dead. And for half an hour, Johanna had been alive to her. Sam had touched her. They'd laughed and cried. Now Johanna was gone, gone, gone again.

And Victor Vigil, she said to herself, that son of a bitch, won't even tell me how Johanna died.

Goddamnit! Sam screamed, and Harpo ran for cover. She grabbed him up and cooed to him. She wiped her tears atop his head; he licked her cheeks. He stared earnestly into her eyes. He needed to go out. She took him, or at least she thought she did. Back in her room, she didn't remember being outside. She paced. She couldn't sit. She couldn't focus on a single thought. She stared into her own eyes in the mirror, trying to see if she was losing her mind. Had she made this all up? Was she dreaming?

Then it dawned on her; all she had to do to know the truth was go upstairs. Then she'd know if Vigil lied. Why, she thought, licking a thumb and erasing tear tracks from her face, I bet Momma's sitting up there wondering where the hell I've gotten off to. Why I'm not drinking coffee with her. Why, I'm surprised she hasn't called me, said, Sugar, where . . .

The phone rang. Sam grabbed it up. "Momma?"

"No, darlin', I ain't your momma."

It was Lavert Washington. Harry's partner in the Rib Shack. A former running back at Grambling University, where Harry had once been The Only White Boy. One-time chef and chauffeur for Joey the Horse of the New Orleans mob. And one of the earth's best people.

"Oh, Lavert, I'm so glad it's you," she cried. "My mother's dead!"

"Whoa. Wait. Hold on. Harry told me about the letter you got from her. But you're saying she was dead when you got there?"

"No, No, I saw her yesterday. My momma. Johanna. She was alive. I think maybe this policeman's lying to me. I can't talk now. I have to go upstairs and see about her."

"What policeman? Never mind. Listen, Harry asked me to check on you, and I'm glad I did. I've got this uncle in Santa Fe. Earl Wisdom. I'll call him. Earl Wisdom. You'll be hearing from him. Earl Wisdom. Write it down."

Sam's heart fell as she stepped off the elevator onto the fourth floor. A uniformed police officer stood there, arms crossed, keeping watch. Down the hall, a trio of officers was gathered outside the open door of 409.

Damn. Damnit it to hell, Sam thought. But maybe it wasn't what it looked like. Maybe it was something else. A burglary. That's it, Momma's been robbed.

So, why did the man say she was dead?

Shut up, she told herself. Don't borrow trouble. Just go see for yourself.

"Can I help you?" The uniform blocked her way.

"My room's down there." Sam pointed. She could see the flash of photographs being shot inside 409. Not a good sign. Not good at all. But still . . . "Is there a problem, Officer?"

"Room number?" he asked.

"Four-eleven."

He pulled a list from a pocket. "Name?"

Shit. This wasn't going to work. But the uniform was still staring at the list instead of at her. Then, down the hall, she thought she caught a glimpse of Rosey Bird, the Indian woman she'd met on the plaza, waving her on. Rosey's face was very sad. Sam blinked, and Rosey was gone. Sam took off running for Johanna's door.

She almost made it too. Probably would have, if it hadn't been for her knees. Just before she reached Johanna's room, the uniform grabbed her from behind. "What the hell do you think you're doing, lady?" He had a good strong grip.

Sam struggled. "That's my mother's room. I want to see about my mother. Let me go!"

Victor Vigil appeared in the doorway of 409. He gave Sam a long look. "Problem, Officer?"

"No, sir. This woman refused to stop. Nothing I can't handle."

Vigil said, "She's the deceased's daughter. Says she doesn't have a clue about her mother's death. Isn't that right, Samantha?"

"Let me see her, you son of a bitch." Sam twisted back and forth, trying to get loose.

"You keep that up, we're gonna have to charge you with resisting arrest." Vigil ran a thumb across one end of his mustache.

"Arrest? Are you crazy? I want to see my mother."

"Forcing your way into a crime scene," Vigil drawled. "That's not something you want to be doing. Get you charged with . . ."

Before he could finish, a little old lady exited Johanna's room. She stopped, looked at Sam, then turned to Vigil. "For Christ's sakes, Victor," she said. "What the hell are you doing?" The woman, who looked to be in her seventies, was a study in mauve. She wore a forties-style dress complete with peplum, purple pumps with matching stockings, and a hat of orchid feathers atop her champagne curls.

"Stay out of this, Lo," Vigil growled.

"We most certainly will not." The woman had a deep Texas drawl. She cocked her head to one side and studied Sam. "Is this Johanna's daughter?"

Thank God, thought Sam. Thank God for *someone.* Anyone. "Yes, I am. I am. I'm Samantha Adams."

"Well, darlin'," said Lo, "we are *so* sorry about your momma." Then she stepped past Vigil and threw a pair of wiry arms around Sam. "Bert," she said to the uniform, "would you please get your hands off Ms. Adams before I slap you with a complaint for excessive force?"

Vigil nodded at Bert, and the man stepped back.

"Lorraine Ellen. Call us Lo," the little woman said, all the while patting Sam on the arm. "We're Johanna's lawyer. Do you want to see your momma, sweetheart? Is that what you came up here for?"

"Now, Lo," Vigil began.

"Don't you start with us, Victor Vigil. There is no reason on earth why this precious child can't see her poor momma except your own meanness and perversity, and you know that."

Vigil began making growling noises in his throat, but

before he could formulate his reply, Lo had slipped an arm through Sam's.

The picture inside Johanna's bedroom was all-too familiar. As a reporter, Sam had seen it hundreds of times. A technician in civilian clothes dusted for prints. Another collected something from Johanna's bedside table and dropped it in a plastic evidence bag. Another was shooting photographs.

Shooting photographs of the corpse lying on the bed.

Shooting photographs of Johanna.

That's what he was doing, the man with his back to her, the man with the camera in his hand. But Sam hadn't yet been able to make herself look at his subject. She stood frozen, arm in arm with Lo Ellen, the photographer blocking her view. Shielding her. Delaying that awful moment.

Sam stared at his back, at his navy gabardine jacket, and she was no longer in this room. A rainy night. San Francisco. Van Ness Avenue. Someone held her arm as cops in rain slickers performed their sad tasks for one of their own. Sean O'Reilly, chief of detectives, SFPD. Sean, her beloved. Tall, red-haired, rangy, his body lay crumpled on its side. He'd been mowed down by a hit-and-run driver, a drunk, it turned out, who'd run a red light.

"I can't look," she'd whispered. But she'd had to. Otherwise, she'd never have believed that someone as alive as Sean could be gone. She'd have forever been expecting him to come ripping around a corner, his raincoat flying, if only she could find the right corner.

"I can't look," she whispered now; and Lo said, "Come on, baby. Let us take you out of here. You don't have to look."

But, once again, she did. Oh, yes, Lord, she had to look. The reason rose up and filled her to almost bursting.

This time, I want to know for a certainty, beyond any reasonable doubt, that Johanna is really dead. Not pretend-dead, like three decades earlier. Not fake-dead. But positively dead.

This time I'll touch Johanna, listen for her breath, lay my fingers on the cold flesh. I'll make sure.

I'll be able to say, absolutely: Johanna's deceased, departed, expired, passed over, breathed her last, sung her swan song, gone to her final reward, kicked the bucket, cashed in her chips.

No doubt about it: Johanna's given up the ghost, signed off, checked out, gone west. She's headed for the big roundup. Popped off. Croaked. It's curtains for Johanna. Adios. Good-bye. Farewell.

This time would be the very last. Ain't no such thing as a third coming. *Don't come back no more, no more.* And I can take measures to make sure. Drill her with a silver bullet. Drape garlic around the bier. Wave a crucifix. Sprinkle holy water. Nail her coffin shut. Bang that sucker, hard. Use lots of big old nails.

Now the photographer moved, shifted around to his left, and there she was. There lay Johanna.

Johanna Hewlett Adams rested lightly in her bed, the covers pulled up over her chest. She was wearing a white nightgown. She looked as if she were sleeping.

Johanna had not hung herself from the shower rod. She had not blown out her brains with a gun. She had not slashed her wrists.

From the looks of it, Johanna had simply closed her eyes, and somewhere in the dark stillness of the night, taken her final leave.

"Momma," Sam cried. "Oh, Momma." A great sob

ripped its way through her insides. I can't bear this, she thought. I can't. I simply can't. Then she stumbled to the side of the bed and stretched a hand out to Johanna's cheek. Vigil lurched as if to stop her, but it was already done. Sam had touched her mother's flesh, and it was cold, oh so very cold.

9

Sometime later, back in her room, Sam climbed into bed. Harpo leaned his feet against the side of the mattress, and she picked him up and tucked him in with her. He sniffed her cautiously, all over. Could he smell death? What did it smell like to him? Then she began to cry again, and Harpo licked her face. She patted him, felt his soft little bones. He snuggled firmly against her hip and began to snore.

I'd give anything, she thought, if I could turn off my mind like that and simply disappear. But how can I do that? I close my eyes, and I'll see nothing but Momma. The two of us laughing yesterday about old times. Momma crying, upset. Momma lying dead. Momma, who Vigil said maybe committed . . . No, I'm not going there. I'm not thinking that word.

Go back home, Sam. Leave Santa Fe now. I want you to leave.

I could use a little help here, she thought. A drink. A drug. Something. Anything.

Opium. That would be good. She wanted to be Julie Christie in the movie *McCabe and Mrs. Miller,* lying on a shelf in an opium den. Mourning for her lover who'd been shot down, his blood making red flowers in the snow. Sam remembered Christie, at the end of the movie, taking a long pull on an opium pipe. The smoke had worked its magic on her sadness. You could see it in her face, as the hard edges, those sharp corners of reality that scrape and puncture and slash the soul, were smudged and blurred and greased by blossoms of limbo.

Oh, what she would give for some smoky surcease. Something to quiet her mind, to ease the chewing on her viscera. Of course, there was always her old friend Jack Daniel's. Now, there was an idea. Call up room service; ask for Jack. Not a good idea, but an idea nonetheless.

With that, her telephone sounded. *No.* Sam shook her head. Negatory, absolutely not. She crammed yet another pillow over her ears, but the ringing wouldn't stop.

"What?" Her voice sounded very far away to her, as if strained through fog soup.

"It's Lo Ellen. We're coming to visit with you. We're having some coffee sent up."

"Thanks. That's nice, but I'm going to pass."

A few minutes later, Lorraine Ellen was perched like a bright parrot at the edge of Sam's bed. Sam lay where she was, propped by pillows. Room service coffee and a plate of muffins sat between them. Harpo had sniffed the muffins and rolled back over. "Does a girl want to talk?" Lo asked.

"I don't know. Mostly I just want this to all go away."

"We know. It's miserable, isn't it?"

"Did you know about me, Lo? Did Johanna tell you she had a daughter?"

Johanna's lawyer nodded. "She told us about a week ago. Before that, we didn't even know a girl existed."

Sam stared at the tiny woman, trying to make sense

of what she was hearing. Lo Ellen spoke a strange language, especially when it came to pronouns.

Lo continued, "It was then Johanna asked us for a meeting. She wanted to talk about her will. She'd written it a long time ago. We had a copy of it, of course, being her lawyer. It left everything to one Samantha Adams. All her money, investments, the house, an old turquoise mine out on the edge of town. Now, we'd never known who this Ms. Adams was, but, then, it wasn't necessarily any of our business. This meeting, though—the one we're talking about—Johanna tells us that she's been thinking, maybe the will's not valid, seeing as how it's written using her alias. 'Johanna Hall,' she says, the name we've always known her by, that's bogus."

"And you'd never had any suspicion she wasn't who she said?"

"You could of knocked us over with a feather. But, you know, Johanna was very private."

Sam said, "I know very little about her, Lo. Until yesterday morning, I'd thought both Johanna and my father died in a plane crash in 1962." She explained about Johanna's letter coming to her house, their all-too-brief visit, the phone request that she leave Santa Fe. Then, this morning, Victor Vigil and his news.

"Good God! This is hard to believe." Lo washed her words down with a big gulp of her coffee. "And that Victor Vigil; we've half a mind to call his momma, Magdalena. She'd straighten Victor right out."

"I don't think so, Lo. You saw the way he was upstairs."

"And you don't know Magdalena Vigil." Then Lo sighed. "The whole police force hasn't been worth shooting since that big brouhaha a couple of years ago. The mayor brought in an Anglo woman as chief. Well, you can imagine, the good old boys on the force got their panties in a twist. Ran her out of town, and now Victor's older brother is the chief. Cops' attitude toward women wasn't exactly improved by the experience, particularly toward white Anglo women with *cojónes*."

"But the man doesn't even know me." Then Sam repeated Vigil's words: *Smart reporter like you.* "How'd he know that?"

"It's hard to imagine Victor doing his homework that quickly. But you never know."

"Johanna wouldn't have mentioned me to him?"

"We doubt it. Like we were saying, Johanna was *very* private. To the point, you might say, of being a little strange." Lo stopped. "Maybe you don't want to hear this now."

"No, no." Sam sat up straighter. "Tell me everything."

"Well, Johanna always kept very much to herself. Hardly socialized at all. We were friends, in addition to our professional relationship, but we knew zip about her past. You could ask a question; she'd give you a look, change the subject. Anyway, this meeting about the will, she says her name's Johanna Hewlett Adams. Samantha Adams, that's her daughter. Wants to make sure we understand that."

"Anything else?"

"Said she'd abandoned you when you were eight."

"Abandoned? That was the word she used?" Sam felt a huge bubble rise up in her chest. She swallowed hard. "What else?"

Lo shook her head. "Nothing. Didn't say why she'd used the alias. We have no idea of where she'd been, what she'd done, how she lived before she came to Santa Fe. Didn't know if she'd been in touch with you or not. She didn't say."

Sam said, "All *I* learned from our conversation yesterday was (a.) she was alive and (b.) my father did indeed die in the plane crash at Orly. Oh, *and* that Johanna had kept tabs on me for a long time. Seemed to know everything about me."

"Really? Did she say how?"

"Private investigators."

Lo sighed. "The hoops human beings make themselves jump through. The pain they cause themselves, as if just surviving this old universe weren't enough."

"There's so much I don't know. Like, why did she contact me now? I can't help but think that it has to somehow be related to why she died. Jesus!" Sam slammed her coffee cup into its saucer. "Look at it, Lo. After thirty-four years of playing possum, Johanna asks me to come to Santa Fe in a letter asking for help. She's staying in a hotel, registered under an alias, not the alias she's been using, Johanna Hall, but yet *another* one, J. Hilton."

"We know, but this doesn't mean—"

"Wait." Sam threw the covers back and climbed out of bed. She stood, ticking off the facts on her fingers. "When I'm talking to her yesterday, she says she called me from time to time. Never talked with me, of course. Hung up after hearing my voice. *'But,'* she says, *'it wasn't even safe to call.'* What does that mean?"

"That she was afraid she'd slip and speak and a girl would recognize her voice?"

Sam was pacing now. "Maybe. Maybe not. There's more. She says the reason she called me here is to answer my questions, but she puts it, *'Mostly'* to tell me everything. What did that *mostly* mean? Why else? For what other reason did she want me here? Because she was in trouble? Because she thought her life was in danger? Then she turns around and warns me off. Says I have to leave town immediately."

"Wait a minute. Where are we going here? Is a girl saying she thinks it's possible her mother's death *really* wasn't on the up and up?"

"Yes."

"That it wasn't suicide?"

"Definitely not."

"That she was murdered?"

Sam wheeled to face her mother's lawyer. "Yes, Lo, that's exactly what a girl is saying."

More coffee had been ordered. Sam sat on one end of the sofa now, Lo on the other. Harpo snoozed in the middle.

"Natural causes," said Lo.

"Let's hear your case."

"Extraordinary timing, we grant you, but there it is. Johanna asks her daughter to come, sees her once, then dies, happily, in her sleep."

"Of what?"

Lo's blonde curls trembled beneath the orchid feathers of her hat as she shook her head. "It doesn't wash, does it? Her health was tip-top. Looked fragile, but she was strong as an ox. Worked harder than any ten men we know. Oh, we could talk with her doctor, Alice Stewart, but Johanna never said a word about any problem."

"Heart attack? Aneurysm?"

"Cancer. Could have been any of those. Timing's still ten million to one, but an autopsy'll clear all that up."

Sam gave Lo a look.

"I know, I know," the lawyer said. "Sometimes an autopsy does. Sometimes it don't. And *sometimes* the coroner delivers his verdict based on what someone else wants that verdict to be. Maybe a little money changes hands . . ."

Yes, indeed. Sam herself had once been involved in a case where a sheriff and the coroner, who was the local vet, declared a man dead of drowning, winking at the huge exit wound in his chest. Sam asked, "Do you have a candidate for that someone who might have a personal interest in the cause of Johanna's death?"

"Nope. We're just saying, as far as understanding how things work, particularly in small towns, neither one of us just fell off the back of a turnip truck. Now, you want to move on to suicide?"

Sam winced.

"It's not something that a girl wants to think about, is it?"

No, no one ever does. And particularly not in this case. Sam couldn't bear the thought. The timing was too macabre. Too cruel. Johanna had come back from the dead just to knock herself off? Yet, Sam had to look at it. "Motive?" she asked Lo.

"We don't know. Probably not her health, like we just said. Her business is sound as a dollar. Booming, in fact."

"I don't even know what her business was."

"Oh, hon, Johanna was a decorator. An interior designer. She did most of the best houses around town."

Sam nodded. It fit. Her mother had been a wonderful amateur painter with a good eye and great color sense. "Okay, say it wasn't her business. Was she depressed?"

"What's depressed? Everyone's down in the dumps these days. Half the country's on Prozac. Johanna was never the most *cheerful* person, but she was getting on with her life. She wasn't lying around pissing and moaning."

"Didn't seem to have anything *unusual* on her mind recently?"

"Well, hell, she had *something* on her mind, didn't she? She checked into La Fonda as J. Hilton. There had to be a reason for that."

"Did I tell you I had to go through a bunch of hocus-pocus with the desk clerk to even make contact with her?"

"Really? Who was that?"

"A young woman named Estela. I definitely want to talk with her."

Lo sighed. "And we probably have to face the fact that Johanna's concern about her will at this particular moment points to a possible foreknowledge of her death."

"Maybe. But was that foreknowledge of her *own* actions, or someone else's? From what we know so far—the aliases, staying in a hotel, the cry for help—seem like strong indicators someone was after her. So, who was that? Who were her enemies? Let's start with her business. Someone, say, she'd swindled in a deal?" In a corner of Sam's mind, a finger scratched. *Business.* Something about Johanna and business.

Lo said, "Johanna was honest as the day is long. And we don't know of anybody who commits murder over a decorating job gone bad, if that's where you're heading."

"A crime of passion?"

"Johanna wasn't romantically involved with anybody, hadn't been, as far as we know, in the five years since she came to town."

"Someone who was jealous of her?"

Lo shook her head. "It's tough to think of anyone. Not that Johanna was the *easiest* person in the world. She knew her own mind. She liked to have her own way. But then, that would describe me. Probably describe you too. But, like we said before, Johanna just wasn't close to many people. She pretty much kept to herself."

"How about someone who worked for her?"

"Carpenters, plumbers, craftsmen—that's what you mean? We never heard her talk about any problems."

"Her secretary?"

"Didn't have one. Worked out of her home. Had moi, her lawyer, and an accountant on retainer." Lo poured herself another cup of coffee. "There was Jesus, of course. But he *adored* Johanna."

"Jesus?"

"Jesus Oliva. Johanna's man Friday."

"Drives an old pickup truck?"

"Drives a whole raft of wild vehicles. Paints them up. Calls them his art. How do *you* know Jesus?"

Sam told Lo about sliding down the driveway on Upper Canyon the night before. "He saved my life. Or, at least, he didn't run over me."

"That must have been Johanna's driveway."

"What?"

"Jesus lives in a casita behind Johanna's house. Second driveway on the left, just after Upper Canyon begins, above Cristo Rey Church?"

"That was my *mother's* driveway? I can't believe it."

Lo shrugged. "Not the least bit strange for Santa Fe. There are *no* coincidences here, m'dear."

"Jesus said he'd been dreaming of me for years. That I'd been sent by Our Lady to make him and his art famous. Is he a little strange?"

"No more than any other artist, or anyone else living here, for that matter. Stick around; you'll find the bizarre, the weird, and the miraculous are the rule rather than the exception in northern New Mexico."

"Okay. You know, I'm thinking, the major disadvantage we have in thinking about foul play is all those blank years in Momma's life. You said she came here about five years ago? That leaves twenty-nine unaccounted for. A lot of time for a lot of people to have a motive."

"True." Lo paused. "You know, Sam, we're following everything you're saying. But Johanna looked so peaceful . . ."

"Cause of death? That's what you're asking? Poison. Suffocation. Bubble of air injected by hypodermic. Alcohol and pills ingested under duress. GHB, or some other designer drug, slipped into a drink. *Tiny* little pick inserted in the back of the neck. There are a million ways to kill someone which leave no readily apparent evidence."

Lo shivered. "We're glad we don't know everything you know. What we *do* know is enough to make us despair of the human race." She reached over and ruffled Harpo's ears. "You know what we think? That we ought to saddle up, right this minute, head straight for Johanna's house. Take ourselves a look. See what we can find." She reached for her purse. "We've got keys. Grabbed them when we left the office, when Vigil called. So what does a girl say?"

WHEN EARL WISDOM HAD BEEN A YOUNG MAN BACK IN Florida, he'd gotten into trouble, spent seven-and-a-half years paying his debt to society in Raiford Correctional, on the edge of the Okefenokee Swamp. When he got out of there—the stinkingest, hottest, wettest place on earth—he had headed for Santa Fe and the high and dry.

Working odd jobs, cutting wood, painting houses, he'd discovered his big hands had the gift of easing misery. He took a few classes, then hung out his bodywork shingle, and one day in walked this famous actor-director who had a place in Tesuque, just north of town. It wasn't long after that the word had spread on the celebrity hot line about Earl's magical hands. The next thing Earl knew he was flying here, flying there, and it wasn't long before Earl found himself being written about in the magazines.

Right this minute, at his bodywork studio, down a little alleyway off Canyon Road, Earl had his gifted hands full of Stuart Wonder. The New Age guru was lying naked, facedown on Earl's massage table. Earl said, "Man, you have got yourself worked into some powerful knots."

"My life has turned to shit, Earl."

Earl laughed his funny laugh—the man a high-C tenor in a body that looked like a basso profundo's. Earl was six-foot-two, broad-shouldered, with muscles to burn even at sixty-one. He inched his great powerful digits down Stuart's backbone, making each vertebra shout hallelujah. Then he said, "I'm sorry to hear that, Stuart."

"I'm way over my head."

"Uh-huh."

"Drowning, you want to know the truth."

"That's not good."

"You want to know what my problem is, Earl?"

Earl said, "No, not really. You don't mind, I'd just as soon you didn't tell me."

"You're kidding."

"Nope. Listen, Stuart, in your line, the guru business, folks come to you, spill their guts, right?"

"Sometimes."

"Mostly women are the ones who want to let their hair down?"

"Mostly."

"That's 'cause men, most of them's not comfortable telling another man what's on their mind. If they do tell, see, then later, they wish they hadn't. Embarrassed, they don't want to see that man anymore. So every time I get a client wants to tell me his most heartfelts, I know I've got to hush him up quick, or I just lost a client."

But talking to women, was that different? Stuart was about to ask, when the door to the massage room pushed wide.

Earl said, "Ma'am, you can't be coming in here." He threw a towel over Stuart's pink butt.

Stuart screwed his head around.

Earl gave the pretty little woman a once-over. She was wearing a black catsuit, not an ounce of flab on her tiny frame.

"*Now* I've got you," she said to Stuart.

"Deborah, what the hell are you doing here?" Stuart asked.

Earl, backing out, said, "Stuart, you know the little lady? Fine. Y'all holler when you're done. I'll be right down the hall."

Stuart reared up. "Oh, no, you don't. I've paid for a massage. Wife or no wife, I *need* a massage."

This darling little woman is Stuart's wife? Hmmmmmm. Earl watched while Deborah circled around the table a couple of times. Was she looking for an opening? A place to stick her knife in? Earl offered to find her a chair; she said, No, thank you, and leaned over, right in Stuart's face. "I wouldn't be here if you weren't such a poot. Locked in your bedroom last night, pretending you were asleep when you knew we needed to talk."

Now, that was interesting, thought Earl. A man like Stuart, spiritual advisor to kings and princes, a multimillionaire, you'd think he could work out the simple stuff. Like, for example, separate bedrooms are not good.

"I told you I'd get back to you when I could," said Stuart. "I have a lot on my mind."

Earl watched Deborah's mouth. When a woman's lips get tight like that, a smart man steps back.

"Stuart, you said the same thing yesterday and the day before and the day before that. You've been saying the same thing for eighteen years."

"So," said Stuart, "why should this day be different from any other?"

"I'll tell you why. Because I had a vision. A vision which told me things were going to change, and soon."

"You *did?*" Stuart flipped over on his back. *Not* a good move, thought Earl, who, for not the first time in his life, thanked the Baby Jesus that he had not been born a white fool. Stuart said, "Let us not forget, Deborah, *I'm* the one in the vision business. *I'm* the Wonder Man."

"Yes, but that doesn't mean diddle, Stuart, because you have no faith. All of our blessings, you think they came to us because you're so slick. But that's not it, Stuart. There really *are* miracles."

"What have you been smoking, Deborah?"

Deborah shook her head. "If people only knew. All those people who think you have a pipeline to the truth, *you,* Mr. Shuck and Jive."

"What do you want, Deb? You're a nonpracticing Jew from the Big Easy. You wouldn't know faith if it bit you in the ass."

"I've found my faith, Stu."

"Oh, yeah?"

Deborah nodded. "In Cristo Rey Church. I go there and sit for an hour every afternoon, right after my tap-dancing lesson. Doors have opened to me."

Earl could really feel himself warming up to this Deborah. He'd always had a soft spot for small wiry women who were a little bit off their nut.

Stuart rolled his eyes. "Uh-huh. You go to this church and then what?"

"I think. I meditate. It's a good place to sit and be quiet. And I love the smell of incense." Deborah's little pear-shaped nostrils widened. Earl had to put a hand on the wall to steady himself.

"A couple of weeks ago, sitting in church, I had a vision that's changed my life. Saint Hyacintha came to me. That's the former Clarice Mariscotti, born 1640, to a noble Italian family. When her parents arranged a marriage for her youngest sister, passing right over Clarice, she had a fit. She nagged her family day and night, until finally they sent her off to a convent, where she was renamed Sister Hyacintha. Okay, she said, she'd be a nun, wear the habit, and live in the drafty old convent, but don't think she was doing without. No sirree. She had the best of everything brought in."

"Saint Hyacintha of Bloomingdale's catalog shopping," said Stuart. "Sounds like your kind of girl."

Deborah ignored that. "Eventually, Hyacintha became a super nun. She raised all kinds of money for the poor."

"Harrumph," Stuart said, and rolled back onto his tummy.

"It was like she was standing right there." Deborah pointed toward Earl. Earl wanted to take that little finger and put it in his mouth. "I heard her voice clear as anything. She said if I'm ever going to find my path, and help people like she did, I have to divorce you. I talked it over with my daddy, and he said, 'Good!' So I've filed, Stuart. I signed the papers this morning. Tomorrow, at the latest, I'm moving out."

"What?" said Stuart.

To where? thought Earl.

"Saint Hyacintha said that I will never find the purpose of my time here on earth if we stay together because you're too greedy and you don't work well with people. So I'm leaving you, Stuart."

Stuart reached for his cell phone and began punching in numbers. "Dr. Morgenstern will get you into Betty Ford; you can chill for a few weeks."

"I don't think so, Stuart. You just give me my half of everything. Now, I know that might be a problem because you've been very very naughty lately . . ."

Stuart dropped the phone. "What?"

"Don't be coy, Stuart. You know exactly what I'm talking about." Then Deborah turned and sweetly said good-bye to Earl.

Earl wanted to pick her up, carry her out, do something *romantic* with her. A picnic maybe. Earl could see it in his mind. But he hadn't gotten past spreading out a tablecloth on the ground, and the little lady was going, going, gone.

Now, being as he himself was famous, Earl had quite a few connections, some of which, he was thinking now, he might need to make use of.

The reason for this? Earl had just been hit upside the head by love. Lust. Infatuation. Whatever. Call it what you will, Earl was feeling it for Deborah Wonder, and God Almighty! it felt good.

The flip side, however, was already dawning on him. Caring about Deborah meant worrying about her too. And Earl was plenty worried.

What if Stuart *did* try to send her to Betty Ford? Or someplace else where they would lock her up and throw away the key? It could happen. Earl had spent enough time around the rich and weird, not to mention his mobster friends in New Orleans, to know that if you had enough juice, you could make people disappear.

Or—and this was more likely, Earl realized—what if Stuart simply screwed Deborah out of every dime? That's what rich men did; they *hid* things the instant the word D-I-V-O-R-C-E was in the wind. Earl didn't want to think of Deborah penniless. Even if she never gave him, Earl, the time of day, he wanted her to have the very best. Saint Deborah of Bloomingdale's, it had a nice ring.

Then Earl remembered what Deborah had said to Stuart: *You've been very very naughty lately.* The little man had gone pale when she said that. That wasn't good. The man was up to something; that much was sure. Hadn't he tried to pour it all out to Earl?

My life has turned to shit, Earl.

I'm way over my head.

Drowning, you want to know the truth.

You didn't let him spill the beans, but it was better

this way, Earl told himself. The man wasn't going to tell the truth, the whole truth and nothing but the truth, anyway. You let him tell his story, his version colors your judgment. Gets in your way.

What Earl was going to have to do was some primary research on Stuart. See what he could come up with. A little leverage. Make sure that Stuart let Deborah go, in style. He was going to get on that right now, he sure was, right after he called that woman his nephew Lavert had asked him to look in on. He had her name here somewhere.

11

IN THE DAYLIGHT, UPPER CANYON WAS A VERY PLEASANT road, turning quickly into a winding rural lane. In no time at all, Sam and Lo were at Johanna's driveway, just past the bridge over the arroyo above Cristo Rey Church.

This, Sam thought, is the driveway where I fell down in the dark. Where I scraped my knees. Where Jesus Oliva stopped just short of squashing me. There's his truck now, parked in the graveled lot, outside the house where my momma lived.

Sam stood before a wall of Johanna's lilacs. Harpo scurried nose down along the brick walk, then circled the green handkerchief of Johanna's front yard. The house was a small simple adobe, its wide brick-floored portal stacked with firewood and bordered with pots of cacti. Double windows, painted blue, framed either side of the front door. It was a dollhouse—tidy, small, and sweet.

Sam hesitated. Do I really want to go inside? To run my fingers across Johanna's things? To try to unearth her secrets? *Be careful what you search for* was a lesson Sam had learned years earlier.

"Come on," Lo Ellen said. "It'll be all right. It's your house now, remember?"

That didn't make Sam any more eager to open the door. Yesterday, she thought, I was all fire and fury, racing for a plane, hurling myself back into the past, forward into the future. The basic Sam Adams—moving, on the go, impatient to know everything—Momma's letter galvanizing as a starting gun.

Now Momma's gone, and here I am, fearful, in my very bones, that somehow my presence in Santa Fe helped push her into her grave. That must be true. The timing was no coincidence.

And what if I hadn't come? Would that have saved her? She must have known that it wouldn't, that either way, she was a goner. So why did she want me to come to Santa Fe? Would she want me to be here now, standing on the threshold of her home, her sanctuary, her most secret places? Maybe *that's* the very reason she did want me here. She knew me. She knew I would snoop. She knew I wouldn't rest until I had the answers to all my questions.

Sam opened the door.

The interior of the little house was like a warm hug. Sam loved it the moment she crossed the threshold. Its thick whitewashed adobe walls, simple unpainted Mexican furniture, bright fabrics, good rugs, all said, Come in, sit down and stay for a while. We'll share a cup of tea and chat by the corner fire. The house smelled of lemon and verbena and lavender.

Front to back, it was divided into thirds. First, a wide center entryhall with a hardwood floor. Behind that, a small kitchen, its countertops dark blue, its floors brown saltillo tiles. Three curved openings that punched through the left wall of the entryway led to a doll-sized living room, small dining room, and, behind a counter, a laundry area. It was light, with many windows. The ceilings were coved, with rough-cut beams, vigas, at the dip of each cove.

In the living room, four chairs covered in mushroom linen sat atop a scarlet oriental carpet. Antique wooden santos, studded crosses, a cow skull, shiny black pottery, all bespoke the Southwest. One large painting hung in the living room: "Big Autumn" radiated with fall colors.

"John Fincher, a local artist," said Lo. "Johanna loved his work." Then Lo did a 360-degree turn, one hand extended. "It's worth close to half a million."

"No."

"Absolutely. The house may be small, but this is prime east-side property, five acres running all the way down to the river. Trees, mountain views, no near neighbors, and it's a six-minute drive to the plaza. Plus, parts of the house are a hundred years old. This is old Santa Fe. Johanna knew what she was doing. She was one smart cookie when it came to money. You want to see the rest of it?"

Lo led Sam through a door to the right of the entryway into a small hall. Johanna's bedroom, in beige and white, was simple as a nun's cell. The bath was tiled in pale yellow. The back study was the busiest room in the house, jammed with bookshelves, file cabinets, a long oak table piled with papers and bills. There was one photograph on Johanna's desk, a framed picture of a barren hill with what looked like a doorframe in the side of it.

"What's this?" Sam picked up the photo.

Lo smiled. "The entrance to Johanna's turquoise mine. It's out near Cerrillos, about a forty-minute drive. She bought it a couple of years ago. All the good stuff's been gone for decades, but you can still pick up turquoise pebbles. She used to have cocktail parties for clients there."

"In the mine?"

"Sure. You ought to go out and see it. It's yours, you know. Everything is yours." Lo opened her hands to the busy room. The house. The grounds.

Sam shook her head. It was too much to think about. So, don't think, she told herself. Roll up your sleeves and get to work. This study was the most likely place to start their search, for whatever it was they were looking for. Something. Anything that would tell them more about Johanna, how she'd lived, why she'd died.

Sam began with a file cabinet. Lo took the table. Johanna had been very organized. All of the materials for each of her design projects for the past five years were carefully filed and cross-indexed. Sam made note of each property-owner's name. Her accounts payable and accounts receivable seemed all in order and told them nothing. Catalogs of materials were filed and shelved alphabetically. Her address book and Rolodex seemed to be business only, though, again, Sam made notes of names that might possibly be personal. There was no personal correspondence. No postcards. No thank-you notes. No letters.

Then, in the back of the bottom file drawer, Sam found half a dozen brown leather-bound volumes. She turned the first one over, and her heart stopped. On its cover, the word *Samantha* was stamped in gold along with the dates, *1978–83*.

"Lo," she said, "come here. Look at this."

Inside, carefully preserved between sheets of plastic, were scores of clips of Sam's stories for the San Francisco *Chronicle*.

November 1978: Jim Jones of San Francisco's People's Temple and the massacre at Jonestown, Guyana. Nine hundred of Jones's followers poisoned with grape Kool-Aid. Sam's follow-up stories about the Fillmore neighborhood, where many of the faithful had lived.

Fast on Jonestown's heels came the assassinations at City Hall of Mayor George Moscone and Supervisor Harvey Milk.

It had been such a terrible, sad time. Sam ran her fingers over those and hundreds of other stories carrying her byline.

Here was an invitation to a dinner in Sam's honor for her award-winning Jamestown coverage and a photograph Sam had never seen before of herself and her friend Annie squinting into the sun outside the Balboa Café.

Another volume was stuffed with pictures from Sam's dance recitals, clips with her name on honor rolls at Girls' State, her high school graduation, a wedding in which Sam had been a bridesmaid. Yet another held her years at Stanford. The last volume chronicled her return to hometown Atlanta and her work for the *Constitution*. Her feature work on the Miss America Pageant. Her series on the Elvis-imitator murders in Tupelo. And, finally, a mention, which had appeared in *Publishers Weekly* only the week before, of Sam's upcoming *American Weird*.

Sam slammed the last one shut, suddenly fighting back tears. "This is breaking my heart, Lo. It's as if Momma were in my life the whole time, and yet I never knew it. She kept me so close to her, and I didn't even know she existed. God, I *hate* this."

Lo stood. "Let's take a break. You go sit out on the back porch, and we'll make some coffee."

A good idea. Out back Sam flopped into a canvas folding chair. Wiping her tears, she stared out at Jesus's small house. It looked to be a studio, two rooms at most, with a tiny walled patio. Sam looked past the fruit trees and aspen and grasses and chamiso and shrubs toward the dark blue bosoms of the Sangre de Cristo. Speak to me, Momma, she thought. Show me where to look. Show me the end of the ball of string, and I'll unravel it all. I know you wanted me to know your secrets. That's why you called me here, isn't it?

Then the bright blue door of the little casita opened. Jesus Oliva stepped out, robed in mourning: black boots, jeans, shirt. His face was filled with grief. He saw Sam, dipped his head in a small bow, then approached. "May I come and talk with you?"

"Please do."

Climbing the porch steps, he held out his hands. "I want to offer you my condolences. It is a terrible thing to lose someone you love. Miss Johanna, she was very kind to me. I feel her loss deeply in my heart." He crossed flattened hands over his chest. *"Corazón."*

I'm going to cry again, Sam thought. Her bottom lip began to tremble. "Won't you sit for a while and have some coffee?" she asked. "Lo Ellen is here with me. She's making some."

A few minutes later, Lo and Harpo joined them on the back porch. Harpo sniffed Jesus's boots, then curled at Sam's feet.

Sam sipped coffee from a blue-and-white cup. "How did you know about my mother's death?" she asked Jesus.

"My girlfriend, Estela. She's a telephone operator at La Fonda. Sometimes she works the desk. She called me."

Sam shot Lo a look. Estela, her inquisitor from last night. The one with the attitude.

"Did you know that my mother was staying at La Fonda?" Sam asked Jesus. "Before Estela called about her death, I mean? Did you know she was registered under an assumed name?"

"Yes. Estela told me. She said that Miss Johanna had asked her to keep it to herself, but she knew that I was worried about Miss Johanna."

"Why were you worried about her?" asked Lo.

"This past week or so, Miss Johanna seemed like she had a lot on her mind. She was not paying attention to her business. Her phone was ringing all the time, and she seemed very sad. That was before she left and went to La Fonda."

"Do you know what was going on?" Sam asked.

Jesus shook his head. "Miss Johanna was not what you would call a happy person. Her spirits were never light. *I* think she was visited by ghosts, but I said that to her once and Miss Johanna, she got angry. She said, 'Jesus, you keep that Catholic hocus-pocus to yourself.' When she said three, maybe it was four, days ago that she couldn't stay in her house here anymore, I knew it was the ghosts. They had driven her out. But I didn't say that. And when Miss Johanna called, to check on things, I didn't let on to her that I knew where she was."

"What did she want you to check on?" Sam asked. "Anything in particular?"

"She just wanted me to look after the house. And, oh, she did ask if anyone had been here."

"Had they?" asked Sam.

"Not that I know of, not while I was home. No one except you." Jesus smiled at Sam. "Did you tell Miss Lo about falling down the drive?"

Sam nodded.

"Miss Sam was brought here," he said to Lo, "by Our Lady. It was not an accident. Let me tell you now about last night. There was a sign that came to me, which told me I should go downtown to check on Miss Johanna." He turned to Sam. "That's where I was headed when I found you."

"What kind of sign?" asked Sam.

"A terrible howling. I reached for my Remington, thinking maybe it was a coyote after Milo, my cat. A couple of times, Mr. Coyote has almost gotten him. So I grabbed up some cornmeal and put it in my pocket.

You have to do that in case Mr. Coyote runs across your path. If Mr. Coyote crosses in front of you, you've got to sprinkle corn pollen or cornmeal in his footprints before you can go on. If you don't, it means certain death."

Lo nodded. "We were late for a trial once, a coyote crossed the road, and we didn't have our cornmeal in the car. Judge said, no problem, he understood."

"But this wasn't Mr. Coyote," said Jesus. "So, I say to myself, maybe it's La Llorana, 'cause I still hear the howling. La Llorana, she's a ghost."

Sam was beginning to think she was having her leg pulled, but Jesus looked serious, as did Lo.

Jesus said, "La Llorana's been roaming northern New Mexico for more than a hundred years, hollering for her lost child. There's different versions about what happened to that child. It wandered off. Someone stole it. It died. But you know what I think? Since Estela called and told me that you had checked into the hotel, and that you looked like Miss Johanna, I'm thinking, maybe this is like La Llorana. Miss Johanna's long-lost child has come."

"Had Johanna told you that she had a daughter?" Lo asked.

"No. Miss Johanna never talked about her old times. I told *her* all about when I was a little kid, when my mama and daddy would bring us to Santa Fe from Truchas. They'd sit us in a booth in the old Plaza Bar. I told her about when you could still roller skate and skateboard on the Plaza and they would not arrest you for endangering the tourists. I told her how downtown was once not all tourist shops, but had gas stations, drugstores, a Sears. Then I would ask Miss Johanna, I'd say, tell me about *your* hometown. She wouldn't say a word."

"But still you thought she had a daughter?" Sam asked.

"Yes. I was certain of it."

"Why was that?"

"The way she looked at little girls, little girls with dark hair. There are many of them in Santa Fe."

Oh, Sam thought. And for a moment it felt as if she were carrying a child, a tiny child in the region of her heart, a child who was turning to show her face. She could see Johanna beaming at a dark-haired toddler, wanting to pick her up, press her to her breast, but stopping herself. The same way she herself had had to hold back when she'd noticed a woman across a room who resembled Johanna.

"Anyway," Jesus said, "last night I said to myself, Jesus, go and check on Miss Johanna. This howling is telling you something important. It's a sign."

"So, did you see her?" Lo asked.

"No. Right after I dropped off Miss Sam, I parked my truck, and I went upstairs and knocked on Miss Johanna's door, but there was no answer. I stood outside her door for a long time, trying to feel her vibration, but I didn't feel anything at all." Jesus paused, his beautiful eyes drawn down at the corners. "Maybe she was already gone."

The three of them sat in silence for a long time, each of them with his private vision of what that meant. Harpo shifted and whimpered in his sleep. Finally Sam said, "Tell me, Jesus, what you meant last night when you said you have been dreaming of me. That I was sent by Our Lady to help make you famous."

"It has to do with Miss Johanna too. But it's a long story."

That was fine, Sam said, and Lo agreed. They could do with some story telling right about now.

"When I was a little kid," said Jesus, "I started painting the blue and green mountain peaks I could see from my front yard. I lived about forty miles north of here in

Truchas, which is a poor town with one narrow street, but we have good land, and we have the mountains. It is here that Robert Redford shot the movie *The Milagro Beanfield War,* when I was twelve. I was an extra in the movie. I painted pictures of Robert Redford and Sonia Braga and Ruben Blades and Melanie Griffith and many other famous people. It was Robert Redford who told me, 'If you keep at this, Jesus, your work will end up in a museum in New York City.'

"So I asked the lady at the bookmobile to get me a book about museums in New York so I could see where my painting was going to carry me. I knew it the moment I saw it. I described it to my gramita Candelaria when she was dying, my grandma who had the gift of prophecy. I told her about the shining white building, shaped like a spaceship. She asked me how my paintings would fit on the round walls. When I said I didn't know, she told me to light a candle to Our Lady of Guadalupe and ask her."

Jesus did as he was told. And that very night, as the soul of his grandmother lifted out of her withered body, Jesus dreamed of the way to best display his talent in that shining white spiral. He saw old Chevys and Mercurys and Cadillacs painted as no lowrider had ever painted them before. He saw himself: the Picasso, the Miro, the El Greco of hot rod art. He saw people waiting expectantly along the sides of the ramps of the famous museum. He heard their *oooohs* as his art began rolling past them.

In that long-ago dream, Jesus also saw the face of the woman who would deliver him and his art to New York City, where he would become rich and famous. Then he would return to Truchas and help his people. It was a noble custom, *el tequio,* to repay the moral debt one owes one's community.

It was two years ago when he first saw Johanna, the

woman in his dreams. He spotted her on the plaza and ran after her. She shied away from him as if he were a robber, and he was crushed. "What do you want?" she asked him. "A job, please," Jesus said, thinking if he could spend time around her, she would realize who he was. To his astonishment, she hired him on the spot, which is how he came to be Miss Johanna's dogsbody, her messenger, her maintenance man, her part-time truck driver, her jack-of-all-trades. And how he learned, at her knee, about color and line and proportion, how to tell good taste from great.

Jesus never spoke to Johanna or anyone else about his dreams. He worked and waited for Johanna to take him and his rolling canvases to New York City. But she never did.

He kept thinking that perhaps there was some test he had to pass. Some task he had to perform. Our Lady hadn't shown him that, but the ways of the saints could be mysterious. And saints had no deadlines. No due dates. Jesus knew that he had to be patient, hoping against hope that he would not be an old man in a wheelchair, rolling down the ramp behind his art, in his moment of glory.

Then last night, he said, Sam, the lady he'd been promised had finally materialized at his very feet. "I realized then that Miss Johanna was not the one. She was the path to you. It was *your* face, not hers I saw in my dreams."

"Oh, Jesus," Sam said. "I don't know much about art. I have none of Johanna's contacts. Until yesterday, I hadn't even seen her since I was eight years old."

But Jesus only beamed at her. He knew what he knew. He said, "If you don't know Miss Johanna, that is why it is good that you came to her house today. Now you must stay here and talk with her."

Sam looked from Jesus to Lo. Lo shrugged. Santa Fe.

Jesus said, "When someone dies, it takes three days before they completely pass over. During those three days, their spirits are still here. They can hear you. You can hear them."

Sam said, "Oh, I see," but she was being polite. She'd been raised Episcopalian, then she'd been a parishioner in the Temple of Booze. In AA, where she was taught about turning over what she couldn't handle to her higher power, she could never get a picture of what that power was. An old man with a beard? She didn't think so. She didn't know what she thought. All-in-all, Sam was about as spiritual as an eggplant. But, still, hadn't she been talking with Johanna just a while ago? Hadn't she asked Johanna where to look for her secrets?

In any case, Jesus was believer enough for both of them. "If you sleep in her bed and think strong thoughts about her before you go to sleep, Miss Johanna will come to you. She's not going back to La Fonda. Her spirit will want to be at home, with her things, with her family. You do what I say, you try talking with her, you'll see. And I'll be right out back here. I'll look after you."

It wasn't such a bad idea, Sam thought, now that she considered it. She'd rather stay here, where Johanna had lived, than the hotel where she'd died. And perhaps, with more time, she might find what she was looking for.

"Now," said Jesus, "I've taken more than enough of your time. But before I go, I have something to give you." Jesus opened the top two buttons of his shirt, fished in, and pulled out a tiny silver key suspended from a slender chain. "Miss Johanna, she said someone might come, someone she hadn't seen in many many years. She didn't say who, but promised I would know her when I saw her. She said, Jesus, you give her this. She'll know what to do with it. Last night in her driveway, I knew you were the one."

Sam took the chain from Jesus and held it gently in her palm. The silver was warm from his body. The key was familiar, but she couldn't bring back the memory.

"Do you know what it opens?" Lo asked.

"No," Sam said, smiling her thanks at Jesus. "But maybe it will come to me if I sleep on it."

12

Sam and Lo poked around Johanna's house for the rest of the afternoon, but to no avail. They found nothing that pointed to why she'd left her house or what, if anything, might have been threatening her. The two of them had dinner at Lo's house, only half a mile away. "Spend the night," Lo said. "We have tons of room, and surely you don't want to be alone." But Sam had insisted that she did. Lo's offer was very kind, but she thought she'd check out of La Fonda and return to Johanna's.

There'd been two messages from George at the hotel. Dear old thing, he was so excited that Johanna was alive, it broke her heart to have to tell him that that was no longer true. When he heard her news, George Adams wanted to jump on the first plane heading west. "I know I can't be of much help, but I don't want you to be there by yourself." Sam insisted that she was okay. She could handle this, whatever it was. "That's the point," said George. "I don't want you handling anything. Give yourself time to grieve, Samantha. This is *fresh* grief, whether you want to see it that way or not. Good God, dear thing, you've just lost your mother all over again." Once more, Sam insisted that she was fine.

But she wasn't, of course, not really. She was pretty rocky, actually. But focusing on the five Ws she'd practiced as a reporter, asking herself those questions about Johanna's death, put it at somewhat of a remove. Pretending it was a story gave her a way of thinking about it that wasn't quite so painful.

After the talk with George, she sat for a while in Johanna's living room. She tried listening to some jazz. Johanna had quite a collection, some of the same albums Sam owned, but even Miles Davis couldn't spirit her away tonight. She lifted book after book from the well-furnished shelves, but couldn't find anything she wanted to read.

Finally she went to bed and tried to empty her mind of everything. Good luck. The questions circled like vultures: *How did Johanna die? Why did she call me here? Why now? Why wasn't it safe for her to call all these years? Why did she want me to leave? Was she murdered? Or did she take her own life? If she did, what could have been so pressing, so awful, so wrong that suicide was her only alternative?*

It was so quiet here, up on this hillside out of town. Quiet and still—and lonesome. Maybe this hadn't been such a good idea. Maybe she should have taken Lo up on her offer. She was wide awake and as wired as if she'd had three cups of coffee, exhausted, but her mind wouldn't shut up. It was clear she was never going to get to sleep.

Maybe she should take a Restoril. Anything would be better than tossing and turning while the hours crept by, reliving that first glimpse of Johanna in her white nightie, so still, so cold, so very dead.

Sam got up and rummaged through her cosmetic bag for her vial of sleeping pills. Then she stared at it long and hard.

Recovering drunks and/or addicts do not take sleeping

remedies lightly. In fact, most don't take them at all. However, for the past year, insomnia had plagued Sam off and on. After talk therapy, acupuncture, and every other nonpharmaceutical nostrum known to modern man, she'd broken her cycle of wakefulness with the help of her doctor and this medication.

Not, however, before talking with her AA sponsor, who'd said, "Take the damned medicine. I don't see any earthly point in your being one of those drunks who's sober for a dozen years, then puts a gun in her mouth because of depression."

Since then, every once in a while, when she hit a very bad patch—and if this wasn't one, she didn't know what was—she'd swallow a pill. But first she'd ask herself, Was this really necessary? Was it going to become a habit? Was it the first step back into addiction? Was she self-medicating simply to escape the pain?

Hell, yes, she was running *and* hiding from Mr. Devil Pain tonight. But she wouldn't tomorrow. Or the next night. Or the night after that. Only tonight, dear God, please let her sleep.

Sam took the pill and climbed back into bed. Don't run the *who, what, why, when, where's* anymore tonight, she told herself, waiting for it to kick in. If you have to think at all, try something concrete. Something simple. Something you can work with.

How about the key?

That's it. Focus on the key Jesus gave you. Johanna wanted you to have it. Forget the convoluted way it came to you. Forget that she didn't simply hand it to you. You don't understand *anything* about Johanna, so let that part go. Let that key float through your mind. Let your unconscious tell you what the key unlocks. Or let Johanna tell you. Isn't that what Jesus promised? If you slept here, she'd talk with you?

Okay, Momma. Let's hear it about key.

Snuggled next to her, Harpo shuddered in his sleep. Sam breathed in his warm dogginess. Then she turned over onto her stomach, facedown, the way she'd slept as a child. And somewhere, toward morning, she dreamed . . .

She and Johanna were once again in Johanna's room at La Fonda, their arms wrapped around one another.

"Momma," Sam said. "Momma, Momma." She couldn't stop saying the word.

"Baby. Sugar. Sammie. I was so afraid you wouldn't come."

"I *had* to."

"I prayed you would. But I didn't have any right to hope. If you only knew how many times I've dreamed of this moment. How many times I wanted to call you. I did, actually," Johanna whispered. "Call you."

"I don't know what you mean."

"I never spoke to you, though. I called and hung up. It wasn't even safe to call."

"Not safe?"

Johanna shook her head, and, in her dream, Sam's focus shifted to her mother's dangling silver earrings, then to the ropes of silver around her neck. Nestled among the heavy silver chains was a large puffy silver heart. It was the locket Sam's father had given to Johanna when Sam was born. Johanna had kept baby pictures of her in it, and later, when Sam was older, favorite bits of Sam's schoolwork, tightly folded. The silver heart locked with a tiny key.

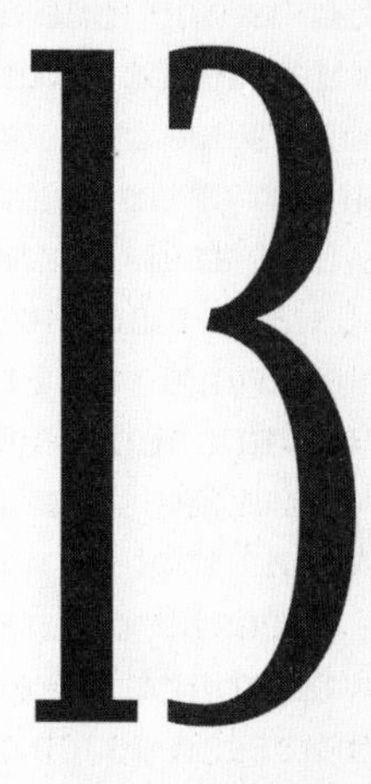

DIGGING UP DIRT ON STUART WONDER WASN'T DIFFICULT for Earl Wisdom. He and Stuart knew many of the same people both in Santa Fe and Los Angeles. Plus, Earl had "resources," folks he'd done favors for, before and after Raiford Correctional. Then there were the Stuart Wonder biographies, both official and unoffical.

In no time at all, Earl had more information on Stuart than he knew what to do with. There was Stuart's real name, for starters. Stuart (Little Stuie) Wunderlich was how he grew up in Great Neck, Long Island, where he was the son of a very successful Cadillac dealer.

From there it got *very* interesting. Stuart had rejected his old man's offer to join him in his business, dropped out of Long Island University where he'd been studying communication arts, and headed for California to grow vegetables on a commune. Then he became a homeless wanderer, worked in Minneapolis as a bartender, and a few years later landed up in Los Angeles studying Zen Buddhism and the Ouija board. At night Stuart worked as a valet for a Beverly Boulevard restaurant, parking Mercedes, BMWs, and, yes, Cadillacs.

By this time Stuart had changed his name from Wunderlich to Wonder and was perfecting a "Wonder" rap. "All is one, one is all. You can have it all if you concentrate on the one," Stuart would say to the tanned high rollers as they tossed him their car keys. Soon, these studio execs, agents, movie stars, were hanging out with Stuart in the parking lot, hungry for more.

Stuart made it easy for them. His message was simple. No twelve steps to master. No diets. No deprivations. It was all about focus. *Really* focus, Stuart proclaimed, on your heart's desire, and it would fall into your hands. Wasn't that Wonderful!?

A gossip columnist ran an item about the "Wonderful Wizard of the Parking Lot," and Stuart was on his way. He began teaching a course he called Wonderful!™ at the New College of Transformation in Santa Monica. His classes mushroomed, and Stuart began renting churches, halls, any place with enough room to accommodate the crowds thirsting for his message.

Then an agent-student got him a book deal, and within six weeks Stuart had produced *Wonderful!*™, a two-hundred-and-twenty-five-page manuscript that explained, in easy-to-read double-talk, about how to properly focus to obtain your heart's desire. Maharishi Mooga blurbed the book. Evangelica Light did too. Stuart was on the spiritual wisdom fast track.

He had the book, the appearance on the *Tonight Show,* the double-breasted suits, but, his agent advised, he needed a wife. A wife would make him more family-friendly. More marketable. He'd take it under advisement, said Stuart. Then, not two weeks later, running through LAX on his way to a lecture in Chicago, Stuart bumped into Deborah Fineman, a New Orleans girl he'd met at a Jewish summer camp when he was ten.

They were married on Maui two months later, as the sun rose above the mountaintops. Halfway through the ceremony, Deborah's father threw up.

Deborah, Deborah, Earl Wisdom mourned when he got to that part in his research. Why couldn't you have waited for me? Then he said to himself, Look for the good part, Earl. Look for the boom to lower over Stuart. Look for where he's gone wrong.

Is it wine, women, young boys, collie dogs, nose candy, what?

It didn't take Earl very long to find out, once he'd called on the son of an old friend of his from Raiford, a young brother computer genius who'd moved to Santa Fe and ran a consulting business out of his million-dollar home in Los Campanas. The whiz kid, who was named Ben, accessed Stuart's financial records as easily as Earl's clients E-mailed him at wisdom@aol.com. He told Earl about Stuart's tax returns, his income, his outgo, his net worth, including the Lear jet, the vintage gullwing Mercedes, the penthouse in Manhattan, the pied-à-terre in Paris, the house and the ranch in Santa Fe, and the man's serious art collection.

"And?" Earl asked young Ben.

"And your jive guru is up to his neck in accounts outstanding. The man is going down for the big count, real soon. They don't make Chapter Elevens this big."

Aha, said Earl. Maybe he'd found it. Stuart was a greedy gut. Stuart was in deep financial shit. That was probably what Deborah was talking about. Stuart had been busy as a little bee unloading the cars, the places in New York and Paris; he'd taken a beating on the Learjet.

But wait. How did that serve Earl? The man's financial catastrophe didn't give Earl any leverage.

Except, he said to himself, when the walls are crashing all around, folks frequently do some pretty stupid things.

"So," he asked Benjamin, "can we find out if Stuart's borrowed money from, shall we say, less than traditional sources?"

"You mean the Italians? It's been my experience that the spaghetti shylocks don't leave a paper trail."

"You're right," said Earl, who ought to know. He was pretty tight with Joey the Horse, one of his regular clients and capo of the New Orleans mob. "But keep looking, okay? Let me know about anything that feels the least bit bent."

Meanwhile, Earl thought, what he needed to do was sniff out Stuart Wonder's passion. What did the man love? Love would cause you to act irrationally, wouldn't it? Why, look at him.

SAM JOLTED AWAKE IN JOHANNA'S SUNNY BED. "YES!" SHE said. Harpo jumped up in a fright, then tipped over sideways in the covers, not awake enough to have the use of himself. "That's it!" Sam crowed. "The key fits Momma's locket." Then she closed her eyes and tried to remember. Was Johanna wearing it when they'd met? No, Sam didn't remember seeing the locket. But she'd been so excited and nervous, would she have noticed that detail?

If Johanna had had it in the hotel, it would have been among her things. The police would have taken it. She'd have to call Vigil and ask him.

No way. Not without searching the house first. This time would be easier. At least she'd be looking for something specific.

She'd glanced through Johanna's jewelry box yesterday. There it sat now, on the dressing table. She flung it open and fingered opera-length pearls, a pair of diamond stud earrings, an assortment of fine Indian pieces inlaid with turquoise and lapis and orange shell. There was no silver heart.

Okay, okay. She'd scour the whole house. Maybe the

cabinets in the bathroom would be a place to start. *After* she'd made a pot of coffee.

Filling the pot, she realized she was feeling much better this morning. Not good, but better. Well, Johanna *had* spoken to her in her dreams. Did she really believe that? Maybe.

Coffee in hand, Sam padded back into the bedroom to find a pair of sweats. Get dressed, get down to it. But then she found herself staring at the view out the windows above Johanna's bed. The early morning sky over the mountaintops was lovely, pale blue, streaked with apricot and gold. She'd never seen skies like this. She was beginning to get a glimmer of why Johanna had settled here.

Then, she thought, she might as well make up the bed while she was standing right over it. She grasped the white-on-white comforter to pull it up, and in the space between the mattress and the wall, something caught her eye.

Her fingers found an envelope, no, two, and pulled them out. They were of the same heavy cream-colored stock as the one Johanna had sent her in Louisiana. They were hand-addressed, in Johanna's careful script, to names Sam didn't recognize.

Sylvia Thissle.

Jayvee Paris.

"Who are these people?" she asked aloud. "Why didn't Johanna mail these notes, letters, whatever they are?" She tapped the envelopes with a fingertip. There was one way to find out.

The notes were dated a week earlier. And with the exception of the salutations, they were identical . . .

Please accept my most heartfelt apology for the pain I have caused you. I'll never forgive myself. There were circumstances . . . but there are always circumstances, aren't there? No excuses, but I have many many regrets.

Forever yours,
Johanna

Jayvee Paris lived on Garcia Street in the historic district, between Lower Canyon and Acequia Madre. His two-story pitched-roof farmhouse of cerulean blue with bright yellow trim stood out like a beacon from its brown adobe neighbors.

"Jayvee Paris?" Lo had said when Sam called. "He's a sculptor, seems to keep body and soul together, which is more than most artists we know. Moved here from somewhere back East five, maybe six years ago. We guess Johanna could have known him. She had professional relationships with many artists. Bought their work, you know, for clients. But we never heard her mention him, not that we remember."

An Hispanic woman answered the doorbell. She was round and pretty in jeans and a white blouse, with a red bandanna covering her dark hair. She carried a feather duster in one hand. "I should say to Mr. Paris that you are?"

"Sam Adams. I called just a little while ago. He's expecting me."

"You will wait here, please." The housekeeper ushered Sam and Harpo into the living room. Its carpet, the same blue of the outside of the house, was scattered with gold stars. Two blue velvet sofas, curvaceous as Dolly Parton, faced one another. A round glass coffee table sat on a base of sandblasted steel. Gold leaf dripped from a baroque mantelpiece. The decor seemed more appropriate for a SoHo loft than this Santa Fe farmhouse.

Footsteps echoed down a wood-floored hallway. Too heavy for the housekeeper's.

The man approaching had wonderful hair, white-blond darkening from ash to light brown. A pink complexion, jolly cheeks, careful eyes the same blue as the love seats. About forty, medium build, a handsome man, who took good care of himself. He held out his hand. "Ms. Adams? I'm Jayvee Paris."

The accent was pure Maine. Sam hadn't picked that up on the telephone, but their conversation had been brief. She had said that she was Johanna's daughter, and she wanted to drop something off for him. Paris had sounded wary but said if she wanted to stop by, fine.

Now they sat opposite one another on the blue velvet love seats. Neither of them made any effort at small talk. Sam pulled the envelope addressed to Paris from her bag. "Johanna wanted you to have this."

Paris took the envelope, then without looking at it, held it against one khakied knee. "I'm curious, why didn't Johanna simply mail it instead of sending you?"

"I take it, Mr. Paris, that you haven't heard that my mother is dead?"

Jayvee Paris reeled back against the blue velvet. "What? What are you saying? I don't understand." His shock seemed like the genuine article.

"There was a story this morning," Sam said. She reached in her bag and dug out the clip from the *New Mexican* that had appeared on Johanna's doorstep. It was short and to the point. Johanna had been found in her bed at La Fonda. Circumstances of her death yet to be determined. The only surprising part was that Sam herself had been mentioned at the end. "Mrs. Hall's daughter, Samantha Adams, of New Orleans, is in Santa Fe." Odd, she'd thought, wondering who had furnished that detail.

Paris looked at the clip, then back at Sam, several times. "Johanna's dead?" He couldn't seem to grasp the concept.

"Yes, she is," Sam said plainly. "As you can see, her

body was found yesterday morning in her room at La Fonda. Now I'm staying at her house, and this morning I found this note addressed to you, and I thought you might be able to help me."

He stared at the note in his hand. "Help you? I'd be happy to, Ms. Adams, but how can I do that?"

"The circumstances of my mother's death are rather strange. She was in the pink of health; then suddenly she's dead. No one seems to know why she was staying at La Fonda rather than at her own home, nor why she was registered there under an alias."

Paris shrugged. "I'm afraid I don't know anything about all that."

"Yes, well, I was hoping you would. Because of your relationship."

"Relationship?" Paris shook his head.

"Yes. I gather that you and my mother were rather close?"

Paris held up a hand as if to ward off her words. "Oh, no, Ms. Adams. I'm afraid there's been some misunderstanding. I didn't know your mother very well at all. We were business associates. She occasionally bought a piece of my work. And that's it."

"Oh, really? Mr. Paris, would you mind reading the note I gave you?"

Paris stared at the envelope in his hand as if it might bite him. He said, "This has been opened."

"Yes. I know. I've read it. Now, please?"

Paris frowned, then slowly unfolded the note. After reading it several times, he said, "I have no earthly idea what this means."

"Really? You have no idea what kind of pain she caused you? Why she was so sorry about it?"

Then Jayvee Paris fixed Sam with his dark blue gaze. As she met it, unblinkingly, the irises seemed to fade until all the color was leached from them. "Really," he answered. "Absolutely. I am one hundred percent sure this note means nothing to me." There was anger in his voice now, white-hot as his glare. He stood, walking in a circle. "I don't understand you, Ms. Adams. Your mother dies, and the next morning you're traipsing around town, calling on a stranger, asking rude questions."

Sam lifted her chin. "Why am I not home grieving? Is that what you mean?"

He turned to face her head on. "It would seem to be the appropriate response, don't you think?"

"We all deal with grief in our own way, Mr. Paris. However, in addition to my grief, as I said, I have serious questions about the circumstances surrounding my mother's death."

"Ms. Adams, let me candid with you. I'm puzzled as to why you're here in my home asking me to think of you *or* your mother's passing. Now, I'm very sorry for your loss, but, as I said, I didn't know your mother very well."

"Then why would she write—?"

Paris didn't let her finish. "I have no idea why your mother would write me this note. Or if she *did* write me this note. It's clear she didn't mail it. *You* could have written it for all I know. Again, I'm sorry for your loss, but, that said, I'm afraid you'll have to excuse me."

With those words, Paris turned toward the front door, ready to usher Sam out. She gathered her things as slowly as she could, stalling for time. She didn't believe a word he'd spoken, but she hadn't figured out a way to trip him up.

Just then a beautiful little girl, six or seven years old, ran into the room from the hallway. She was olive-complexioned with dark eyes and long dark curls. "Hi, Jayvee," she said, grabbing onto his hand. "I just got back from the park. I'm ready for my lesson." And then she spied Harpo. *"Ooooooh,* what a cute dog. May I pet him?"

Sam smiled at the little girl. A diversion. An opportunity, perhaps. "Of course you can. Harpo loves children. But first, put your hand out gently and let him smell it."

Harpo licked the little girl's hand, and she squealed with delight. "He is *so* cute. I'm going to get a dog, aren't I, Jayvee?" She jogged up and down.

"When your mother thinks you're old enough. But, let's not keep Ms. Adams, Isabel. She was just leaving."

"I *am* old enough," Isabel protested.

"Isabel," Sam said brightly, holding her ground. "What a pretty name. My name's Samantha."

Isabel said, "There's a Samantha in my class. *She* has a dog named Grady. A cocker spaniel."

"Isabel, really." Paris edged closer toward the door.

But Isabel wasn't done petting Harpo. Still looking at the dog—in fact Sam wasn't sure to whom the little girl was speaking—Isabel said, "*I* am Isabel Martinez. I'm pleased to make your acquaintance."

With that, the housekeeper appeared around the corner and hurried into the room. She leaned over Isabel, grabbing her shoulder. "Isabel! Come with me. You know better than to interrupt Jayvee."

"I'm not, Mom. Look at Harpo. Isn't he cute?"

Paris said, "Isabel, that's enough. Go with your mother, please, and I'll be right along for your drawing lesson. Ms. Adams?" Once again, he gestured toward the door.

There was nothing more that Sam could do, short of collapsing onto his starry carpet and feigning some kind of fit. Was it possible that Jayvee Paris truly didn't understand Johanna's apology? That he didn't have a clue? She hardly thought so. He'd been way too upset at the news of Johanna's death. He knew what the note was about. She was sure of it.

"Bye, Samantha. Bye, Harpo." Isabel waved as she pranced from the room ahead of her mother. "Are you and Harpo going to come and see us again?"

"I don't know. Maybe," said Sam.

Paris swung the door wide. "Ms. Adams?" Sam reluctantly stepped through it, Harpo trailing behind her.

"Isabel, come," the housekeeper repeated.

"You look like somebody I know." Isabel's words floated down the hall.

Sam turned and stuck a foot in the closing door.

"My Auntie Johanna," Isabel called. "You look *just* like her, but you're younger. And taller. She's going to give me a dog when I'm old enough. She promised."

Sam stood toe-to-toe with Paris, who was flushed, the red creeping up his neck. She stared him in the eye. " 'Auntie Johanna'?"

He smiled, coldly. "Isabel is a very friendly child. And an imaginative one. She has a very rich fantasy life, Ms. Adams, as I suspect you do." With that, Jayvee Paris opened the door wide and, reaching out, shoved Sam so hard she tumbled backward, right off the porch.

Earl Wisdom, waiting to make a left onto Cabra, had a lot on his mind. He'd been trying to reach this Samantha Adams woman. But she'd checked out of her hotel, and he hadn't been able to connect with his nephew Lavert to see if she'd left town, or what. The main thing he was thinking about, of course, was Deborah Wonder. Earl was like a lovesick teenager, obsessed.

Sitting in his old black Mercedes coupe, he'd driven this loop three times already today, from his house on El Caminito through back lanes to cruise past Cristo Rey Church. He had no idea what kind of car Deborah drove, but he was sure he'd know it when he saw it.

And, now, he did. He spotted a black Infiniti with a license plate that read 2WONDER. How sweet it was. Earl wheeled in beside Deborah's car. He jumped out, ran a hand along the Infiniti's smooth lines as if they were Deborah's thighs, then headed for the church. Once he'd slipped through the side door, he stood for a minute in the back of the sanctuary, taking it in.

The church's interior was peasant simple. Its towering ceilings were laced with split cedar shakes and supported by massive vigas. The stations of the cross were marked by rustic oils framed in pressed tin. The concrete floors were painted tan; the wooden benches were plain and hard. On one of them, up front, sat Deborah, his heart's delight.

Earl cleared his throat, not wanting to startle her. She turned, then raised a hand and waved at him. She smiled. Earl thought his heart would burst. He hurried down the aisle and slipped in beside her. "How you doing?" he said.

"Good. How about you?"

"Oh, real good. Great. Fantastic, in fact."

Deborah laughed. Golden notes to Earl's ears.

"Do you come here often?" She fluttered her eyelashes.

"Nope." He was grinning like a fool.

"I didn't think so. I've never seen you here before."

"Yeah, well, you know, yesterday you said you stopped in here sometimes. I thought maybe if I dropped by, I might run into you."

"Oh, really? And why was that?"

"Well." Earl cleared his throat again, this time because of nervousness. What was he going to say: Because I'm head over heels crazy for you? I've thought of nothing but you since the moment we met? He didn't think so. Not quite yet. "I was wondering, you know, I couldn't help but overhear that you were leaving Stuart, moving out you said, and I wondered, well, if you needed any help."

"That's awfully sweet of you, Earl, but I pretty much have it under control."

"Yeah, well." Earl played with the hymnal in the rack on the back of the pew. "I just thought I'd like to offer my assistance, if I could." He cleared his throat again. "You know, I guess I didn't much like the sound of what Stuart was saying about sending you to Betty Ford."

"Oh, don't worry about that. Stuart's not going to do

anything that stupid." She leaned closer to Earl. Her hair smelled like spring flowers. "I've got him by the short and curlies."

Now *that* made Earl sit up straight. "You don't say."

Deborah had a very sweet smile. It showed him lots of even little teeth. "Yep. Stuart's been a very bad boy. He's not going to screw with me, if he knows what's good for him."

"I see. So you think you're going to be okay? Physically, financially, all of those ways? I mean, I know it's none of my business, you don't even know me, but it just got my dander up the way he was talking to you. I thought, I hope he's not going to take advantage of this lady."

"I appreciate your interest." Deborah had dimples a man could get lost in. "And it's true that financially Stuart's already got us well on the road to wrack and ruin. The man is crazy when it comes to money. He cannot stop spending it. He'd own the earth if it were for sale. Such a greedy gut."

Exactly the words Earl had picked himself. He *was* on the right track. He stopped for a moment to congratulate himself. Then he said, "Really, that's a shame."

"But believe you me, I'll get half of what's left. Plus I'm asking for the ranch. Rancho Maravilloso. I have plans for it. You see, having had my life turned around by Saint Hyacintha, I want to return her favor. I want to help the poor, especially needy children, and I think the ranch could be useful in that way."

"Well, I think that sounds real nice, but . . ."

"No ifs, ands or buts about it, Earl. I'm going to get that ranch. That's probably the thing he'll be the most difficult about. But I'm not above blackmailing Stuart to do it."

"Blackmailing?"

"You bet your sweet bippy. See, Stuart's gone too far

this time." She leaned closer to Earl's ear. "Promise you won't tell a soul?"

He snuggled nearer. "Cross my heart and hope to die."

"Stuart's been receiving stolen goods. Big time. Something the feds are sniffing around."

"You're kidding."

"I'm not." Then Deborah poked out her bottom lip. "The problem is, I'm not *exactly* sure what it is. Or how much that might be worth to me." She rolled her big brown eyes at him. "I guess, if you really wanted to, you could help me with *that.*"

16

DRIVING DOWN GARCIA STREET, SAM TALKED TO HERSELF. "I'm going to get that son of a bitch. Don't think I won't. Jayvee Paris is toast." Then she slammed on the brakes, realizing she'd almost blown past her next stop. She turned sharply into the parking lot of Downtown Subscription. She hadn't realized when Sylvia Thissle had given her the address that it was just down the block from Jayvee Paris's house.

"Sylvia Thissle's a realtor who's done very well for herself," Lo had said. "A showy kind of woman, loud, blonde, fiftyish—you know the type."

Well, Sylvia Thissle had better watch out, she thought. Jayvee Paris had already taken the shine off her slightly improved mood. Her rear end ached from the tumble she'd taken off his porch. That, coupled with her skinned knees, meant she limped past the slackers littering the coffeehouse's wide portal. Inside, she grabbed herself a cup, then made her way into the garden. Harpo followed.

Downtown Subscription's side yard was a pleasant oasis of shade on this brilliant day, a bevy of umbrellaed tables sprinkled among fruit trees, surrounded by a low wall. At one table, a group of young women laughed together, their heads inclined toward one another like bright tulips. Three huge dogs and a cowboy with a laptop commanded another table. Sam was aiming for an empty spot toward the rear, when someone called her name.

She looked up. She didn't know this man standing and motioning to her. He was handsome, in his late forties, his thatch of dark hair winged with silver. His expensive fawn slacks and white shirt draped well on his muscular frame. "Antonio Pomodoro," he said, coming toward her now, extending his hand. "You *are* Samantha Adams? Johanna's daughter? Or am I mistaken?"

"Yes, I am." Sam paused, puzzled. How did this Antonio Pomodoro with the warm baritone, the trace of an Italian accent, know who she was?

"Forgive my forwardness." He bowed formally. "I knew Johanna. We were friends. I was *so,* so sorry to read about her passing in the paper this morning." Sam nodded her thanks at his condolences, and he continued. "And now I was just thinking about her. Then I looked up and saw you and remembered that the notice said her daughter was in town. The physical resemblance is so strong, I thought I'd take the chance. What a coincidence, no?"

Yes. Sam's life had always been rich with such chance meetings. And Sylvia Thissle had said that Downtown Subscription was the central clearinghouse for Santa Fe, the place where you'd eventually see everyone you knew. Or, perhaps, were about to know.

Pomodoro gestured toward a chair. "Won't you come and sit with me? I'd understand if you'd like to be alone, but . . ."

"No, no. Thank you, I will." She was eager to speak with anyone who had known Johanna, and when an opportunity presented itself like this, she could hardly refuse. "I'm meeting someone in a little bit, but we can visit until then. Do you mind the dog?"

"I love dogs. And this one's particularly handsome."

Harpo gave Pomodoro's offered hand a sniff and, finding it of no particular interest, searched out a shady spot beneath the table.

"So, Mr. Pomodoro," said Sam, settling herself, "tell me how you knew my mother."

"We did business together, back in New York. That's where I live, actually. I've known her for, oh, maybe fifteen years. I'm an art dealer with a gallery in SoHo, and Johanna seemed to like the work I show, as did her clients, luckily. We'd become friends, over time." Pomodoro ran a hand through his thick hair. "I simply can't believe she's gone."

Sam nodded. "I know. It's hard. It was so . . . unexpected."

"Yes, I saw her only a few days ago. We had lunch together."

"Really? How did she seem?"

"Fine. Perfectly fine. The same old Johanna. In good spirits, I thought." He paused. "Do they know yet . . . ? Or perhaps you don't want to talk about this. Of course you don't. I'm so sorry."

"The cause of her death? No. I don't. Toxicology reports can take quite a while." Sam wondered about his saying Johanna had been in good spirits. Jesus had said she was distracted, out of sorts. "I'm curious, Mr. Pomodoro—"

"Antonio, please."

"Antonio. When you saw Johanna, did she happen to mention, was she staying at La Fonda then?"

"At La Fonda? Oh, that's right. I remember now, reading that in the paper. I wondered why she wasn't in her own charming house. I thought, well, maybe she was having it painted or something. Though she was there, at home, when I first contacted her about lunch."

"And at this lunch, you said she seemed fine? In good spirits?"

"Yes, yes. The usual Johanna, up on everything as if she had only left New York moments earlier. She didn't talk about herself, of course."

"Of course?"

"Come, come, Samantha, you must know that Johanna never spoke of herself. That was part of her mystique. Though, of course, she was probably different with you."

"And did she speak of me often?"

"Well." Pomodoro seemed flustered. "You know how it is; you know someone through business . . ."

"She never mentioned me, did she? You didn't know she had a daughter until you read it in the paper, did you?"

Now he was uncomfortable. "No, I'm afraid I didn't. But her secretiveness, that was part of her charm."

Sam smiled encouragingly. "Tell me about *your* Johanna."

"Well, we used to tease her, my friends and I. We said that she liked being a woman of mystery. Such a trait can be a positive, you know." Pomodoro rushed on, seeming to want to make up for the awkwardness he'd perceived in the mother-and-daughter relationship. "I have always found that when people are not forthcoming, others become obsessed with knowing more about them. We're drawn to the secretive, aren't we? You'd see people who'd known Johanna for years listening to her conversation very carefully, looking for the slightest clue, waiting for her to make the tiniest slip about her private life. Her past."

"And did she?" Sam asked. "Did she ever slip?"

Pomodoro paused. "Only on purpose, I think. Occasionally I'd hear her mention something like a garden she'd loved, somewhere in the south of France." He paused. "Did she ever live there?"

Sam shrugged and gave Pomodoro an enigmatic smile. "Please go on. Tell me more."

"Well, when she did throw out a tidbit, her inquisitors, those who were dying to know more—would *pounce.*" Pomodoro made a claw of his hand and dropped it, ever so briefly, atop Sam's. "They'd poke and prod for more. Of course, had their curiosity been satisfied, they'd have been bored within a minute, just as they were bored with everything else."

"I see." And then, feeling that perhaps she'd learn even more if she was open, she told Pomodoro she'd had no contact with Johanna for many years.

"Oh, my dear Samantha. And now she's gone. How *awful* for you. And not even knowing the cause of her death."

"Yes," she said. "There are millions of questions I wanted to ask her. We lost so many years, so much opportunity . . ." They sat quietly for a few moments. Then Sam said, "Tell me, Antonio, do you remember my mother wearing a large silver heart on a chain?"

"Of course." He brightened. "She wore it all the time."

"Was she wearing it when you saw her for lunch?"

"I'm not sure. Why do you ask?"

Sam pulled the slender chain and the silver key from beneath her blouse. "She gave me the key, but not the locket, and I haven't been able to find it so far."

"She didn't tell you where it was?"

"No."

"Have you looked through her things?"

"I've begun to. I'm staying in her house."

"Well, you must find it. If Johanna wanted you to have the locket, it must have been important."

"My father gave it to her as a gift when I was born."

"I do wish I could help you. In fact, I'd like to be of any assistance I can. You'll be around for a few days?" Pomodoro reached into a pocket for a thin gold case, pulled out a card, and wrote a number across it. "I'm staying at the Eldorado. Call me anytime. Please don't hesitate if there's anything at all you need."

Pocketing the card, Sam looked up and saw a heavyset blonde standing in the doorway of the coffeehouse. She was wearing a long full dress of hand-painted blue silk and fit Lo's description of Sylvia Thissle. Her blonde hair was done in an upsweep. She was fiftyish, with an attractive face and beautiful skin, but there was something fevered about the woman's china blue eyes.

"Antonio"—Sam turned to him—"I think this is the person I came here to meet."

"In that case, let me go." He half stood.

On an impulse, Sam grabbed his arm. "No," she said. "If you have the time, please stay." She raised a hand, and the woman saw her and started toward them. Yes, it might be helpful to see someone else's take on Sylvia Thissle. And, another's presence might diffuse the situation if Sylvia were to react as negatively as Jayvee Paris.

Pomodoro nodded. "Certainly. However I can be of service."

Now the blonde was upon them. "Hello! Are you Samantha Adams?" she boomed, pumping Sam's hand. "So good to see you. I'm Sylvia Thissle. And I *love* to welcome new people to Santa Fe." Sam thanked her, then introduced Pomodoro. At his name, Sylvia clutched a hand to her substantial bosom. "You are *kidding* me. *Count* Pomodoro? My God!"

Pomodoro said, "Guilty as charged." He turned to Sam with a look of embarrassment. "I don't use my title."

Sylvia leaned closer and waggled a red talon in Pomodoro's face. "I've been hearing your name all over town.

I was beginning to feel left out that I hadn't made your acquaintance yet, and *here* you are. Well, as we say in Santa Fe, there are no coincidences. I'm a realtor, you know, and I have a couple of clients who are great collectors. I'd *love* to have you meet them."

"Perhaps," Pomodoro said politely, "that can be arranged."

"Perhaps? Do you hear that?" Sylvia trilled. "The count is *so* coy. *Perhaps* he likes to be pursued. Did you know, Samantha, that Count Pomodoro is a famous art dealer from New York? He's been visiting all our little galleries, haven't you? I wish you'd let *me* show you around. I could tip you to some things *no one* ever sees."

"I'm sure that would be very nice." Pomodoro smiled.

Lo had been right about Sylvia. She was pushy—and more than a little pathetic.

"Good, good," Sylvia said. "I'll give you a call. You're staying at the Eldorado, aren't you?"

Pomodoro was startled. "Why, yes, I am."

"Now, don't act so surprised. Santa Fe's a tiny place. Everybody knows everything. And you're the talk of the town. Surely you know that."

"Well, no, I can't say that I do." Pomodoro didn't seem pleased.

"A handsome man like you? On the loose? Come now, Count Pomodoro."

Pomodoro chose to make no comment. Wise move, Sam thought. Any encouragement would be like blood in sharky waters.

"Now, Samantha here," Sylvia said in a voice that carried throughout the quiet garden, "is interested in buying a house in Santa Fe. Maybe you'll want to consider making this a second home too. There's lots of art bought and sold in this little place. Third largest market in the country. But I'm sure I don't have to tell *you.*"

"You're buying a house?" Pomodoro turned to Sam.

"I'm afraid Ms. Thissle misunderstood me on the phone." She'd realized that at the time, but Sylvia had hardly let her get a word in, and she'd thought, just as well. "Actually, I'll be selling one."

Sylvia's face fell. There were far more sellers than buyers in Santa Fe. And then she smiled, trying to recoup. "I see. So where is this house?"

"It's on Canyon. Upper Canyon. Just up the road from Cristo Rey Church."

"Well, that's good," said Sylvia. "Prime old east side."

"It's not a very big house," said Sam, "but it's quite lovely. My mother had very good taste."

"Your *mother's* house. I see."

"Yes," said Sam. "My mother was Johanna Hall. I'll be inheriting the property."

"Johanna Hall?" Sylvia's mouth opened and closed like a fish.

"Yes." Then Sam added lightly, "You knew my mother, didn't you, Sylvia?"

Sylvia Thissle craned around wildly as if the correct answer to the question lay somewhere in the garden. Then she said, "Of course, I did. Yes, I knew Johanna."

"You were friends?" Sam ventured.

"No, no. She did floss-ups for me when big properties were on the market. You know, if a place needed the cosmetic treatment, Johanna was the best." Sylvia licked her lips. "That was how I knew her." The tongue flicked again. "Professionally. We weren't social friends, if that's what you mean. I'm sorry," she floundered on. "I *was* sorry, to read about her passing. It was terrible, terrible news."

"Thank you," Sam said. "You're very kind. But, you know, Sylvia, I was wondering if I could ask you about the misunderstanding between you and Johanna?"

Sylvia blanched. "What do you mean?"

Sam pulled the envelope inscribed with Sylvia's name

from her bag. "I found this addressed to you in my mother's house. It's a note of apology. I was sure that you would want to have it. I wonder, though, could you tell me how she offended you?"

Sylvia Thissle blinked, then blinked again. She looked from the envelope to Sam's face, to Pomodoro, and back at the proffered envelope. But she didn't raise a hand to take it. Instead, Sylvia Thissle grabbed her bag, then pushed sharply back from the table. The table tipped, and coffee cups spilled, rolled, and fell to the ground. Harpo yelped. And Sylvia Thissle ran.

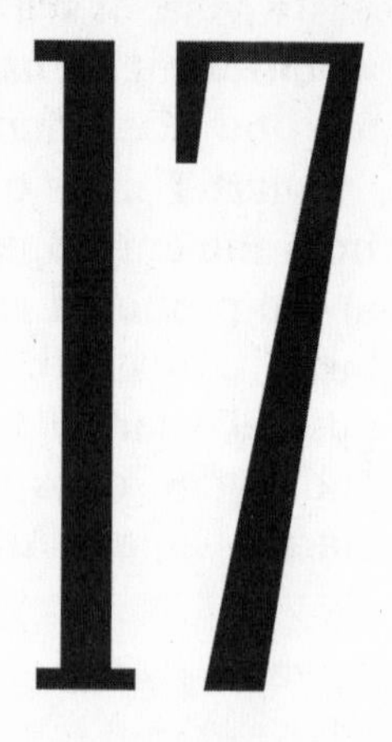

WHAT THE HELL WAS GOING ON? JAYVEE PARIS LYING about how well he knew Johanna, then shoving Sam out the door? Now Sylvia Thissle heading for the hills as if Johanna's note were a rattlesnake. Sam couldn't wait to get together with Lo and chew over her day.

But before she did that, she had thought she'd make one more stop. She wanted to visit with Estela, Jesus's girlfriend, the young woman behind La Fonda's desk who'd acted as Johanna's go-between. Who'd fielded Johanna's calls. Sam had quite a few questions for Senorita Estela.

Now she was stopped at a traffic light on Paseo de Peralta, the street that looped around the center of town. She was trying to remember which street to take to access La Fonda's parking garage when she realized a blue light was flashing behind her. A police gumball atop a midnight blue sedan. Damnit. What now?

Sam pulled to the right and stopped. The four-door Chevy sedan cozied in on her tail. As a man climbed out, she recognized him. Shit, it was Victor Vigil.

Sam rolled down her window. "Yes, Detective Vigil? How can I help you?"

"I was looking for you," he growled. "You checked out of your hotel and didn't leave a number."

"That's right. I did. Is that a problem for you?"

As he leaned into her window, Sam smelled onions and garlic and something else, some rankness specific to Victor Vigil. "I needed to know where you were," he said, and rested a beefy forearm on the window frame.

A thrill of fright zigzagged through her. His sleaziness was one thing, but this went way beyond that. There was something malevolent about Victor Vigil. She could smell his disregard for others' pain. Lo had implied that Vigil was a momma's boy? She'd have to see that to believe it.

"Did you have something you wanted to tell me?" Sam made an effort to keep her tone neutral.

"I thought you might want to know"—Vigil's mustache stretched wide above his smirk—"your mother committed suicide."

Sam's world went black. It whirled. Bile rose in her throat. She gripped the steering hard and hung on. "What are you saying? How could you know?"

"I'm telling you, she had enough sleeping pills in her stomach to kill a horse. Washed down with half a bottle of Scotch. It's a wonder she didn't throw up, choke to death. Sometimes they do."

Sam struggled with the temptation to jump out of the car and punch the son of a bitch in the face. She flung her words at him. "I don't believe you. They couldn't know this soon."

"Oh, yeah? Well, it's easier when we tell them what to look for. Which wasn't too hard, considering we found the pill bottle and the Scotch in her room. Gives the lab boys a head start, know what I mean?"

Sam leaned her forehead against the steering wheel.

I'm not going to cry in front of this man, she told herself. I'm not going to give him a goddamned thing.

Vigil hitched up his pants. "So that's why I needed to get in touch with you. Makes it hard, you disappear like that. Running all over town."

"When are they going to release her?" Sam whispered.

"What?"

"When is the M.E. going to release my mother's body?"

"Tomorrow morning, I 'spect. That's one of the things I wanted to ask you. Where you want it shipped?"

It? Sam's head jerked up. The one hundred pounds of flesh and bone that had once given her life? Where did she want *it* shipped?

"I'll have to make arrangements," she said flatly, her mind flying from morgue slab to funeral home to cemetery. Familiar territory.

"Fine. Now, you want to tell me where you're staying?" Vigil pulled out the greasy notepad he'd been carrying the day before.

Or was it the morning before that? Whenever *that* was. Time had become a shape-shifter. Neither was space reliable, the bottom falling out. Nothing seemed substantial anymore. She was beginning to feel that she'd tumbled into a nightmare she couldn't rouse herself from. She stared at Vigil? Was he lying to her? Had Johanna killed herself? Was *he* even real, or was he part of the nightmare? Maybe she'd wake up. She squeezed her eyes tight and willed herself to do that.

". . . phone number in case we need to get in touch with you again," Vigil was saying. "Death, you know, even an open-and-shut case like this, it ain't always that simple."

Sam couldn't respond. She stared at the cheap watch the detective wore. She watched the second hand move. Tick. Tock.

"Where you're staying?" he repeated.

"My mother's house," she managed, her mouth dry, her tongue stuck. "I'm staying at my mother's."

"Uh-huh. That'd be on Upper Canyon?"

"Yes."

"Now, you want to follow me?" Vigil said.

Follow him?

"You need to come into the station house. Fill out some paperwork."

"I don't understand."

Vigil crooked a finger. Don't question. Just follow.

"The feds?" Ben, the computer whiz, said to Earl. "His wife said the feds are after Stuart Wonder?"

"That's what the little lady said."

"For stolen property, but she didn't know what kind?"

"She overheard a phone conversation Stuart was having with someone privy to the situation."

"Interstate," said Benjamin. "Got to be interstate, whatever it is, if the Fibbies are involved."

"Yep."

"She didn't have anything else for you?"

"She did say Stuart mentioned a woman's name in the conversation. Christina. And she wouldn't be Stuart's squeeze, according to Deborah. She said he was too afraid of the tabloids, his good name, to be screwing around. Now, Deborah could be wrong."

"Well, gee, Earl, that's a big help. So all I have to do is a search for all the Christinas on earth."

"Only the ones you can find on the Web, young Ben."

Police headquarters were in a small industrial complex on a circle off Rodeo Road, way out at the south edge of town. Two-storied, the featureless building that housed the Santa Fe Police Major Crimes Division could have been home to any number of small businesses.

Vigil ushered Sam into a reception area. A pretty Hispanic woman was chatting on the phone behind a desk busy with photographs of three children. Glass-topped partitions marked off hallways on either side that branched to a number of small offices. "Have a seat," Vigil said, pointing to a butt-sprung chair upholstered in blue. "I'll be right back."

"So I said to her," the receptionist said, "that she ought to be ashamed of herself, she couldn't do any better than that. I took her kids the last three times in a row. I *told* her, Candelora." Fifteen minutes passed, while the receptionist and her friend chewed over their respective mothers-in-law. Meanwhile, in her head, Sam talked with Lo.

"I just can't believe that Johanna brought me here to witness her suicide. No matter what happened to her, no matter how she might have changed, the woman I met at La Fonda was still the mother I remember, and she wouldn't do that. Not unless someone was holding a gun to her head.

"Look at it. She asks me to come here to help her. Urgent, she says. Then tells me it was unsafe *to call me all those years. She's afraid to stay in her own house, checks into a hotel under an alias. Has Estela put me through a whole routine to make sure I was her daughter and not someone else. Someone was after her, Lo. Threatening her. And someone killed her. I don't care what Detective Vigil or anyone else says, Johanna Adams did not kill herself."*

The receptionist raised her voice. "She never thinks about me. She's only concerned with what her sons want. So I said to her, 'You get sick, you think your sons are gonna come and cook for you? Clean your bedpan?' "

"Miss?" Sam raised a hand.

"Just a minute."

Long minutes passed before the receptionist hung up the phone. Then she began rummaging in her desk.

"Miss? Detective Vigil went to get some paperwork for me. That was almost half an hour ago."

"Uh-huh."

"Do you know where he went?"

"I'm afraid not."

"Well, can you check?"

"Sure." With that the receptionist stood, jerking down her short red skirt. She grabbed her coffee cup and disappeared along a hallway.

Another twenty minutes idled by. Then, finally, the receptionist reappeared, plopped down at her desk, and picked up the phone.

"Excuse me," said Sam.

"Yes?" The receptionist looked at Sam as if she'd never seen her before.

Do not scream at this woman, Sam told herself. Do not bash her head in. "You went to see where Detective Vigil had gotten off to? With my paperwork? I'm Samantha Adams," she said as evenly as she could.

"I don't know."

"Then where did you go?"

"Excuse me?"

"Didn't you go to find Detective Vigil?"

The woman shrugged. "I think maybe he's in a meeting."

"Then can *you* get me the paperwork? For having my mother's remains released?"

"I don't know anything about that."

It had been an hour now since Vigil had disappeared. I'm going to have a fit, Sam thought. Lie in the floor and flail. What is *wrong* with these people? Is the whole police force involved in some kind of conspiracy to drive me mad?

Just then, a man in a navy suit who bore a strong resemblance to Vigil entered the office through the outer door. "Any messages, Maria?" he asked.

"A whole bunch, Chief." Maria, the receptionist, smiled sunnily. "They're in on your desk."

Seconds after his brother the police chief headed down the hall, Victor Vigil appeared from around a glass-topped partition with a single piece of paper in his hand. "Here you go, Miss Adams," he said.

GODDAMN VICTOR VIGIL. GODDAMN THIS WHOLE HIDEOUS business. Sam stopped at a minimart and dialed Lo's office number on a pay phone. Lo was at the courthouse, her assistant said. Could she get back to her?

Sam stood and stared into the minimart, past candy bars, pretzels, Cheez Whiz. She didn't see any of it, thinking of Jayvee Paris, Sylvia Thissle. Victor Vigil waving Johanna's suicide at her, playing with her. She'd had a gutful, thank you very much. Estela could wait. Sam needed a break. She needed a rest. She needed . . . Her gaze focused on the cash register, then the display of cigarettes above it.

"A pack of Marlboro Lights and some matches, please," she heard herself saying to the clerk behind the counter.

Within moments, she was out on the sidewalk, sucking down death. God, did it taste good. She couldn't wait to get back up the hill, park herself on Johanna's back porch, and smoke her brains out.

When she wheeled down Johanna's drive ten minutes later, Jesus's truck was nowhere in sight. Good. She didn't want to talk. Just smoke, smoke the whole pack.

She grabbed up the small bag of groceries she'd bought. Soup. Bread. Cheese. Milk. Her Marlboros. What else did a person need?

The name of a good funeral home. Somewhere for the M.E. to ship her mother's remains.

Other than that, hey, she was on top of the world. She puffed, then held the cigarette out from her, inspecting it. She was great. Yes, sirree. Doing just dandy. Check out her brave face, her game face. Does this woman look like she's got a ghost sitting on her shoulder?

Ahead of her, Harpo ambled toward the house, pausing to pee on a stone. He turned and gave her a look. Was she unlocking the door, or what?

"Yes, sir. Right away, sir." She caught up with him. Then, as she went to slip her key into the lock, the door swung open.

Uh-oh. What was this?

The door swung wider. Oh, shit.

The entryway looked as if it had taken a bomb. It was showered with papers, books, broken flowerpots, a jumble of canned goods, a sun hat, a watering can.

Sam stood, her heart pounding. A wise person would head back to Jesus's casita to call the cops, or even better, hightail it down the road.

She stepped inside.

The view was no better there. Every single book had been ripped from the living room shelves. A tide of crockery, Cheerios, spaghetti, cans of beans, soup, and chili, flowed across the kitchen countertops. The freezer door gaped, its cool curling like smoke.

The back of the house took the worst hit. Johanna's study was a blizzard of paper and files. Her bed had been stripped, the mattress flipped and tossed to the floor.

Why? Was this the work of kids wilding? Thieves?

The obvious targets still stood in place: television, VCR, computer, sound system. Even the cameras and Johanna's jewelry box were intact.

Someone was looking for something.

What?

What was so valuable?

She closed her eyes. What was valuable to her?

Johanna's scrapbooks!

She dashed back into the study and yanked out the drawer where she'd left them. It yawned, empty.

Goddamnit!

She whirled, her fury rising. She bumped into furniture. She slammed file drawers shut. Damnit! Enough. Enough, already. Then the bile began to rise, and the saliva pooled beneath her tongue. She swallowed and swallowed again, then dashed for the head. Made it just in time.

Afterward, she sat there on the cold tile for a long time. Stretched out on it, in fact. Took herself a little rest. She'd been robbed before. It was always a violation. It always felt like a form of rape. It was very creepy, knowing that someone had been in your space. Touched your things.

Finally, she pulled herself up to rinse her mouth, wash her face. It was then that she saw the message scrawled in lipstick on the bathroom mirror. *"GO HOME!"*

"So, what'd the police say?" That was Lo, later, on the telephone.

"I didn't call them. Look, I know you'll think I'm crazy, but I don't see any point in involving the police." Then Sam told Lo about her meetings with Paris and Thissle and about Vigil's stopping her in the street. She told her about the suicide verdict Vigil was so pleased to announce to her.

"No!" said Lo. "We don't believe it."

"I don't either, Lo. I think the man's full of shit."

"*That* we know. But . . . God, it's hard to believe that even Victor would lie about something like this."

Sam told her about her trip to headquarters. "He kept me waiting there for an hour. Plenty of time for him to toss my house, come back, and give me that shit-eating grin of his."

"Yes, yes, that sounds completely plausible. But, on the other hand, there's Jayvee. Sylvia. Both of them, either, strong candidates, from what you've said. Sounds like you made both of them plenty nervous."

"Okay, say it was Jayvee or Sylvia? What help is Vigil going to be? The man clearly has a hate-on for me, and it's not as if I can go whining to headquarters about him, can I? Not when his brother's chief."

"You're right. Which reminds us, we'd forgotten to tell you the Vigil family once owned Johanna's house."

"She bought it from them?"

"No. There was another owner in between. But the interim owner was also Hispanic."

"So?"

"There's mucho resentment in the Hispanic community about outsiders, especially Anglo outsiders, coming in and buying property. That's one of the reasons the Historical Committee, we call it the Hysterical Committee, is so tight-assed about renovations."

"And that's why Vigil's being such a jerk? It's all about the house?"

"Maybe. Plus he *is* a jerk."

"And what about his brother, the chief?"

"Eduardo's more together than Victor, but you know, we have this saying in Texas, all hat, no cattle."

"Gotcha. I don't know, Lo. The whole thing beats me. Vigil's a son of a bitch. Paris and Thissle both acted like scalded cats at the mention of Johanna's name. The only person I met today who wasn't weirder than hell, who actually fessed up to knowing and *liking* Johanna, was Antonio Pomodoro. His name ring a bell?"

"Pomodoro? Sure. We met at a party a couple of nights ago, one of the gallery owners gave. He seemed like a nice man. He knew Johanna?"

"Johanna bought art from his gallery in New York."

"You don't say? He didn't mention that. But then, we didn't really talk very long. We do think we remember his saying he had a gallery, though."

"Well, he had a lot to say about Johanna."

"That's wonderful. Listen, why don't you let me and Flora, my housekeeper, come over there and help you clean up?"

Sam declined. It was a generous offer, but the idea of the two talkative women in her little house was not one Sam wanted to contemplate. "Many thanks, but I can take care of it."

"Ah. You probably could use some time alone. We understand. Now let us let you go." But before she hung up, Lo added, "Sam? You asked about a place for Johanna?"

What? Then she remembered, a mortuary. Of course. She had to choose one and inform the police.

"Johanna was very clear in her wishes," Lo said. "She wanted to be cremated. No service. No church. No burial. That's what she said. In fact, we have it in writing."

Lo's words twanged an old chord. Sam closed her eyes, and she was eight again, standing in the cemetery with George. Before them, on the bright green turf, sat two tiny caskets, bearing what they believed were the charred remains of her mother and father. Sam was holding a basket of rose petals. George's hand rested on her shoulder.

"We've contacted Sombra's Mortuary for you," Lo said. "Delfina Sombra is expecting your call. She'll take care of everything."

Wouldn't that be nice, Sam thought, if Delfina Sombra *could* take care of everything? If she could mend my heart and ease my mind?

Why did Johanna die? How? What was this "GO HOME!"? What hornet's nest had she stirred up? What about Johanna's scrapbooks? What the blithering hell was going on?

Whatever it was, Sam didn't think she had the strength for it. Not this minute, anyway. Sitting on Johanna's back porch, she said, "Uncle," to the hills in the distance. "I give. Enough." She leaned back in the canvas chair and closed her eyes. But, there, inside her lids, waited the image of Johanna's body. Stretched out. Still. *Whoa.* Stop right there, she told herself and jumped up. Cigarette, she thought. I'll smoke. Yes. She was hunting for her pack when the phone rang.

George. She told him about the suicide ruling. She didn't mention Jayvee Paris or Sylvia Thissle or Victor Vigil. Nor the break-in, the warning scrawled on the bathroom mirror. Nevertheless, what she did tell him was enough for George to insist, "Come home, Sammie. Come to Atlanta. It's over, whatever it was. I can take care of all the arrangements by phone."

Sam stared at her fingertips. She didn't want to tell him of her conviction that Johanna had been murdered. He'd come and get her, for sure. "I've got to stay through the cremation, George. It's the least I can do."

"I don't agree, and I don't like the way you sound. Not one damned bit. You ask too much of yourself."

"I owe Johanna this, George."

There was silence on the other end of the line. "Okay. I hear what you're saying. That doesn't mean I like it, though." Then he added, as if to himself, "I wish Harry were there."

Yes, she said. She understood his feelings. Yes, she would check in with him tomorrow. Then she hung up and found her cigarettes. She smoked as she picked up the worst of the mess, straightening the bedroom enough that she could sleep in it. If she could sleep. She fed Harpo—she had no appetite herself—and took him out for a last pee. Jesus wasn't home, his truck nowhere in sight. Then she smoked another couple of cigarettes, or three, sitting in the living room, and downed two sleeping pills. She wasn't making a habit of it. Two nights, even in a row, did not constitute a habit. She just needed the rest. Otherwise, she'd stay up all night smoking and rerunning the same goddamned questions over and over.

Finally, she headed for bed.

Half a mile away on Caminito, Earl Wisdom's phone rang. It was Ben.

"Yes?" Earl said.

"You want to know how many Christinas I pulled up on the Net?"

"I know you want to tell me."

"Four hundred thousand and thirty-nine."

"And?"

"One that fits our parameters? A Christina that might possibly be related to Stuart Wonder's receiving stolen goods? The FBI? Goods which would have crossed state lines and/or belonged to somebody heavy?"

"Uncle Earl isn't a patient man, young Ben."

"Okay, okay. How's this? 'Christina in the Desert,' a painting by Joseph Mars, a septuagenarian primitive who trekked out of the Arizona desert about five years ago and took New York by storm. 'Christina in the Desert,' a billboard-sized female nude. 'Christina in the Desert,' a babe on her back, crucified sans cross, her arms stretched wide, her tender parts exposed to prickly cacti, red rock towers, the spire of an Hispanic chapel. 'Christina in the Desert,' mouth soft, tentative, slightly open. You want me to send you a copy?"

"You already got me hard, son."

"Our 'Christina' was the centerpiece, the showstopper, of Mars's first New York exhibition. She was purchased by one Langford Milton, a gazillionaire collector, who couldn't resist her charms, and, *ta dah,* here's the good part: A month ago, 'Christina' was nabbed from Milton's Philadelphia mansion. Does this sound like a possibility?"

Over on Upper Canyon, Sam was drifting. She and Harry were sitting in a johnboat, turning slowly in the bayou. Spanish moss made lacy curtains overhead. It was hot. A white crane high-stepped off the bank.

Sam floated with the little boat. . . .

In her dream she was somewhere on the edge of Jayvee's living room. Johanna and Jayvee and Sylvia sat facing one another in a triangulation of blue velvet sofas. They screamed questions at one another while a figure Sam couldn't make out crept through the room's shadowy corners. Someone tapped her on the shoulder. She turned and saw Rosey Bird, the Indian woman from the plaza, beckoning to her. "Come on," Rosey said.

Meanwhile, in Johanna's living room, a figure sat in one of the mushroom-colored chairs. The figure lit up one of Sam's cigarettes, stared off into space, then, with great deliberation, dropped the burning butt down between the cushion and the frame.

Sam grunted and turned beneath Johanna's white quilt. Deep, deep in the Land of Nod, she slept dreamlessly now, while in the living room, the cigarette smoldered.

In about forty minutes the flames would flare, and the smoke would billow. Another five minutes of sucking down the fumes and smoke, Sam and Harpo would be dead.

19

AIEEEEEEEEEEE! AIEEEEEEEEEE! A WOMAN WAS SCREAMING in Sam's face.

Nope. Think again. Someone was holding a catcher's mitt over her nose. So where was the noise coming from?

"Hey, Sam," a huge man spoke, a gigantic Native American. "Howya doing? My name's Dan. Dan Bird. You're gonna be just fine."

It was then that Sam realized that *she* was the woman screaming, or trying to, and the thing on her face was an oxygen mask. She lay on a gurney in an emergency vehicle that was speeding along a road. Blue lights flashed. Sirens blared.

"You're doing great," said Dan, the Goliath, leaning over her. He wore the black shirt, yellow pants, scarlet suspenders, and big black boots of a fireman. "We'll be at the hospital in just a couple of minutes. You've got a little smoke inhalation, but no burns. The fire was contained in the living room. You were real lucky."

She was? Sam blinked, and once again she heard Harpo barking, then a crashing, and finally, the wail of fire engines. *"Sam! Sam! Sam!"* someone cried, lifting her.

She tore the mask from her face. "Where's my dog?"

"Right here." Dan the giant pointed to another fireman, who was cradling a wriggling Harpo in his arms. "He's right as rain. Deserves a medal, this little guy. He was barking his head off, the guy said, the one who found you."

"Who? Who was that?"

"Jesus Oliva. Said he lives in the casita behind your house."

Once again, Jesus had come to her rescue. Sam fell back onto the gurney. "And is he okay?"

"Oh, yeah. When we left, he was pulling stuff out into the yard—a mattress, some upholstered chairs. Wasn't that bad, really, just some smoke damage. He said for you not to worry about a thing." The EMS vehicle lurched as they turned a corner. "You were real lucky, you know. The chair where the fire started was out in the middle of the living room, not near curtains or anything. But that smoke, it'll still get you."

The fire had begun in a chair. How had that happened?

"You smoke?" Dan asked.

Sam shook her head. "No. I used to."

"Huh. Maybe somebody visiting you, then? Right before you went to bed? Sure looks like one got wedged down between the cushion and the frame. Happens a lot." Dan paused. "There was a pack on the coffee table, along with some matches."

Oh, God. Of course, she *had* been smoking last night. Then she'd taken a sleeping pill and smoked, a lot. And then what? Talk about sucking down Mr. Death.

The ambulance slowed. Dan announced, "We're headed for St. Vincent's, almost there. They'll check you for CO-two levels, soot in your respiratory passages and lungs, but I'm sure you're just fine. Jesus got you out of there in the nick of time." The ambulance turned, rolled to a stop. Someone threw open the back doors, and the cool evening air poured in. It felt wonderful.

Two men lifted the gurney onto a concrete apron. Dan said, "They'll take good care of you here. And we'll run Harpo by a vet I know near here, just to be sure he's one hundred percent. I'll leave the vet's number at the desk."

Sam's limbs went to Jell-O. "Thanks, Dan Bird."

It wasn't until she was in the emergency room, the EMS vehicle already gone, that it struck her: Dan Bird, Rosey Bird—was that another one of those Santa Fe noncoincidences?

20

EARL THOUGHT, FOR A WOMAN WHO HAD JUST LEFT HER HUSband and moved out of her house, Deborah Wisdom was incredibly cool. Look at her now. She wore a frilly white apron over a little black catsuit. There was something very Folies-Bergère about the outfit. Saint Hyacintha goes Las Vegas. Oh, yeah, thought Earl, sitting at the dining table in the Quail Run condo that Deborah had rented. Miss Deborah, she was the very definition of cool.

"I hope you like *migas,*" she said. Eggs scrambled with crumbled tortillas and cheese, topped with a red chile sauce. Black beans on the side. More tortillas. Rich black coffee with a hint of chicory.

"I love *migas,*" said Earl. *And I love you.*

"I'm really glad you could come for breakfast. I'm sort of embarrassed about being here." She waved a hand—gated community, white as rice, all of that. "But I wanted to be somewhere Stuart can't just come barging in. I gave all the guards at the security gate pictures of him. 'Do not admit,' I said."

"He can tag along with somebody playing golf. You know that."

Deborah nodded. "Sure, but this makes it a little tougher." She wiped her mouth daintily with a napkin. "So, Earl, where's that picture you wanted to show me?"

Earl pulled out the image of "Christina in the Desert" that young Ben had downloaded. "Ever see this?"

"Sure. It's hanging in Stuart's office at the house on Monte Sol."

After the docs at St. Vincent's had pronounced Sam A-OK, she'd called Lo, and together they'd rescued Harpo from the vet. Sam had spent what was left of the night at Lo's. Lo hadn't pushed her about the cause of the fire, for which Sam was grateful. The thought that she could have incinerated Johanna's house, that she had almost killed herself and Harpo, made her cringe with shame. How could she have been so careless? Self-destructive?

At first, standing in front of Johanna's after Lo dropped her off, Sam saw no evidence of the fire except for Johanna's mattress and the upholstered chairs littering the grass. Inside she found Jesus Oliva sweeping up soot, washing windows.

Sam threw her arms around him. "Jesus! How can I thank you? You've saved my life twice now."

"Anyone would do the same." He tucked his head with embarrassment.

"They most certainly would not. Wouldn't want to be responsible for me. Did you know that, Jesus? You save someone, you're responsible for them forever. That's what the Chinese believe."

"That would be fine with me, Miss Sam."

He was so sweet; Sam was glad Johanna had had him in her life. She reached out and touched Jesus's shoulder. He smiled shyly, then said, "I think you want to let it air for a few days. Then maybe call the carpet-cleaning people." Jesus didn't ask her how the fire had started. He was a model of reticence and tact.

Victor Vigil had neither of those admirable qualities. He came rolling down the graveled driveway minutes after Jesus drove out to see about business of his own. At the sight of him, Sam's paranoia stood up and saluted. Had Vigil been lying in wait, wanting to catch her alone? Standing out on the portal, she looked first right, then left. There were no neighbors close enough to hear her scream, should she have reason to scream.

"Detective Vigil, it's you again." She watched him make his way down the brick walk. "How can I help you today?"

He grinned. His gold tooth blinked in the sun. "Looks like you're the one needing the help. I understand you set your house on fire?"

A flood of shame washed over her. Then she stuck her chin out. Maybe, she wanted to say. I don't remember. How about you? Do *you* remember tossing it yesterday afternoon? Tearing the place six ways to Sunday? Did you find what you were looking for? Was that you, Detective Vigil? Do you want me to GO HOME!? To shut up? To leave things well enough alone? Or was it Jayvee or Sylvia? So far, my money's on you, Detective Vigil. You're the meanest. The scariest.

"I set my house on fire?" she asked. "What makes you think that?"

Vigil shrugged. "Fires, we get reports of all of them. Most we ignore, trash cans, y'know, stuff like that. But this one, the guys said it was a cigarette dropped in a chair? Well, it makes a person wonder."

"Wonder what, Detective?"

He hitched up his pants. He was dressed in the same tired jacket and slacks he'd worn when he'd awakened her to tell her Johanna was dead. He was like a vulture, this man. Bad news, he was right on it. He lunched on other people's pain.

"Well, you know, I wonder about the timing," he said. "You come to town. Your mother kills herself. Then you almost burn yourself up. It's interesting, you know?"

Sam felt her anger rising. She might be wary of this son of a bitch, but that didn't mean she'd let him push her around. "Interesting, you think? Might your *interest* be a tad personal, Detective Vigil? Might it have something to do with your family's history with this property?" There. She'd put it back at him.

Vigil had snake eyes. They didn't blink. His mouth stretched wide, his lips thinned into a rictus of a grin. "You know, Miss Adams, an awful lot of stuff seems to be happening around you. It *does* make a person wonder."

"Really?" She couldn't keep the sarcasm from her voice.

He didn't like that. "Let me tell you, girlie, northern New Mexico's a funny place. In some ways, it's still not part of the United States." He spit into the yard, making a snail track on the dusty grass. "We got the law, hell, I *am* the law. But we're a kind of throwback to the old days. The conquistadores. You know what I mean?"

Sam didn't answer. But she didn't look away, either.

"Yeah, now *those* were the days. A man was a man. Dudes rode in on big, strong horses, *hombres* in armor. Didn't put up with any crap from anybody, especially not women." Vigil spit again. Bull's-eye, smack atop his earlier offering. "No women out here, back then. Except the squaws, of course, good for the one thing." He paused. He seemed to be considering whether to continue or not.

Sam had had enough. She turned back toward the house. "I'm kind of busy here, Detective Vigil, straightening things, you know, after trying to burn my house down. Was there a reason you stopped by?"

"Yep. Wanted to tell you the meat wagon's coming up from Albuquerque."

The meat wagon. Of course. Carrying Johanna's remains. She looked away so he couldn't see her tears.

"Yep," Vigil said. "Be here any minute. Sombra's, that's the funeral parlor you chose?"

Sam nodded, wordlessly.

"I thought so. Well, listen, anytime you want to come by the station, pick up her stuff, we'll be waiting for you." Then Victor Vigil hawked and spit again. Another bull's-eye.

Earl had wanted to run right over to Stuart's house to see this "Christina in the Desert" for himself. But Deborah had called, and Stuart was home. "Wait," she said to Earl. "We'll do it later when he's out playing golf." So Earl scooted down to the teen center to shoot some baskets with the kids who gathered there every morning. Deborah wasn't the only one interested in working with the youth of Santa Fe.

When Earl got there, all the teenagers were gathered around Jesus Oliva. He was helping them design a mural they were going to paint on a bank building downtown.

"Qué pasa?" said Jesus.

"Not bad," said Earl, and the men slapped five.

Then the kids' voices rose. They were arguing about who was going to be the featured player in the mural. The girls wanted Selena. The guys wanted the Barrio Boys.

"My money's on the girls," Jesus said. "Women are *strong* these days."

Earl nodded, thinking of Deborah. Yes, indeedy. Little bitty woman using him to help her get what she wanted.

He knew that. He didn't mind, not one bit. Let him be her vessel. Let her use him up. He was willing.

Jesus was leaning up against the side of one of his glory-colored vehicles, this one an ancient Mercury. "My girlfriend Estela's maybe getting *too* strong," he said. Earl pictured Estela, her dark curls, her pretty face. "I think Estela's stepping out on me."

"What makes you think that?"

"She's got this new gold ring; it's got a big square red stone in it, a garnet. She says a friend gave it to her."

"A friend, huh?"

"That's what I said. She said, if I didn't trust her, I could go fuck myself."

"Estela said that?"

"No, but, you know what I mean. She said, like trust me or forget it. But I know what I know. My cousin Pablito—he's a busboy in the restaurant in the lobby of La Fonda, where Estela works—he said there's been this old guy chatting her up. Hanging around. I'm going to find this guy, tell him to lay off. Call him out. Damn gringo *turistas,* they come here, throw their money around, think they own the town. I hate their guts." Jesus punched his fist into the side of his Mercury. But softly. A painter needs his hands. "Find him, I'll call him out."

It was Earl's own rash behavior that had caused him to be locked up in Raiford years earlier. He didn't want his young friend Jesus going down the same path. "Hold on, man," he said. "You're sure he's the one who gave Estela the ring?"

Jesus shrugged. "Estela says I'm confused, because I have so much going on in my life. I don't know, man. Miss Johanna, my boss, has died. Her daughter, Miss Sam, came to stay in her house, and last night the house caught fire, and . . ."

"Whoa! Wait up. Did you say 'Sam'?" How many women named Sam could there be in Santa Fe?

Sam had been about to head down the hill to Sombra's Mortuary when Johanna's phone rang. It was Antonio Pomodoro.

"A fire!" he exclaimed. "That's terrible! What can I do to help you?"

Nothing, Sam said. Not a thing. Though, on the other hand, Lo was busy in court, and the visit to Sombra's wasn't something she relished doing alone. . . .

"Give me the name of the place," he said without skipping a beat. "Better yet, I'll pick you up."

When they got there, Johanna's remains still hadn't arrived. So, the business at the mortuary was relatively straightforward, until they got to the part about the urn. . . .

The three of them sat in Delfina Sombra's dark paneled office: Sam, Pomodoro, and Delfina, a sultry woman in navy. Elevator music purred while Sam paged through the funerary catalog.

Who'd ever thought there'd be such variety? First came the metal containers: silver, brass, brushed steel, chrome, nickel, copper, fourteen-, eighteen-, and twenty-four-karat gold. There was the china series: Wedgwood, Limoges, "Ming dynasty," a little adobe chapel that resembled a cookie jar. Or one could choose to disguise her loved one as a humidor, picking among teak, ebony, rosewood, mahogany, burled walnut, heart-of-darkness tulipwood, or the more rustic knotty pine. Then there were the sporting trophies: golf, bowling, basketball, tennis, croquet, polo, volleyball, shuffleboard, weight-lifting, wrestling. Or the gamesplayer's ashes could be placed in chess pieces, Scrabble tiles, checkers, Boggle squares, dominoes. Or name-your-own-fantasy: the dead could be ensconced in a replica of a workshop, a sewing machine, a fishing boat, Elvis, Marilyn Monroe.

Sam closed the catalog. "I'm having a little trouble here. I haven't the slightest what sort of thing Johanna would have wanted."

"Let's think about her house," Pomodoro suggested.

Sam closed her eyes and imagined Johanna's living room, when it was still intact. "She did have a collection of Indian pottery. Several of the pots are black, dull-finished with shiny details. Do you know what I mean?"

"Maria bowls, probably," said Delfina Sombra. "The work of Maria Martinez from Santa Clara Pueblo; they're quite valuable. We could work with one of those."

Then Sam remembered her friend Suzie from Stanford, and the death of Suzie's mom. "What if I decide to scatter the ashes?" she asked.

"Then you don't really need an urn at all. In that case, we can provide you a temporary container for the remains."

It had been the seventies when Suzie's mom had run her Corvette off Highway One. It had soared, then exploded on the beach below. Suzie swore that her mother had had premonitions of her death and had insisted that, when her time came, her ashes be scattered. The *where* of it she left in Suzie's hands, which was unfortunate, for decision-making wasn't Suzie's strength.

Sam and Kitty, her roommate, had spent many an hour considering the possibilities with Suzie. Lots of folks flung their loved ones from a plane out over the Pacific, but given Mom's death, that seemed repetitive. Muir Woods? Off San Francisco's Coit Tower? The Golden Gate? Not bad, but there was that Pacific thing again. Meanwhile Mom's ashes languished in the trunk of Suzie's MG, just in case she happened upon the perfect site.

After almost a year, it came to Suzie. She'd take Mom

to a Dead concert—Mom had adored the Dead—and somehow finagle the ashes backstage to Jerry Garcia, who she was sure would oblige her by flinging Mom out into the crowd. Sam and Kitty weren't convinced, but they did give Suzie points for daring. Whether or not she would have succeeded became a moot point when Suzie's MG was stolen the night before the concert. The car was recovered about a month later, but Mom . . . ?

"If scattering is what you choose, the temporary container is about this size." Delfina's hands outlined a half-gallon container. "A plastic bag inside a thick cardboard box." Yes, Sam said. Definitely. That would do it. Anything to get out of this room. Now.

21

MORE THAN A MILLENNIUM EARLIER, INDIANS HAD MINED turquoise from the Cerrillos Hills south of Santa Fe. They held the blue-green gem sacred for its powers to bestow a long and happy life and exported tons of it, even as far as to the hands of Montezuma. The route southward from the mines toward Mexico became known as the Turquoise Trail. It was this road that Sam and Antonio Pomodoro traveled now.

"What would you think about taking a drive?" Sam had suggested, once they'd escaped Sombra's. "I could do with a little break. Some fresh air. And it seems that Johanna owned a turquoise mine. . . ."

Pomodoro had been game, enthusiastic, in fact.

And so they found themselves heading out into land that grew progressively flatter and drier and more desolate. Here and there little hills, *cerrillos,* popped up like solitary mushrooms. This was the same landscape where Sam, driving up from Albuquerque, had thought Death bided his time.

Now Pomodoro pointed toward a huge volcanic outcropping off to the right. Just there, according to Lo's directions, was the turnoff onto a narrow paved county road. Behind the craggy outcropping, they passed a lonely pink adobe ranch. Beyond that, the road curved, then seemed to disappear.

"Looks like we're running out of blacktop," Sam said. Gravel spun up from their tires.

This was good, she thought, getting out into the country, away from the smell of smoke and death. And she was so glad to have company. Thank God for the kindness of strangers. Thank God for Jesus and Lo—and Pomodoro. Where would she be without them?

Pomodoro felt her glance and smiled. Suddenly Sam found herself blurting, "They declared Johanna's death a suicide, you know. The police told me just before you called."

"I can't believe that!" Pomodoro stomped involuntarily on the accelerator, and the black Jeep lurched. "Suicide? Not Johanna, surely."

"Pills and alcohol, that's what they claim. They said there were empties of both in her room."

Pomodoro eased off the gas. Then he reached for Sam's hand and squeezed it tight. "I am *so* sorry."

"Thank you. And thanks for not believing them. *I* don't. They can say what they want; that doesn't make it true."

"Then what *do* you think?"

"I'm not sure. I certainly have a lot of questions. And I'm not going to stop asking until they're all answered."

Pomodoro nodded silently. Then he said, "That could take some time."

"I know. And I do have family obligations. But *this* is one also."

"I'd certainly say so. I certainly would."

Pomodoro's hand continued to rest atop Sam's. And for a moment, she thought of Harry. Sweet Harry. She *did* wish he were here. Then she found herself telling

Pomodoro about the missing scrapbooks, the fire, her suspicions of Vigil.

"Very puzzling," said Pomodoro. "Most upsetting too. And, you say you still haven't found this locket of Johanna's?"

"No. It could be with her things that the police impounded at the crime scene. Maybe, if you don't mind, we could stop by and pick them up on our way back into town."

"Of course. Whatever I can do to be of help."

"You're very kind." Then Sam turned back to the directions. "We were to make two long turns, and we've done that. Then we go past the marker to Rancho Maravilloso. Stuart Wonder's retreat."

"Do you know Wonder?"

"No, I haven't met him. But I sat by his wife on my flight from New Orleans."

"Really? What a coincidence."

"*No coincidences in Santa Fe.* Isn't that what they say?"

"Do you believe that?"

"I don't know. So much has happened in the brief time I've been here I don't know *what* to think anymore."

Rounding the next curve, they found themselves at the ranch's gate. Sited just back from the road, Rancho Maravilloso was a re-creation of the main street of a Western town of more than a century earlier. There was a bank, a saloon, a dry goods store, a Chinese laundry, a ghost house—maybe twenty buildings in all—plus a barn, a stable, a blacksmith shop.

"Well, *this* is something, isn't it?" said Sam. "Under different circumstances, I wouldn't mind visiting."

"Maybe you can do that. Do you want to get out now, take a look around?"

"No, let's go on toward the mine. It shouldn't be far."

And sure enough, a half-mile further, Sam pointed out a red gate that was marked on the map. "Yes, and there's the cattle crossing. We're here."

Pomodoro pulled off onto a dirt-and-gravel washboard road. They drove a rough quarter mile to the red gate and parked off to the side, though the difference between road and not-road was marginal. There were no habitations, as far as they could see, with the exception of Rancho Maravilloso behind them. Miles of sparse scrub, tumbleweed, and greasewood ranged toward the Ortiz Mountains.

"I'll get the padlock," Sam offered, cramming on her sun hat and jumping from the Jeep. But the lock wouldn't budge, even after three tries. Then Pomodoro got out and carefully logged the numbers as she recited them out, but still no luck.

Sam studied the rough map that Lo had sketched. "According to this, it's only three-quarters, maybe a mile down this road. You see that hill straight in front of us? That's here on the map." She tapped the spot. "There is the entrance to the mine. What say we leave the car here, climb the fence, and walk?"

"Why not?"

Once over the gate, they trudged slowly down the dusty road. The heat and the altitude made the going tough. After fifty yards, they were both panting.

Sam said, "Don't you think it's strange, Johanna buying a mine? It's not like having a summer cabin or a fishing camp. Something you could really enjoy."

"Oh, I don't know," Pomodoro answered. "Johanna was always quirky. It was part of her charm. She could have owned a rice paddy outside Bangkok; I wouldn't have been surprised."

"I guess you're right. Even when I was small, I realized Johanna was different from my friends' mothers. So full of high spirits, and she *painted*. But we always idolize our parents, don't we? When we're children, we think they're gods, even if they're deeply flawed. Like my father . . ." Sam paused.

Pomodoro waited.

"My father was a drunk. A binger," she explained. "When I was a little kid, I thought it was perfectly normal that he would go along for months being quite wonderful, and then he'd go off on a toot. He'd drink everything that wasn't locked up. Then he and Johanna would fight. They had some doozies: stomping up and down stairs, screaming behind locked doors, throwing china. The whole nine yards."

"Really? Who threw the china?" Pomodoro asked.

"Johanna mostly. When she was angry, she could destroy some crockery, big time." Sam stopped and wiped her brow on an arm.

"So she *was* violent," Pomodoro said.

Sam stopped dead in the dirt. "Violent? What do you mean?"

Pomodoro blinked. "Throwing china? That sounds violent to me."

"I've never thought of it that way. I guess I excused her because she was provoked. When *I* drank, I was such a jerk I'm surprised people didn't lob whole china cabinets at me."

"I disagree. I don't think there's ever any excuse for that kind of behavior." Pomodoro's voice was cold, tamped down.

Sam was taken aback. "Have I said something to upset you? I just meant that drunks can be so obnoxious that I can understand if other people sometimes overreact."

"No." Pomodoro shook his head fiercely. "I don't think they should."

Sam was growing increasingly uncomfortable. There was something going on with Antonio Pomodoro that she didn't understand. "Maybe we should change the subject."

"You're right. *I'm* the one who's overreacting now." He smiled sheepishly and grazed her hand with a fingertip. "Please forgive me. I'm thinking of my *own* family, not yours."

"It's okay, really. You don't have to explain."

"No, no, I want to. You see, when I was a kid, my parents fought all the time. And my mother, well, she was very excitable, and she'd get carried away. She was a good woman, but sometimes . . . Anyway, when I was fourteen, they were having this big row—my dad was a drinker, like yours, and he'd come home soused—and she was mad, and she picked up something, a silver pitcher, I think, and hit him in the head. She'd hit him before, but this time, he collapsed and died."

"Oh, Antonio, no!"

"I'm afraid it's true."

"I am so sorry. That's a terrible story."

"I know. I really loved my old man. He had his faults, but I loved him."

"I loved my dad too. And Johanna. I miss them both, terribly."

They stood there for a long moment, under the blazing sun, their eyes shining with tears. Then Sam tapped his shoulder. "Let's see the mine and then go back into town and grab some lunch. Suddenly I'm starving. What do you think?"

The tall tan hill looked no different from any of the others around—barren, sparsely dotted with chamiso and scrub—except for a dark opening in its side, framed with rough wood. The mouth of the mine looked exactly as it had in the photograph on Johanna's desk.

Sam reached the entrance first. "Come on," she called to Pomodoro trailing behind. "What are you doing?"

He stood trying to balance on one foot. "Just a minute. I've got a pebble in my shoe."

Sam turned, then stepped inside the doorway and looked down a dark narrow tunnel that began just beyond where she stood. The temperature dropped immediately. It was impossible to make out much detail in the blackness, especially after the brilliant sunshine, but it looked as if the rock walls and floor were slick with damp.

She stepped out again and walked back into the white heat toward Pomodoro, then reached for the water bottle strapped to his shoulder. After a long drink, she said, "Lo told me that Johanna had cocktail parties inside. Can you imagine?"

"I didn't know she *ever* had parties, but . . ." Before he finished his sentence, something raced across the ground between them and the mine shaft. Something gray-beige and swift.

Sam jumped back, startled. "What was that?"

"Nothing. A dog." Pomodoro straightened up and reached for her arm.

"No," Sam said, suddenly uneasy. She squinted out across the brush and chamiso. "I don't think it was a dog. It was a coyote."

"Whatever; it's gone now. Shall we?" He dropped a hand to the small of her back.

But Sam wouldn't budge. "Nope," she said. "We can't do it."

"What are you talking about?"

"It's not safe." She recalled Jesus's words: *If Mr. Coyote crosses your path, you've got to sprinkle corn pollen or cornmeal in his footprints before you can go on. If you don't, it is certain you will die soon.*

Pomodoro smiled indulgently. "You don't believe that. You don't strike me as a superstitious woman."

"Well, given my luck the past few days, I'd rather be safe than sorry."

Pomodoro's smile faded. "But we drove all the way out here. I can't believe you want to turn around now when we're only a few yards from the mine."

"Maybe seeing it wasn't the point. Maybe the drive was. You know, the journey? Besides, we can do this another day."

"But we're here now."

"I just can't do it, Antonio. Call me crazy, but I can't." She turned and looked back down the deserted road. She didn't see the coyote now. In fact, nothing moved for miles. There'd been no cars in Rancho Maravilloso's yard. This was such desolate country anything could happen out here and no one would know. She turned and patted Pomodoro on the shoulder. "Tell you what, let's run by police headquarters and pick up Johanna's things, and then I'll buy you that lunch I was talking about."

AMONG JOHANNA'S THINGS THAT THE POLICE HAD TAKEN from her hotel room Sam found silver bangles and bracelets inlaid with turquoise, four pairs of silver earrings, a silver squash blossom necklace that looked to be valuable and quite old. But there was no silver heart locket. Sam stood alone in a small property room and sifted through the jewelry, a few clothes and underthings, a couple of paperback novels. It was upsetting to touch these last belongings of Johanna's, and soon she found herself awash in tears once more.

But tears were good, she thought. It was good to cry, to grieve, to mourn. Lo had told her that, as had George. And at moments like this she believed it, and she gave in to it. Though there was always that voice that said, Buck up. Find out what *really* happened to Johanna. Later, there'd be plenty of time for tears, back home.

Outside, she rejoined Pomodoro, who was waiting in his car. "Now for that lunch, I promised you," she said.

"We don't need to, if you'd rather be alone."

"*I* need to. But could we just eat?"

He nodded yes. They didn't have to talk of Johanna.

"Let's go to my favorite place," he said. "I think you'll like it."

She did indeed. Café Escalara, in the heart of old Santa Fe, was a long simple room, modern and cool and serene, all white with two sets of French doors and mirrors along one long wall. The hostess, who looked like Buddy Holly's sister, greeted Pomodoro warmly, then led them to a table for four. She made the extra place settings disappear as if she'd waved a magic wand.

And Sam, despite her ever-shifting moods, found that she did indeed have an appetite. She devoured her salad and eggplant with roasted tomato sauce and tasted Pomodoro's linguine with Manila clams.

It was on her way back from the ladies' room, through the bar, that she paused at the sound of a vaguely familiar voice. A woman was saying, "Tell me about Christina, Stuart. I want to know the whole story." Sam turned.

Deborah Wonder, her companion from the plane, stood talking with this "Stuart," who must be her husband. Seated on a barstool, he was staring straight ahead. He was small, pudgy, but nice-looking, green-eyed, with a headful of sandy curls. "Mind your own business," he said to Deborah.

"This *is* my business," she said. "I'm going to find out about your Christina, don't think I won't."

At that Stuart threw some money on the bar and blew past Deborah, out the door.

"I won't be put off that easily, Stuart!" Deborah called, following close on his heels.

What was that? Sam wondered. And here she'd just been talking about these people out at Rancho Maravilloso. Then she glanced at the video monitor behind the bar on which a pretty young brunette was doing card tricks. A caption scrolled across the bottom of the screen. *"What you see ain't what you get."*

A finger of premonition tickled the back of Sam's

neck. Okay. So, *why* did she see Deborah and Stuart Wonder now? And *what* did she see?

Then someone brushed her shoulder, and Sam turned. Dear God, it was Rosey Bird, cutting quite a figure in a full three-tiered skirt of black trimmed with red.

"Rosey!" Sam exclaimed. "What are *you* doing here?"

Rosey said, "It was good that you didn't go in the mine. That would have been very dangerous. It's good that you listened to the coyote."

What the hell was going on? "I don't understand. Were you there? I didn't see you." She looked out from the bar toward Antonio Pomodoro, as if to seek his concurrence. When she turned back, Rosey Bird was gone.

After lunch, Pomodoro dropped Sam back at Johanna's and she packed up her clothes. She couldn't stay here now, and it wasn't just the smoke. She was deeply ashamed of her carelessness and more than a little uneasy with Johanna's ghosts. No matter what Jesus said, she'd be much more comfortable over at Lo's.

"Hey, little dog!" she greeted the twirling Harpo at Lo's door.

"He's a very sweet dog," said Flora, Lo's housekeeper, bustling out of the kitchen. "But he wouldn't eat. I think he wanted to wait for his mama. I tried to feed him some eggs, but, no."

"My little lifesaver. My picky eater." Sam held him to her chest, and they did their favorite waltz. "You want to go for a walk? For a ride in the car? Want to go to the store for some Mighty Dog?"

Yes, yes, and yes.

"Where's the closest grocery?" she asked Flora.

"Well, there's the Albertson's on Cerrillos or over by de Vargas Mall. Then there's Furr's on Saint Michael's. Johnny's Market is just down the road, but I don't know about dog food. Then there's . . ."

Harpo could starve by the time Flora explored all the possibilities. "Where does Lo shop?" Sam asked.

"Ah! Miss Lo, she trades at Kaune's on Old Santa Fe Trail. You head down Cabra to Canyon, make the left onto Monte Sol, then right on Acequia Madre. . . ."

It was at the intersection of Acequia Madre and Garcia that Sam saw Isabel Martinez dawdling along the road in front of Downtown Subscription. "Look, Harpo," Sam said to the little dog who was standing on her lap. "It's Isabel, your number one fan in Santa Fe." Then she called hello to Isabel.

"Harpo!" the little girl shrieked. "Harpo! Harpo!"

"I think," Sam said to the dog, "that God wanted us to stop and buy this little girl a soda. Pump her about Jayvee Paris and her 'Auntie' Johanna. What do you think?"

Settled under the shade of an umbrella in the coffee shop's garden, the three of them—Sam, Isabel, and Harpo—tucked into their drinks. "You're sure your mom won't mind that you're here?"

"Nope," said Isabel. "I come here all the time. I *am* six. I can go wherever I want to." She paused. "As long as I don't go off the block."

Sam smiled. When she'd been Isabel's age, she'd had the same boundaries.

"Besides," said Isabel, scratching at a scab on her elbow, "Momma's gone to the store. She's shopping for food to take up to the ranch."

"You're going away?"

"Just up to Abiquiu."

Georgia O'Keeffe country, Ghost Ranch, Black Mesa. Somewhere up north of Santa Fe. Sam knew that much. "You spend a lot of time up there?"

"Uh-huh. We're leaving tonight. Jayvee said we were

going to, right after that lady left this morning. He said to Momma that it was a good time to go."

"What lady?" Sam asked casually.

"Sylvia. That was her name. Do you know her?"

"Not really. But I've met her." Sylvia Thissle. Had to be. *Very* interesting.

Isabel lurched on. "We ride horses at the ranch. I have a pony."

"You do? I always wanted a pony, but I never had one."

"Mine is all white. His name is Snow. He's not mine, really; he belongs to the foreman. But he's mine when I'm there."

This was the opening Sam was waiting for. "My mother was afraid of horses. One ran away with her when she was a little girl. My mother is your Auntie Johanna." Sam suspected that Isabel didn't know of Johanna's death.

"Really? I *told* you you look like her. And you know what?" Isabel peered over the side of her chair at Harpo and made a face at him. She waggled her hand at him, and he licked her fingers. "Auntie Johanna told me one time that I look like her little girl. She said that's one reason why she liked me so much." Isabel popped back up and gave Sam a big grin. She was missing a front tooth. "So, I look like you!"

"I noticed that the first time I saw you."

Then, Isabel's thoughts leapfrogged backwards. "Jayvee didn't like Sylvia."

"Really?" Sam said. "How do you know?"

"I heard them yelling in the living room. Then Sylvia left, and Jayvee said we were going to the ranch, and Momma went shopping for groceries." Isabel sucked loudly through her straw. "Does Harpo like chocolate milk? I could give him some."

"No, dogs can't have chocolate. It makes them very sick. They can't digest it."

"Oh. Does he like peanut butter cookies?"

"Loves them. You may give him a very small bite, if you want."

Isabel broke off a piece of her cookie and handed it down to the little dog, who took it gingerly with his black lips. "How old is Harpo?"

"He's four. I've had him since he was a puppy."

"When's his birthday?"

"January eighth. Elvis's birthday. Do you know who Elvis is?"

"Of course. *My* birthday's May sixteenth. Where was Harpo born?"

"In San Francisco. I used to live there. Have you ever been there?"

"*I* was born in Truchas."

"Oh, really? I know someone else from there." *There are no coincidences in Santa Fe.* "Jesus Oliva; he's a friend of Johanna's, come to think of it. Do you know Jesus?" She hadn't asked him this morning about Jayvee Paris or Sylvia Thissle. She'd been too busy thanking him for rescuing her from the fire. And then he'd gotten away, and Victor Vigil had come calling. . . .

"Uh-huh," Isabel was saying. "Jesus paints pictures on cars. He took me for a ride in one of his cars once, a convertible. I sat up in the backseat and waved at people."

Sam could just see that. Isabel doing the Junior Miss America wave. She proceeded carefully. "Sounds like you're good friends with Johanna and Jesus. Do you ever go to Johanna's house?"

"Lots of times. *One* time I slept over. Auntie Johanna told me stories and drew pictures for me. I slept in the bed with her. It was fun."

Sam's heart turned over. Sam had adored sharing Johanna's bed when she was a little girl. When her father had been away on business, she and Johanna had tucked into her parents' high bed with piles of pillows, cookies, and hot chocolate. They'd stayed up late, and Johanna had told her stories about when she was a little girl. . . .

Isabel reached up and touched Sam's cheek. "Why are you crying?"

"I'm not. I've got something in my eye."

"That's what my momma always says when she cries. Grown-ups are weird."

"You can say that again."

"Grownups are weird." And then Isabel threw her head back and roared with laughter.

Sam could see why Johanna had loved her.

EARL WAS ON THE PHONE WITH DEBORAH WHEN STUART'S call beeped through.

"Sure, I can take you," Earl said to Stuart. "Of course. That's what I'm here for, my man. To give you relief, reduce your stress."

Then Earl switched back to Deborah. "He's coming right over."

Jesus, just then walking in his door, answered the phone on the fourth ring.

"Jesus," Sam said on the other end, "I was just talking with a little girl who said she was a good friend of yours. Isabel Martinez?"

"Isabel! One of my favorite people." Then he paused. "One of Johanna's too."

"So you know Valentina Martinez and Jayvee Paris?"

"Sure. Miss Johanna was fond of them all."

"They visited often?"

"Often for Miss Johanna, though around the time, a week ago or so, I told you when Miss Johanna started seeming so upset, about then, Isabel stopped coming over."

"Did you ask Johanna why?"

"I did, but she wouldn't say anything."

"What do you think? An argument with Jayvee, maybe? Or Isabel's mother?"

"I don't know about any arguments. But Valentina is not Isabel's mother, Miss Sam, if that's what you mean."

"I beg your pardon?"

"I know because Valentina is from Truchas. She's older than me, but Truchas is a little town. I knew Valentina, growing up."

"So whose daughter *is* Isabel?"

"Who is her mother, that I don't know. But I know her father. Jayvee Paris is her father."

Sam was speechless.

"Yes, Mr. Jayvee Paris, he came driving through Truchas with Isabel when she was a tiny baby. He stopped at the church and talked with the priest. He said he was looking for someone to come with him to Santa Fe, to help him take care of Isabel. Now the priest knew that Valentina, who was about eighteen at the time, was dying to leave Truchas. And she was a good girl. So, the priest gave Jayvee her name. He went to her house and visited with her parents, and they said she could come. But when they got to Santa Fe, Mr. Paris told Valentina he wanted to pretend that the child was hers instead of his."

"Jesus, are you sure of this?"

"Miss Sam, why would I make it up? If you don't believe me, you go and look in the church records in Truchas, see if Isabel's name is written there. Go ask Jayvee. Ask Valentina. Miss Johanna knew their secret, and you are her daughter. I'm sure that they would talk with you about it."

"I don't think so. Jayvee Paris told me that he barely knew my mother."

"No, no. You must have misunderstood."

"Perhaps." She paused. "Tell me, does anyone else in Santa Fe know about Isabel?"

"People from Truchas, for sure. Some Cordovas. A few Lopezes. Some Vigils."

"Vigils?"

"Oh, yeah. There's Vigils all over New Mexico."

"The family of Victor Vigil, the police officer?"

"Oh, yeah. Victor's from Truchas. He and his brothers moved down a long time ago. One of their uncles, you know, he used to own Miss Johanna's house."

Sam sighed. The more she learned, the less she understood. She already knew of Victor's relationship to Johanna's house, but what did this new information mean? And why had Jayvee lied? *Dear Jayvee. Please accept my most heartfelt apology for the pain I have caused you.* What the hell was going on here?

She asked Jesus, "Do you think Isabel knows Jayvee's really her dad?"

"Oh, no. No one ever talks about it."

"But, Jesus, doesn't it occur to you that there must be some *reason* why Jayvee would go through this pretense about his daughter? Who *is* Isabel's mother? Why doesn't Jayvee want anyone to know? Doesn't anyone ever ask these questions?"

"The past is the past. Mr. Paris is a good father, in his way. Valentina is happy. Isabel is happy. Who would want to upset a little girl?"

Well, *I'm* going to ask, Sam said to herself, approaching Jayvee Paris's house. Jayvee's old blue Toyota Land Cruiser squatted in his drive. She pounded on the door. There was nothing but silence inside. "I know you're in there, Jayvee Paris!" she called. Still no answer.

Okay, he wanted to play it like that. Fine. She stepped back on the porch, took a deep breath and yelled at the windows, "You lied to me about knowing Johanna. And

I think I know why. It's about Isabel, isn't it?" She stopped. How far was she going to go? Isabel shouldn't hear this from her. But how else was she going to push Jayvee Paris hard enough to get him to talk with her? "Isabel and Truchas? Don't make me do this, Jayvee. Come out and talk with me."

Somewhere upstairs someone threw up a window. Sam stepped back off the porch and looked up. Valentina Martinez stood pointing a pump shotgun straight at her heart. Sam knew the weapon, which took a three-inch magnum slug.

"Go away," Valentina said quietly.

"Look, I just want Jayvee to talk with me."

Valentina racked the shotgun, a sound ominous as a diamondback's rattle. Sam walked backwards, hands up. "Don't do this, Valentina," she said.

"Don't tell me what to do. You come to my house and threaten my daughter." The barrel tracked Sam's heart.

"I'm not threatening Isabel."

"Get off our property. Go home and leave us the hell alone."

STUART WAS SOAKING WET WHEN HE WALKED THROUGH THE door of Earl's studio. The man was sweating like a hog in one of the driest climates on earth.

"Stuart, my man," said Earl. "What's up? Uh-oh. Look at your shoulders, all scrunched. You're going to kill yourself, worrying."

Stuart ripped off his clothes and threw himself on the table, facedown. "Help me, Earl."

"I'm glad you called, Stuart. You've come to the right place." Then Earl set to work, beginning with Earl's neck, kneading the knots that practically glowed in the dark. Loosen those up, Stuart would talk.

Stuart moaned, "Oh, that's so good. Earl, you wouldn't believe the troubles I've got."

See? Earl started on the man's shoulders.

"I've got hell coming after me."

Earl leaned into Stuart's trapezius. "IRS? Lots of my clients got problems with the Internal Revenue. Ain't so unusual."

That pricked Stuart's pride, piqued his competitive spirit. Earl could feel it in the way his muscles tightened again.

Stuart said, "I wish. I mean, them too, but, no, this is even worse."

"Uh-huh." Earl rolled a thumb across Stuart's right deltoid.

"Can you keep a secret, Earl?"

"Oh, you bet. Don't you know that a masseuse's table is as private as the confessional booth?" He knew that Stuart wouldn't remember that he'd told him, only a couple of days earlier, he didn't want to hear his troubles.

"Well," said Stuart, "there's this deal I did. Traded something for something I really wanted; now it's turned around, bit me in the ass."

"Uh-huh. Kind of a barter thing, that's what you're talking about?"

"Yeah. But big-time barter. Mega-barter. You know what I mean?"

Earl grabbed up a handful of latissimus dorsi. "Not exactly. But, a man of your stature, I'm sure it was something huge."

"It was colossal. It was, well—now, this is real hush-hush, Earl."

"My lips are sealed."

"There was this painting I really wanted, see?"

"I hear you have a world-class collection, Stuart. That's what everybody says. Says, that Stuart Wonder, can't nobody shine a candle to him when it comes to art. Except maybe a Getty, one of them."

"Yeah, well, the Getty people would have loved to get their hands on this one. But somebody else beat them to it. And then somebody else relieved that someone of the painting. . . ."

"Hot art. Is that what we're talking about here, Stuart?"

Stuart waggled a hand. Sort of. You might say so. In the ballpark. Warm. Close. Yeah. Stuart's pride in his wheeling-dealing had obviously outruled his discretion.

Not that Stuart had been reticent to begin with; he'd been a braggart since he was three.

"So what happened?"

"Well, you know, like I was telling you the other day, I have a few financial woes. I've been buying too many toys, you know what I mean?"

"I do. It's easy, once you start."

"Yeah. Anyway, I wanted this painting, but I didn't have the scratch, so what I did, I traded a piece of property I owned out in Southampton."

"Uh-huh." Earl didn't need to be told about the Hamptons or the value of the property. Earl had clients with Long Island mansions. They imported him to the South Fork the same as they brought in caviar.

Stuart said, "So everything was hunky-dory until Hurricane Archie."

"Don't tell me."

"Yep. Goddamned hurricane ate that lot right up."

"Yeah, but that ain't *your* problem. You made the trade. Over and out."

"That's what I said. But the man I did business with, he didn't see it that way."

"So now he's squeezing you."

"He is, Earl, he is. Between that and Deborah doing her Saint Hyacintha number, well—you heard her the other day—I don't know which way to turn."

"Just tell the man to take a walk."

"I tried that. But, it didn't work. This man, he's got me all involved in some shit I don't *even* know what's going down. Like I said the other day, Earl, I'm drowning here. Way over my head."

"You want me to talk with the man?"

"Oh, no. I don't think so."

"Might be good idea, Stuart. Might be just the thing."

"Mmm," Stuart said, sounding less sure of himself. "I don't . . . *aaah.*"

Earl smiled as he took two big handfuls of deltoid and began to knead. He could feel Stuart begin to relax. Oh, yeah. He could work this little sucker, all right. Stuart was putty in his hands.

Okay, calm down, Sam told herself, back in her car. Valentina didn't shoot you. She warned you off, but she didn't shoot you. Did you *think* she was going to shoot you?

Yep.

Yep. Yep. Sure did.

She thought you were threatening Isabel. Even if she's not Isabel's natural mother, it was her maternal instinct that made her pick up her rifle. She had to protect her child.

Sam stopped.

She hadn't thought of that possibility for her own situation, that some terrible thing had wedged itself between Johanna and *her* child. Or some terrible someone. Was that it? Had their years of separation been set in motion by someone Johanna needed to protect her from? Was she still protecting her when she was killed? Had Johanna realized that in calling Sam here, she'd put her in some kind of final jeopardy? Was that why she'd tried to shoo her away?

The only way Sam was ever going to know was to keep asking questions, even if it meant facing down shotguns, the likes of Victor Vigil, and God knows what else. With that, she threw her car into gear. She wasn't giving up on Jayvee, not by a long shot. But right now, she had her sights on Sylvia Thissle.

Jesus sat in his '60 Fairlane, waiting in the drive before the steps of the Eldorado Hotel. He was waiting for El Gringo, his blood enemy, the rival for Estela's affections. Jesus had tracked him down with the help of his cousin

Pablito, who'd described El Gringo to him in the first place.

The man was staying in room 510. A suite. That's what Pablito had said. He'd also described the man's car. Now Jesus watched a couple climbing out of a silver Lincoln Continental. He'd seen a million *turistas* like them in Santa Fe. The woman, a blonde, good-looking in a hard kind of way, her face thick with makeup. Her husband, balding, a pretty good paunch, red-nosed—he'd go a bottle of Scotch a day, easy. The two of them, and this was the part that killed Jesus, had only just arrived—there was their car and their luggage—and already they were wearing what looked to be ten thousand dollars' worth of Southwestern gear. The blonde sported a concho belt with intricate and delicate inlay, a squash blossom necklace, turquoise bracelets with gigantic stones. Hubby wore the belt, the boots, the hat, a jacket dangling fringe and feathers. Did they wear this stuff back home?

Now the couple was halfway up the steps, a porter struggling with their wagonload of luggage, and Jesus turned his mind back to El Gringo. He'd been thinking about this moment for a while.

When the man appeared, Jesus was going to call him out.

Pistols in the plaza at dawn.

Jesus liked the ring of it. The plaza was the by-God-we-made-it end of the gut-ripping drive on the old Santa Fe Trail. Before that, it was the place where show-off conquistadores wheeled around on their steeds. Put your ear to its earth, and you could, even today, hear echoes of braves dancing. *Eeee-wa-ha.* Nope, you couldn't do much better than the plaza for a display of manly pride: it reeked of valor, gunpowder, and testosterone. Santa Fe's plaza was the epicenter of the Wild West.

A black Jeep Grand Cherokee pulled into the drive and stopped right in front of Jesus's Fairlane. Jesus tightened his grip on the steering wheel as a big handsome man with wings of silver in his dark hair handed the vehicle over to an attendant. He turned toward the steps, this man who had to be Jesus's foe, the man moving like a lion, as if he could buy and sell the whole town before lunch.

Jesus jumped from his car, drew himself to his full five-six, add another two inches for the lifts in his boots, and stepped in front of El Gringo, clicking his heels.

Sylvia wasn't at her office. Yes, said the receptionist, Sam could leave a message, but Sylvia didn't seem to be picking them up today. She'd said she was coming down with a cold. She might have gone home. No, she couldn't give Sam, Sylvia's home number. Nor her address. But Lo Ellen's crackerjack of an assistant could.

Ten minutes later, Sam was pulling into Sylvia's driveway. The house on East Palace was a rambling old estate Sylvia'd picked up at a fire sale. The grounds were park-like, and the white stucco Mediterranean-Spanish house included, among other things, five bedrooms, a gym that Sylvia never used, cavernous public rooms, and four outbuildings.

Right now Sylvia was standing in the blue-and-white kitchen, surrounded by luggage. What had she forgotten? She'd grabbed up clothes, cosmetics, lots of cash. Well, old girl, she told herself, you're leaving this town the same way you arrived. Running. Hiding. But this time—she patted the full money belt beneath her dress—you know a little bit more about surviving.

And with that, Sylvia Thissle opened the kitchen door and slipped out the back.

"Sir?" Jesus gave a small formal bow to El Gringo. He could see himself, as if in a movie. He could hear the mariachis, the rising clatter of the castanets.

"Yes?" said El Gringo.

"I am Jesus Oliva. I have come . . ."

But before Jesus could finish his sentence, the man was staring past him at the Fairlane. Stepping past Jesus now. Walking toward the car. "Good God," El Gringo said, and extended a hand respectfully, as if he were about to touch a *santo*. "Look at this wonderful vehicle! This magnificent piece of art!"

Jesus tried to see the Fairlane through the other man's eyes, and yes, if he did say so himself, the car was quite something. It was filled with passion. This painting was much much more than its technique. This was a work of Jesus's soul.

Last spring, he had spent a week at Christ of the Desert Monastery in the red rock country near Abiquiu. Every day Jesus had fasted and prayed and hiked. On Good Friday, ten miles into one of his sojourns, Jesus had heard men screaming as if in agony. He rounded an outcropping in a red rock canyon, and there he saw a circle of Penitentes, a cofraternity of the Catholic Church. A dozen men, they were stripped to the waist, flogging themselves. Flutes wailed. Chains rattled. Blood streamed down their backs, then fell, black, into the dust. Behind the Penitentes rose a rough cross, upon which the most fortunate, the chosen, of their number would be bound and hung.

Jesus had stood transfixed. He'd closed his eyes to wipe the sweat from them, and when he opened them, the Penitentes were gone. There'd been nothing before him but the towering rocks and the whistling wind.

Upon his return to Santa Fe, Jesus had done his best to capture his vision, with the Fairlane as his canvas.

"This is magnificent," said El Gringo. "The color. The agony of these figures. And their joy. It's fabulous. This is genius."

"Thank you," said Jesus.

"This is *yours?* You did this work?"

"Yes," Jesus said simply, though within him, a great thrumming had begun.

"Do you know what a marvelous gift you have?"

Jesus nodded. *Twenty,* he finally managed to say. *I have done twenty more cars.*

The man grasped Jesus's hands, then gave him a great hug. He pulled a card from his pocket and said, "Listen, I know you are thinking, who is this man? What do I care about his opinion? So I'm going to tell you. I have a gallery in New York, a very good gallery downtown in SoHo. I would love to see the rest of your work. And, if it's anywhere as good as this, I want to talk with you about a possible show at my gallery. Is that something you might consider? Is that something we could discuss?"

Jesus stood wordlessly smiling. Inside him, the chant began, a rosary of thanksgiving. *Thank you, Blessed Lady. Thank you, grandmother. Thank you, Robert Redford, Miss Johanna, Miss Sam. Thanks be to you all.*

Okay, Sam said to herself, pulling her car into La Fonda's parking lot. You can't find Sylvia Thissle, who had a screaming argument with Jayvee Paris, according to Isabel. Valentina, who's *not* Isabel's mother, has threatened you with a shotgun. Victor Vigil is a pig and a creep. *Someone* rifled Johanna's house and stole her scrapbooks. *You* set her house afire and almost burned yourself up.

Sam froze.

The thought had never occurred to her until now. What if she hadn't set the fire? If she hadn't dropped the cigarette? She had a vague remembrance, this flickering image somewhere in her mind, of someone else sitting in that living room.

Whoa, she told herself. Hold on. A lot of crazy stuff was going on, but that was no reason to get paranoid—said the paranoid as the killer had him by the throat.

Get out of the car, Sam. Go talk with Estela.

Sam found Estela at her perch behind the front desk in La Fonda's lobby.

"Yes?" Estela smiled brightly.

"I'm Sam Adams. Do you remember me, Samantha Adams? Johanna Hall's daughter? I'd like to talk with you."

Estela's mouth tightened. "I'm afraid I can't do that now. I'm on duty."

"I've called several times. You didn't answer any of my messages."

"Yeah, well. I've been busy." Estela rolled her eyes.

Sam leaned across the desk. "I've been busy too, *awfully* busy trying to figure out what happened to my mother."

"I'm sorry. I cannot help you." Estela twisted the garnet ring on her finger. She also wore gold hoops in her ears and a gold chain around her neck. This was a girl who liked bright shiny things.

Sam opened her wallet, plucked out a hundred-dollar bill, and laid it on the desk between them. "I realize that your time is very valuable. Would it be possible to pay you for a few minutes of it? Perhaps a meeting in the coffee shop?" Sam inclined her head in that direction.

Five minutes later they were settled into a corner table. Sam was saying, "When my mother checked into the hotel, she made this arrangement with you, that you were to ask anyone who wanted to ring her a series of questions?"

"That's right."

"It was sort of a test?"

"I guess." Estela couldn't seem to keep her fingers off her garnet ring. She twisted it back and forth.

"Did she say why she was doing this?"

"No. And I didn't ask her. She gave me a hundred-dollar bill." Estela raised an eyebrow at the irony. "I didn't ask any questions."

"I see. And what about when you weren't on duty? What happened then?"

Estela shrugged. "Maybe she had the same arrangement with the other desk clerks and phone operators. I didn't ask. She told me, she said, 'Estela, don't talk with anybody about this.' "

"Did you know my mother before she checked into La Fonda?"

Estela shook her head.

"But you knew that Jesus worked for her?"

"Uh-huh. But I never met her."

"You never went over to Jesus's house?"

"No. I have my own house. Why do I need to be going over there?"

"I don't know, Estela. It's something that people do sometimes, go over to their boyfriend's house."

Estela gave her a hard look, and Sam moved on. "And the name of the chambermaid who discovered my mother?"

"Manuelita. She called downstairs; she was screaming in the phone." Estela raised her hands to her ears.

"And you went right up? You didn't call security? Didn't call the cops?"

"I told you. I didn't know then what the problem was. Manuelita, she just kept screaming."

"Okay. You went upstairs, and my mother was lying in the bed. Let me ask you, Estela, did you notice what was sitting on the bedside table?"

"I didn't see anything."

"A liquor bottle? A prescription vial?"

"I didn't notice. I was just looking at Manuelita jumping around screaming over this dead lady."

"How did you know she was dead?"

"She looked dead. She wasn't breathing."

"Did you take her pulse?"

Estela made a face at the idea.

"Okay. Another thing. Did you notice if my mother was wearing a silver locket? A big puffy silver heart on a chain?"

Estela pushed back from the table. "Is *that* what you want? You think I stole something? You're not paying me enough money for me to sit here and listen to you accuse me of being a thief."

"I'm not, Estela. I'm just looking for the answers to some questions that . . ."

But before she could finish, Estela said, "Screw you, lady," and flounced out.

25

EIGHT O'CLOCK, SAM AND LO HAD FINISHED DINNER AND were sitting out on Lo's patio. "I feel terrible about it," Sam said. She was talking about having put the question of Isabel's parentage out in the street. "But no one was answering the door. Jayvee wouldn't talk with me. Maybe Isabel didn't hear. Maybe she wasn't home."

"Someone points a shotgun at us, we don't think we'd be so et up with a guilty conscience."

"I know, but still—"

"When people make decisions to hide things like that, they have to know that someday they may be sorry. There can be some awfully dire consequences to keeping secrets."

"You have any children, Lo?"

"Nope, we never married, though we know that's not a prerequisite. Had plenty of beaux, though. Then we came out here, discovered girls."

Sam's head swiveled.

Lo laughed. "Oh, yeah. There's lots of that going around in Santa Fe. It's a grand place for the ladies. Our last lover, Claire, died two years ago. We were together twenty-one years."

"I'm really sorry," said Sam.

"Yeah, me too. Guess the only thing we missed about never having hitched up the conventional way *was* the kids. Wouldn't mind having a passel of grandbabies running around about now. How about you? You still could, assuming that train ain't left the station."

"Forty-two, it's a little late to get started. And, you know, Lo, my history with motherhood, well, I guess I just never had the inclination."

"What do you mean, 'cause your mother died when you were little? That's what you thought anyway, up until a few days ago. You didn't have any idea of otherwise, so how could that make any difference?"

"But maybe I did know. Maybe deep down somewhere inside, I suspected something wasn't quite right. Maybe that made me shy away from going down the baby trail myself. Not to mention, of course, I never exactly met the right man."

Lo snorted. "You expect us to believe that?"

Sam rocked for a few moments. Out to the west the setting sun turned the sky the most amazing shade of flamingo. She told Lo about Jimmy, her one-and-only husband, and definitely not the right man. Then there was Sean. "I thought he was it, but he died before we could get to the babies."

"And no one since?"

Sam smiled. Well, yeah, there was Harry. The next thing she knew, she was telling Lo about Harry's songwriting, his barbecuing, how funny he could be. His physical bravery, his slow smile, his gray eyes, how the lid of the left one drooped just a tad.

"Sounds sexy," said Lo.

"You'd be right."

"Where is he now?"

"I'm not exactly sure. Somewhere in China. He's on a river-rafting trip. Exploring virgin territory."

The phone rang. Lo picked it up. "Why, yes," she said. "She sure is." Then she laughed. "Same back at you. Well, you'll have to come see for yourself." Then she handed the phone over. "It's for you."

One of the things Sam had always loved about Harry was his exquisite sense of timing.

"I'm looking at some awfully interesting country," he said. "Wish you were along."

"Where *are* you?"

"In Kunming, about eight hundred miles northwest of Hong Kong. To get to the river, we've got a three-day drive through some pretty spectacular mountains. This is the last chance I'll have to connect with Ma Bell for about a week and a half, so I thought I'd take it."

"How'd you *find* me here? Wait, don't tell me; you called George."

"He said things weren't going as smoothly there as you might have hoped."

Sam felt a lump begin to rise in her throat. "It's been hell."

"I'm sorry about your mom, Sammie."

She'd forgotten how soft Harry's voice could be. How comforting. It was awfully good to hear from him. "I am too," she said. "I'm really sorry."

"They know the cause of death? I asked George, but he was a little vague."

"They're saying it was suicide." Then, once again, Sam found herself pouring out the tale. The only thing she held back was the fire.

Harry waited until she was done; then he said, "You ought not to be dealing with all that alone. You just sit tight. I'm grabbing the first flight out of here."

"What are you talking about? You just traveled half-way around the world to run this river."

"These guys, they're world-class. They only asked me to come along to carry their gear."

"That's not true, and you know it. Besides, what do you think you're going to do when you get here?"

"Hold you in my arms. Dry your tears. Beat the crap out of that jerk Victor Vigil. Shake the truth out of those other two. What do you think?"

Sam couldn't answer. She could only nod her head. Yes, please come.

"We're too far apart, Sammie. Been like that for way too long."

The lump in her throat was now a tennis ball. She was so touched by Harry's concern. But then, he knew her. Talking to him was like going home. Yet, as much as she wanted to feel his arms around her right now, she didn't trust herself. Was she sure she'd feel the same way a month from now? She didn't want to play with Harry, use him either.

He said, "I had stewed sharpei puppies and boiled rat for din-din. How about you?"

She managed a laugh. "Nothing that tasty, I'm afraid. Just some green chili and cheese enchiladas Lo's housekeeper, Flora, made for us. You'd have loved it."

"Now tell me what you're wearing."

"A T-shirt and jeans. It was ninety degrees today, going to drop into the fifties tonight. What else do you want to know?"

"Which T-shirt?"

"Elvis saves Green Stamps." She pulled it out from her chest, looked down. "I can hardly read it anymore."

"That 'cause I rubbed the Elvis off, long time ago."

"Harry," she warned.

"Don't 'Harry' me. Listen, here's the deal. No matter what you say, I'm flying back, first plane I can grab."

"By the time you get here, I'll be long gone, back in

Atlanta, visiting with George. Blowing out those birthday candles."

"You lie. You'll stick in there till the last dog is hung. I know you, Sammie, and I don't like the sound of any of this mess. Your poor momma. This Vigil creep. Jayvee Paris. Your momma's house trashed. Secret passwords with some desk clerk. And who the hell's this Pomodoro character?"

"He's a nice man, Harry. He was a friend of Johanna's. He's been really helpful."

Harry was silent. About twenty dollars' worth of long-distance time hummed past.

Finally, Sam said, "If it'll make you feel any better, Lavert assigned one of his Mounties-to-the-rescue relatives on me. An uncle named Earl Wisdom. He called; I've got to get back to him. Right after you finish sweet-talking me some more."

Earl Wisdom. Lavert Washington. Slaughter Phipps, a cousin of Lavert's Sam had met in Tupelo. What was with this family that made them the most taking-care-of-business men on earth?

"You know what?" Earl said to Sam after they'd talked for a bit. "I'm gonna go speak with Jayvee Paris myself. See if I can get him to change his tune. And Sylvia, I'll track her down. I know Sylvia. I sure do. The woman's a piece of work."

Sam said, Sylvia, all right; she'd be happy to turn her over to him, but she really wanted to deal with Jayvee herself.

Whatever she wanted was fine with Earl. Then he asked, "Now, about your momma's locket. You think Estela, she took it?"

"I'm leaning in that direction. I spoke with the other desk clerks and operators, and Estela's the only one sounding like she's got something to hide."

"I really hate to hear that. I'm friends with her boyfriend, Jesus. *You* know Jesus. He's the one who told me how to get in touch with you."

Then Earl asked her to tell him everyone she'd talked with. She ran down the list, then said, "And there's Lo, of course. And Deborah Wonder, a woman I met on the plane coming here, but I haven't seen her since. Well, I saw her yesterday at lunch, having words with this man I think was her husband, but I didn't speak to her. And Antonio Pomodoro, who's an old friend of Johanna's who's been very kind to me. But he doesn't live here. He's from New York."

Uh-huh, Earl said. Earl Wisdom was cool. He didn't like to be going and speculating aloud about things and folks until he knew what was what, who was who.

Now one thing Earl did know for a certainty was that—when he called Deborah at the Quail Run condo and she said, "Can you come right over?"—he could do that.

She was wearing a little slip of a black dress when she met him at the door. No shoes. Just the dress and a big smile. Great legs.

"Earl!" she crowed. Her saying his name like that warmed places in Earl that had been shut down for years. Now, opening his arms and feeling Deborah step right into them, he thought, Maybe I've died and gone to heaven. So he pinched himself. Nope. He was alive, all right. He took a deep breath. Deborah's curls smelled sweet and fresh. He said, "You won't believe what all I've—" But before he could finish, Deborah laid a finger to his lips. *Shhhhh,* she said, taking him by the hand and leading him into the living room, where the only lights were a couple of candles on a low table. The two of them sat on the sofa, side by side. Earl knew he was dreaming now.

"Would you like some wine?" she murmured. "Or maybe some cognac?"

Cognac. That'd be just fine. Keep that warm feeling going. Cognac, that'd be good. Then he said, "Don't you want to hear what Stuart—?"

No. There was that finger again, to his mouth. This time, Earl opened his lips just wide enough to touch that finger with the tip of his tongue. *Ummmmmm,* said Deborah, turning her finger. Gently giving it to him, tip first. Earl sucked that little finger in. Let it go. Sucked it in. Oh my. My my my. Deborah moved closer. She was like a warm little animal. Earl's eyes filled with tears.

"I've been so lonesome, Earl," Deborah whispered.

"Well, you don't have to be lonesome no more." Earl ran his hand slowly down the tenderness of her neck.

"I'm glad. Have you been lonesome, Earl?"

"Something terrible."

"I have something to tell you," she murmured.

"Umm-huh."

"I decided to run on over by myself to the house to see about 'Christina.' It was the same painting, all right. Then I tracked Stuart down at Escalara, wouldn't give up until he told me *who* the deal was with. Who's bothering him for the money which, goodness knows, ought to be mine. I mean, what's with this Antonio Pomodoro?"

Whoa. There was that name again, the same one Stuart had told him. Of course, he didn't necessarily believe Stuart. He could be lying to the both of them, him and Deborah.

Deborah said, "So, Pomodoro made a deal. Now he's trying to renege on it. Stuart said that there were extenuating circumstances. He said Pomodoro was driving him crazy. He said he was thinking he ought to give Pomodoro whatever he wanted. Said I'd have to understand. I said, 'You just tell him, Take a walk, Mr. Pomodoro.' "

"Deborah, Deborah, you are a woman after my own heart."

"Yes, and, you know, it makes my heart hurt, thinking about the waste of two people like us, loving people, not being together." Then she turned and kissed him. The kiss was like a snowflake on his lips. Earl was stunned. It was as if he'd never been kissed before. It took him a minute to gather himself and say, "Yeah, but we're together now. No more hurting hearts. Not a single solitary thing hurting here now."

Deborah looked up at him from under her lashes. "Nothing you need to kiss? To make it well?"

"Now, wait." Earl reared back and took a long look at her. Looked until he had his fill, for now. "I wouldn't go that far." Then he kissed the tip of her long, thin nose. "I'd say maybe there's two or three things need to be fixed with a kiss." He kissed her eyes, her dark lashes fluttering like butterflies. "Maybe four." He ran his tongue along one perfumed earlobe. "Or five." Kissed the hollow of her throat. "No, ten." Ran his tongue just below that hollow. "Twelve." Felt the swell of her small breasts begin beneath his lips. "Thirty-eight." Nuzzled an inch lower. "About four hundred and sixty-two things to be kissed, that would be my best estimate."

Deborah had a great laugh that started somewhere deep in her belly. Earl waited for that laugh to subside, and, then, a few minutes later, all the counting ceased. Everything that had to do with cerebral functioning shut right down. Logic was unnecessary on this sofa. Deborah and Earl were acting on instinct here. Their bodies led them like homing pigeons toward the best places and those rhythms that swung the most.

It was an awful shame, Earl thought—a couple hours later, when his brain began to function again—that he had this damned late-night errand to run.

* * *

Meanwhile, over on Picacho, Sam was happily tucked into Lo's guest room. It was a snug, safe place with pale blue linens and adobe walls sponged the softest gold. Lo had brought her a glass of warm milk and a plate of chocolate chip cookies.

"Watch out. I'll never leave," Sam said.

"Good."

Who needed Restoril with milk and cookies? Sam was definitely going to sleep tonight. She managed only a couple of pages of a mystery novel she found on her bedside table before she drifted off.

In her dreams, she and Harry lay together on a chaise out on his French Quarter patio. All around them was a rushing river. Lots of whitewater. Little rapids. Flooding across their knees were Narvin Kimball's banjo and jazzy ragtime notes from Preservation Hall next door. Harry smothered her with kisses.

"I can't breathe," she said.

"*Shhhhhhhh.* Don't talk." It was Harry who said that, but he was speaking in Earl Wisdom's lovely high-tenor voice.

Sam said, "I can't wait to meet Earl."

Harry kissed her clavicle. "I love this place," he whispered, kissing it again. Then, "I hope you don't fall in love with Earl."

Sam giggled and pulled her Elvis T-shirt over her head. "Why would I do that?"

"You always fall in love with Lavert's relatives. All fourteen hundred of 'em you've met so far. Especially the uncles and cousins."

"That is not true," Sam said. She ran a finger into Harry's belt buckle, loosening it. "I didn't fall in love with Antonio."

Harry pushed up on the chaise, his arms stiff, and stared down at Sam. He stared hard. He said, "Lavert doesn't have an uncle named Antonio."

EARL HAD THOUGHT ABOUT IT FOR A WHILE AND HAD DEcided that he didn't want to meet this Antonio Pomodoro anywhere inside. Earl's years in jail had given him a touch of claustrophobia. Whenever anything made Earl the least bit uptight, he could see Maginnis, the dude with the dead eyes who'd run his dorm at Raiford, backing him into a corner. Pulling a shiv. Telling Earl he didn't do like he said, Earl was gonna die.

So Earl said on the phone, "Mr. Pomodoro, I understand from our mutual friend Joey the Horse that you enjoy a good cigar. I've got a couple of fine Dominican stogies in my pocket; wonder if I could invite you out for a stroll?"

"Why sure," Pomodoro said. "When?"

"Right now, if it's convenient. Not too late for you, I hope."

After he'd left Deborah, Earl had called Joey the Horse in New Orleans wanting to know if there was any way to get a line on this Pomodoro dude. "Antonio Pomodoro?" Joey had said to Earl. "Sure. Antonio. Tony Tomato. I heard of him. New York, that's right. Lucky Brancati, the Garibaldi crew, he's the one mentioned

Tony, I'm pretty sure. Fancy art dealer, right? I don't got the details right here at the tips of my fingers, but you give me a day, I'll be back to you."

Earl hadn't waited. Knowing that Pomodoro was somehow mob-connected, he figured, hell, that was enough to get him in the door. And, the way Earl saw it, time was an issue here. Stuart was getting crazy. There was no telling what the man might do next to put Deborah's financial situation in jeopardy. Earl wanted to be Deborah's knight in shining armor. Right now. Man, he said to himself, hanging up from Joey, see how you let it do you. A little sweet pussy, four or five cognacs, man, you got the impatients. Yes, you do.

So now Earl and Pomodoro were smoking their ten-dollar Avo cigars, walking down East Palace, away from the Eldorado. "So that's how you know Joey?" said Pomodoro. "You're his masseuse?"

"Yeah."

"You must do one hell of a job—you here, Joey in New Orleans. Him taking the trouble to fly you in."

"I like to think I'm pretty good." Earl's chest swelled a little.

"So, you say you and Joey were talking, and my name came up? How's that?"

Earlier, when Earl was thinking how he'd play this thing, he'd decided he'd start with something that didn't mean shit, then work his way up to the Stuart connection and the "Christina" fiasco with the beachfront lot. Then he'd see if he could somehow wave the man off, get him to ease back on pressing Stuart, for now. Until Deborah got what was hers. After that, well, it was none of his concern.

So he said, "How'd your name come up with Joey? Well, see, like I said, Joey knows my nephew Lavert, and Lavert called me a few days ago, says to give a hand to his friend Samantha Adams. Then I'm talking with Sam, and she says that *you've* already helped her out. Says that you did business with her mother in New York. So, it's like, I say to Joey, it's a small world."

Had he played that right? Earl was asking himself, when *ka-boom,* he tripped on a chunk of buckled sidewalk. It was hard to see, the street pretty dark now that they'd crossed the Paseo and were strolling through a residential neighborhood. Pomodoro grabbed onto Earl's arm to keep him from falling, and held on, a friendly gesture. "So, you mentioned me to Joey, Joey says, 'Call him up? Say hello?' Is that it?"

"Pretty much. Yeah. That's what he said."

"We have any other acquaintances in common?" Pomodoro still had Earl's arm in his grip.

Earl thought about the question for a minute. Which way should he go with this thing? Art. That was where he wanted to be heading. So maybe he'd slide into it sideways. "Jesus Oliva. I'm talking with him, he says you ran into him, told him you liked his car art. He's real excited. It's nice you can do something to help him out. Real nice."

"So Jesus is a friend of yours." Pomodoro puffed thoughtfully on his cigar. "I think young Jesus could be very successful. How about his girlfriend, Estela? You know her too?"

From what Jesus had said, Pomodoro was coming on to Estela, so Earl didn't want to go there. He wondered why Pomodoro had brought it up. Earl was beginning to feel that he'd stepped into quicksand. He wasn't sure what was safe, what wasn't. So maybe he'd just cut to the chase. "Actually," he said, "when I was talking with Joey, he said you might be the man to talk with if a person were interested, just a theoretical, of course, in moving some merchandise that might have some *urgency* about it." It was then that Earl noticed that they had stopped right outside the wall of Sylvia Thissle's house. He'd told Sam that he would talk with Sylvia. He needed to get on that, tomorrow morning for sure.

Pomodoro leaned toward Earl, one hand on Sylvia's gatepost, the other resting on his gold belt buckle. He said, softly, "What are you talking about, Earl?"

"Business. You know, business."

Pomodoro lowered his left hand, so now both hands were caught at his buckle. "Business, huh? Same kind of business Sam's mother and I were involved with back in New York?"

"I don't know about that," said Earl.

"But she did believe that lie, didn't she?"

"Lie? What do you mean?"

Pomodoro stepped closer. "Sam believed Johanna knew me in New York?"

"So what are you saying? You didn't know her? I don't know what you mean, man."

"I knew Johanna *way* earlier than that."

"And?"

"Oh, we went *way* back. Back to the old country."

"Oh, I see. So I guess this earlier business was something you didn't want Sam to know about. Her momma was dirty, that's what you mean? Maybe brought some merchandise in from . . . what, Italy?"

Just then, a cloud moved across the moon, and again the night grew inky black. Pomodoro pulled the tongue of his belt away from the retaining pin of its gold buckle. That buckle was also the handle of a short, stubby knife with a double-edged blade of 440-C steel. The handle protruded now, razor-sharp, between Pomodoro's first and second fingers. He said to Earl, "You know, Earl, I think you ask way too many questions." The cloud cover shifted again, and in the silvery moonlight, Earl spotted the knife. He lurched back, arms up, but it was far too late for that. Pomodoro had already lunged with his right hand high, the full force of his body leveraged forward into the attack. Pomodoro was a powerful man, and he hit Earl's jugular, pulsing wildly beneath ebony skin, with the first blow.

An hour later, driving out the Turquoise Trail, Antonio Pomodoro puffed on a second cigar, one that he had pulled from Earl Wisdom's pocket. He'd said, "Thank you, Earl," to the corpse. Then he'd given Earl a little salute. Antonio Pomodoro was feeling fine.

It was a great night, he thought. Cool, even though the thermometer had registered ninety today. Dry. A few scudding clouds, one occasionally cloaking the moon. Otherwise, a big sky full of stars. He'd never seen so many stars in his life.

His father, Orlando, had loved the stars. When Pomodoro was a little boy, the two of them would sit side by side out at their country place, Orlando pointing out the constellations and telling him their stories.

"See that one there? That triangle? That's my father, your grandfather. That's where I'll go when I die, where I'll wait for you, Antonio, until you come and join me. You'll fill in that space, starting with that bright red star."

Now Pomodoro blinked twice. Even after all this time, he couldn't think about Orlando without tears.

Jesus, he'd loved his father.

"Everything, Papa" he whispered now, into the New Mexico night. There was no need to whisper, though. Earl Wisdom, wrapped in black plastic garbage bags in the back of the Jeep Cherokee, couldn't hear him. "Everything, Papa, I've done, I've done for you."

Not that this latest thing, killing Earl, had been something he'd planned. But Pomodoro had had his blade—

he'd named it Vendicatóre—at the ready, just in case, since that terrible night when Papa had died.

He'd let Papa down once. Never again.

So now, when Earl Wisdom had come along with his questions, Pomodoro had seen that Earl could get in the way of his paying his final respects to his papa. And Antonio had been prepared. He'd showed Earl he couldn't do that, that he loved his papa too much.

"See, Papa," he said now, peering through the windshield at the star-studded sky. There was the triangle. There was Papa, waiting for him.

Just after his stargazing papa had been murdered, when Antonio was just a boy, Antonio had become a creature of the night. He slipped out of his family's ancient palazzo to wander the Palermo streets looking for anything to salve his grief. He stalked through the skeletons of palaces whose roofs and walls had fallen victim to Allied bombs. Palaces, once rich with chapels, theaters, libraries, boudoirs of gilt and mother-of-pearl, now lay in ruins. No one cared about them. No one saw the fires Antonio built there except the homeless squatters, and they ran from the flames, and from Antonio—the crazy boy.

Somehow, Antonio found, the fires made him feel better. And, eventually, he began dragging home souvenirs from the flames: seared frescoes, blackened bits of marble, scorched wood. From them, he built a monument to his father in the abandoned ballroom of his palazzo.

It was this burnt offering to his papa that caught the imagination of his uncle Gioacchino, his mother's brother, when he came home to Palermo for a visit.

Gio, who was a painter, saw past Antonio's strangeness to his talent, and when he returned to New York's SoHo, he took the boy home with him.

Antonio proved to have a wonderful eye and to be both nimble and quick, so in not so many years had opened his own place, the Pomodoro Gallery, in the heart of SoHo. In a building owned by the Brancati family.

One of the two Brancati brothers was a priest. The other, Lucio, was a capo in the Garibaldi family of the Cosa Nostra. Antonio adored both brothers, though he loved Lucio more. And Lucio "Lucky" Brancati was amused by the idea of having a son of Palermo's aristocracy as a tenant. Back home, the grand old families tolerated the Mafia or pretended it didn't exist, though they might call upon a capo if they had a very pressing need. Here, Antonio called Lucky his uncle, invited Lucky to his dinner parties and gallery openings and treated him with respect. Lucky was proud of Antonio. Also, Lucky could smell the penchant for darkness that never ceased to run through Antonio like a burning vein of coal. And, occasionally, as one thing or another came up in Lucky's business, he offered Antonio an outlet for his dark side. It was a sort of favor to Antonio.

Now, suddenly, Pomodoro turned the wheel of the black Grand Cherokee hard to the right. He'd almost missed the road to Johanna's mine. Here was the volcanic outcropping off to the left. Here was the lonely pink adobe ranch. Gravel spun up from his tires now, just as it had yesterday when he'd driven this road with Sam.

Ah, Samantha.

He'd lost Johanna, the murdering bitch. She'd slipped away from his grasp.

But the gods had been generous with him. They'd given him a second chance to avenge his papa's death.

They'd given him Samantha.

Here was the red gate. Pomodoro braked, climbed from his car, snipped the padlock, and drove on through and up to the mouth of the mine. He would bury Earl here. After all, the man's death had been Johanna's fault.

Cause and effect. It all made sense. There was a symmetry to everything. Pomodoro could see the patterns zigzagging across one another. Riches and loss. The quick and the dead. Across the plain, the mountains of the Sun and the Moon gazed over the burial site. Pomodoro reached for his shovel. He would plant the black man on this dark night where soon, under the bright blue sky, he would bury the shining Samantha. Dark and light. Yin and yang. Symmetry. Just so.

SAM AWOKE IN A START. IN A SWEAT. IN A PANIC. WHERE was she? She saw sunlight on soft yellow walls, a parade of wooden saints across a low chest, a hammered tin cross upon the wall. Lo Ellen's guest room. She was safe.

But someone wasn't. Dread plucked at her from the sleep she'd just escaped. She fell back against the pale blue linens and let fragments of her dream fly past. She saw a little girl. Pretty. Brunette. It was Isabel, and she was running from someone. She raced through the desert, glancing fearfully back over her shoulder. She ran as fast as she could. Her young knees were going spongy beneath her. She was staggering now, collapsing. The man grew closer. She could hear his breathing. Her own breath tore from her lungs like fire. She couldn't keep up this pace. She was going to fall. He would catch her. His fingers would close on her thin legs. And, through it all, looping around the action, a counterpoint to the pounding of Isabel's feet, was a woman's mournful wail. It was La Llorana, grieving for her lost child.

Dear God! Sam's eyes flew open. In the blurry, slip-sliding way of dreams, she had *become* Isabel. Her own heart pounded, her stomach heaved. Dread threw itself around her like a cloak.

Sam reached for her Filofax. She found the number she was looking for and dialed it.

Headed down the hill, Sam felt her confidence eroding. So she'd convinced Jayvee to give her five minutes. Thirty seconds after you get your foot in the door, she thought, he's going to toss you out.

And you don't know shit. For all your poking around, you haven't learned a damned thing. Okay, Isabel is Jayvee's daughter. You know that. But what makes you think Jayvee's going to believe in your premonitions, that your nightmare concerning Isabel is going to get you anywhere?

It wasn't. She could tell that from the look on Jayvee's face as she sat now across from him and Valentina on the blue velvet sofa. Then Valentina said, "I don't like this. These kinds of dreams are no good. La Llorana. Isabel. I don't like this at all."

"No, Valentina." Jayvee shook his head. "Don't go down that path."

"She *knows* about Johanna," Valentina said. "She knows Johanna was Isabel's godmother. She knows what Johanna did."

Sam held her breath. What did Johanna do? What was Valentina talking about? Her hands grew clammy. She surreptitiously wiped them on the blue velvet.

Jayvee continued to glower at her. Sam remained quiet and still. Come on, she thought. Come on, Valentina. Spill it all.

"This could be a sign from Johanna," Valentina said. "She's sorry now for what she did. This dream is a warning she's sending us from the grave."

At that, Jayvee exploded. "Witches, ghosts, red fireballs, flying cows, earth babies, and now, messages from the grave. Is there no end to your crazy superstitions?"

Valentina drew herself tall against the sofa back. Her dark eyes narrowed. "Don't tell *me*, Jayvee Paris. You come here from your Maine." She waved a dismissing hand. "You don't know us. You don't know our ways. You don't know *anything* except you want someone to help you with Isabel."

At her words, Jayvee's anger vanished. His voice went soft. "No, Valentina, please."

But Valentina would not be stopped. "You don't get only what you ask for, not with that precious baby. You get it all." Valentina pounded a fist softly over her heart. "You get my fears for her. *I* have to protect her too."

Jayvee laid a hand on Valentina's arm. "I know. I'm sorry. Truly, I am."

Sam stared down at her feet. Her heart felt fluky in her chest. Whatever this was, whatever they were talking about, she was beginning to think she didn't want to hear it. Then Valentina said, "So, do you think Johanna told someone else about Isabel? Someone else who's going to ask us for money?"

Her words were a blow to Sam's gut. Had Johanna extorted money from them? *Blackmailed* them? Is *that* what Valentina was saying? It took all her strength to keep her gaze steady as she said, "No, I have no reason to think that."

"But isn't that why you're really here, Samantha?" Jayvee's anger was back as he spat the accusation. "To follow in your mother's footsteps? To befriend us, then bleed us?"

Sam shook her head, No. Her ears rang. Her mouth went dry. *Momma, Momma, Momma, what did you do?*

Valentina said, "You're not going to threaten to find Isabel's grandparents? To help them take Isabel away?"

Sam shook her head. Her voice was frozen deep down inside her. But her tears flowed freely. *Johanna, how could you? You threatened to take away their child? Who* were *you?* Finally, she whispered, "I would never do that. I'm so sorry. I'm truly sorry."

Valentina wiped away tears of her own, while Jayvee gave Sam a long, assessing look.

Then the story poured out, Jayvee and Valentina taking turns recounting the tale that they thought Sam already knew, filling in details they thought she might not have.

Johanna had loved Isabel from the first moment she saw the child, Jayvee said. He had stopped by Johanna's, the year-old Isabel in tow, to show Johanna sketches for a project.

It had been a long while before Johanna told him that she had a daughter of her own who had looked much like Isabel at that age. After that, they'd become best friends, constantly in one another's pockets, visiting back and forth between their houses. Jayvee couldn't remember the exact moment he'd told Johanna about Isabel's mother.

Mirta was her name. Jayvee had loved her more than life, and when she died, in childbirth, he'd almost lost his mind. Mirta's parents had offered to take the infant, just for a little while. A few days later, when he went to collect his daughter, Mirta's parents said no. They'd hired a lawyer and were collecting documentation of every drink Jayvee had ever taken, every joint he'd ever smoked. They were certain they would find a judge to rule that Jayvee's life as an artist made him unfit to raise a baby.

Jayvee went crazy. He slugged his father-in-law, then he tried to wrest the baby from their arms. After his own lawyer warned him that the legal battle could go on for years and that she couldn't guarantee the outcome, Jayvee was desperate. While the in-laws were at the movies, he tricked the babysitter, grabbed his baby, and ran.

"Of course, Johanna didn't know the details," Jayvee said, "but she'd already doped out the broad outline. Maybe it was because she had her own closetful of skeletons."

"She was such a good friend," said Valentina. "We never thought she would betray us."

"What happened, exactly?" Sam had to know.

A little more than a week earlier, Johanna told Jayvee that she needed $150,000. He said he'd love to loan it to her, but he didn't have that kind of money. She said she wasn't talking about a loan.

"And you don't know why she did this?" Sam asked.

"Not a clue," said Jayvee. "It was like one day, she was our best friend, the next day, our worst enemy. But we did what we had to do. We mortgaged and sold and scraped together the money. And then, Johanna seemed to change her mind."

Valentina said, "She told us she'd made a terrible mistake. She was so sorry. She was leaving town because she couldn't face what she'd done. Good, I told her. I said, You *should* be ashamed."

Something had possessed her, thought Sam. She didn't do this out of greed, out of malice. Something *made* her do this. Or someone. Please, God.

Jayvee said, "I told Valentina, 'You know something must be wrong with Johanna. Maybe she had a small stroke or she's in the beginning stage of Alzheimer's. This isn't the Johanna we know. We've got to help her.' "

"So I agreed." Valentina's words tumbled over Jayvee's. "Then, before we could reach out to her, a young woman called and said that Jayvee was to meet Johanna in a room at La Fonda." Then she added, "This was the night she died."

Jayvee had seen Johanna that night?

"Her call came around seven. I was told to go to her room immediately, which I did. She was drunk, drunk and kind of crazy. Reeling around the room. She kept apologizing, saying what a terrible person she was, how she hadn't meant to be, but this was what she deserved. . . ."

"What was the *this* she was talking about?" Sam wanted to know.

Jayvee shrugged. "I couldn't make sense of what she was saying. I didn't know what she was going to do, if she were going to threaten us again, or what. At that moment, I felt so many things. I was sorry for her, I hated her, I felt disgust. But I couldn't find room in my heart to forgive her. She'd frightened me too badly."

"Did she ask you again for the money? Had she changed her mind again about that?"

"No, this wasn't about the money. I never knew exactly what she wanted. I guess"—and then Jayvee's face softened—"considering that that was the night she did away with herself, that maybe she didn't know either. Looking back on it, I'd have to surmise that in her last hours, she was racked with guilt."

Jayvee's words were the final nails in Sam's heart. No, please, no, she thought. Please don't let it be true. I don't want to know that Johanna really was a blackmailer, that maybe Vigil was telling the truth. That maybe Johanna, filled with shame for what she'd done, *did* commit suicide.

Jayvee was talking again. "It was after I left, when I was heading down the stairs, that Sylvia Thissle saw me. I didn't see her, but she caught a glimpse of me, she said, just as the stairwell door closed."

"Sylvia. Yes, Sylvia," Sam said, trying to follow where Jayvee was headed. But it was too much. She heard his words and her own as if she were underwater, lying on the bottom of a pool.

"Sylvia came here, to talk with me after she'd met with you," Jayvee said. "I hadn't known until then that Johanna was blackmailing anyone else. I hadn't thought about the possibility. We were just so concerned about Isabel. Johanna had also asked Sylvia to La Fonda and had gone through the same routine with her: apologized, ranted, and raved." Then he remembered he was speaking to Johanna's daughter. "I'm sorry, Sam."

Sam shook her head, her eyes squeezed tight. There was no way to soft-pedal this story.

"Sylvia reacted differently than Valentina and I did at the news of Johanna's death," Jayvee continued. "We were, well, I'm afraid we were *relieved*. Sylvia, however, seemed to be even *more* frightened. She was frantic."

"She was very very angry too," said Valentina. "She said terrible things. She scared me." Then Valentina looked at Jayvee, hard.

"I taped our conversation with Sylvia," Jayvee explained. "I didn't know what she wanted. I did it for our protection. I thought maybe *she* was going to try to blackmail us too."

Please accept my most heartfelt apology for the pain I have caused you. I'll never forgive myself. There were circumstances . . . but there are always circumstances, aren't there? No excuses, but I have many many regrets. Forever yours, Johanna.

Jayvee said, "Do you want to hear it?"

Hear the tape? No. Yes. Sam didn't know what she wanted. She didn't know if she could stomach any more truth. But, finally, she voted yes, let's get it out. Get it over with. Hear it all.

Jayvee punched a button. First, there was silence, and, then, there it was, Sylvia's voice shaking with rage. Sam could see the woman, blonde and blowsy, too much makeup, her eyes damp, her mascara running.

"Johanna suckered you in, didn't she? The mysterious

Johanna, she sat there in that chair of hers, smoking and listening, and you poured out all your secrets, thinking that if you laid your heart at her feet, that she would give something back to you. Because she had that air about her, didn't she? Which made you feel she knew something wonderful, a secret that would make everything all right. But she didn't give you a thing, did she, Jayvee? That's because Johanna was a taker. Gimme, gimme, gimme, that's what Johanna was. And now her daughter's here, sniffing around. She's on to us, Jayvee. Johanna told her, told her everything about us, and the next thing you know, she'll be coming after us. She's going to want what Johanna wanted, or more. We've got to stop her. Stop her before she destroys us."

The tape ended. Sam sat, stunned. The silence stretched. Finally she said, "So, did you try to help Sylvia stop me? Did you trash Johanna's house that afternoon? Steal Johanna's scrapbooks? Did you write *Go home* on a mirror, hoping I would?"

Jayvee shook his head. "No, though all of that would have been tempting, had I thought of it. All I did was ask Sylvia to leave our house. I told her I wanted to forget about all this. She called yesterday and said she'd decided she was leaving town, indefinitely."

Sam didn't know whether to believe him or not. Even if he had trashed her house, she couldn't say, given the circumstances, that she blamed him. But what if he had set the fire?

Sam realized that Jayvee was staring at her. He shook his head, in wonder. "You didn't know about the blackmail, did you? You didn't know any of this."

"No," Sam whispered. "Like I told you before, I hardly knew Johanna at all."

Meanwhile, on the south side of town, Jesus Oliva sat waiting in his Penitente Fairlane outside his girlfriend Estela's house. Estela was still mad at him. She hadn't returned his calls since he'd accused her of stepping out on him with the garnet-gifting gringo, who'd turned out to be Count Antonio Pomodoro, of course. His benefactor-to-be.

Jesus wanted to tell Estela about his good fortune: how Our Lady's blessings to him had passed from Robert Redford to his *abuela* to Miss Johanna to Miss Sam and now to Antonio Pomodoro. For half an hour this fine August morning, Jesus had been watching the front door of the house Estela shared with three other girls on the southeast edge of town.

Suddenly, here she came, gorgeous in her red off-the-shoulder blouse and short black skirt. In her high-heeled sandals Estela was just tall enough to reach his shoulder, but a firecracker who held a black belt in karate. A smart man wouldn't mess with Estela.

Jesus leapt from the Fairlane. "Estela, yo!"

She just kept walking toward her old faded yellow Toyota, didn't even turn her head.

"Wait!" he called. But Estela was revving up the Toyota and backing out. Jesus wasn't about to block her way with either his body or the Penitente Fairlane. He did, however, follow her.

Estela motored along, headed out of town, never even glancing in her rearview mirror. She turned onto Old Las Vegas Highway and passed the pickup trucks on the side of the road selling red chile *ristras,* coyote fencing, and paving stones.

As usual, she didn't signal when she made the left into the lot of the Sunset General Store.

Jesus was always getting on her about her failure to indicate what direction she might be headed. "I do," she insisted, looking at him as if he were nuts. She was looking at him that way now. Pausing on the store's steps, she said, "Is there something you want, Senor Oliva?"

"To talk, Estela. I've called you a million times."

"Yes, you have," she agreed. "You are really getting on my nerves, Jesus." And then she hauled her pretty little butt on up the steps and into the store.

The Sunset General Store was eccentric, even for Santa Fe. Out front it sold gasoline and ice cream. Inside, the left half of the market was stocked with canned tomatoes, SpaghettiOs, motor oil, cleaning supplies, fishing tackle, miscellaneous dry goods. To the right, were lychee nuts, ginseng, cellophane noodles, fish sauce, rice steamers, six tables, and a sushi bar.

Estela stepped up to the front counter and ordered a coffee and a croissant.

Jesus said, "Make that two, please," and paid the tall, pretty Korean woman behind the cash register, then joined Estela at one of the tables. Estela made a fence of her newspaper. "You don't trust me," she said. "I don't like that."

"I *do* trust you. I just don't trust this Count Antonio Pomodoro, that is, as he relates to you."

"And how do you know his name? You've been snooping, Jesus. I can't stand jealous men. They go crazy on you. Next thing I know, you'll be following me, then you'll be shooting up somebody."

"Me, Estela? Jesus? Who are you talking about?" Estela didn't answer. "Okay," he said. "I want to tell you my good news. Everything else aside, I have decided to do business with Count Pomodoro. I'm going to let him show my work in New York."

Estela gave him her big eyes.

"No, it's true. Count Pomodoro loves my cars. Yesterday, I took him over to Pablito's garage, and you should have seen him. He was practically jumping up and down. Money, he said. Together we can make lots of money."

"How did you meet Count Pomodoro? Answer me that."

She had him there. He couldn't tell her the truth, that he'd tracked the count down with the intention of challenging him to a duel. "I was driving my Fairlane down Palace, and he waved me over at a red light."

"I don't believe you, Jesus Oliva. You're a terrible liar." Estela pushed back from the table. "You've been bothering Antonio. I'm sure of it."

It pierced Jesus's heart, the way she said the man's Christian name. "I have not been *bothering* the son of a bitch!" Jesus slammed his fist down on the table, and their coffees jumped.

Estela held up her right hand, showing him the offending garnet. "I suppose you didn't ask Antonio why he gave me this ring. Which means Antonio didn't tell you that he is a special agent of the CIA which has been tailing your precious Miss Johanna. Do you want to know why?"

Sure, said Jesus. Of course. He always wanted to know why the CIA had been following his employer. Miss Johanna, his benefactress, who'd done so much for him.

"You think you're so smart, don't you? Well, you don't know that your Miss Johanna was buying plutonium from scientists she was blackmailing at the Los Alamos lab and selling it to those crazy militia people in Idaho."

Really? said Jesus. Wow.

"*Plus*, she was blackmailing other people here in town."

"Why would she do that?"

Estela stopped. "I don't know that part. But I've been keeping an eye on her for Agent Pomodoro. She was a dangerous woman, your Miss Johanna."

What a load of crap! Jesus couldn't believe that Estela would be so dumb. "*Who* was Johanna blackmailing?" he asked.

"I'm not sure of all of them. But I know it was Jayvee Paris and Sylvia Thissle. I helped Agent Pomodoro set up a meeting with those two and your Miss Johanna in her room at La Fonda, for surveillance purposes. That's how I earned this ring, Jesus." Estela leaned closer. "It once belonged to a famous woman Russian spy."

"Estela, Estela, Estela," Jesus mourned.

At that, Estela drew herself to her full five-foot-two, if you threw in her stiletto heels. "Please do not patronize me, Jesus Oliva." Her back was stiff as a marine's salute as she marched out of the Sunset.

What she didn't tell Jesus was that she was meeting in a little while with Antonio Pomodoro. He'd called her early this morning and said he had another gift for her. *But,* he said, and this part had shamed Estela deeply, he would give it to her only if she brought him Johanna's silver heart in exchange. How had he guessed that she had taken it from Johanna's room before the police arrived? But then, why wouldn't he? He was Count Antonio Pomodoro, Special Agent Extraordinaire. Estela had seen him work his magic before.

Busy, busy, busy, Antonio Pomodoro said to himself a while later as he watched Sam pull out from Jayvee Paris's house. Not that he hadn't been busy himself, on the phone early this morning, then meeting with Estela. Now *there* was a dumb little twat. He'd cruised by Earl's house, to see the dead man's black Mercedes still sitting in his driveway. So Earl had walked to their meeting at the Eldorado. That was good. But then, as he'd been making the circle back out Earl's street, he'd passed Deborah Wonder driving in. That wasn't so good. But, on the other hand, what was she going to find?

Now Pomodoro slowed for a minute and let a garbage truck pull in between him and Sam up ahead. The way she was driving, she probably wouldn't see him anyway, but he didn't want to take the chance. Surprise! That was what Pomodoro had in mind for Sam today. Surprise!

The garbage truck stopped, and a man jumped off and began hauling cans from behind a hedge. Now Sam was getting way ahead. Maybe this hadn't been such a good idea, except he knew where she was headed: back to Johanna's house or Lo Ellen's on up on Picacho. Where else?

Pomodoro puffed on his cigar and watched the garbage men haul and lift. His friend Lucky Brancati had been in garbage, back in New York, where garbage was a *seriously* lucrative enterprise. . . .

One night, Antonio must have been around twenty-eight or so, toward the close of an opening at his gallery Pomodoro, Lucky had dropped in at the gallery for a drink. Antonio got a big kick out of introducing the capo, a little too dapper in his green silk suit, to the uptown crowd. After Antonio had tucked the last sable-wrapped matron into her limo and locked the gallery doors, Lucky invited him to come along to a little private party. Antonio grabbed his coat.

First, they stopped for dinner at a joint behind a joint on Mulberry Street. There, over a plate of ziti with sardines and currants and pine nuts the likes of which Antonio hadn't had since he was a boy in Palermo, he and Lucky talked about that ancient city. How much they loved it, hated it, missed it. They laughed and talked until almost midnight, drinking a bottle and a half of a fine Barolo. Then Lucky invited Antonio to join him at a business meeting.

The meeting was being held in the meat-packing district in the West Village, on Gansevoort Street. The guest of honor was one Eddie "The Mouth" Molinara. When Lucky's driver pulled his black Lincoln up in front of Grimaldi Pork Products, The Mouth and three of Lucky's men were waiting, squeezed like sausages into the cab of a green giant of a garbage truck that read BRANCATI BROTHERS CARTING. Lucky and Antonio and the other four men climbed out and stood in a circle on the cobblestoned street. The Mouth's stance was tenuous, his ankles roped together and his hands tied behind his back. Silver duct tape held the apple that had been stuffed into his mouth.

Lucky introduced Antonio to his three men: Little

Joey, Moosh, and Sixes, who had an extra digit on each hand. It seemed that this meeting was to deal with The Mouth's having cut himself too large a slice of the Garibaldi garbage-hauling pie.

"We thought this'd be good," Lucky said, pointing out the Grimaldi Pork sign to Mouth, "seeing as youse was making a pig of yourself." Mouth tried to answer, but the apple prevented that. "You know," said Lucky, sharpening on a steel an already-keen carving knife he'd pulled from the trunk of his car, "the thing that was so good about pigs, Gramma always said—they raised them back in Sicily—was that you could use every single little piece of them. There was nothing that went to waste." And with that, Lucky stepped forward and, with one lightning-quick swipe of the knife, sliced off Eddie the Mouth's right ear.

Eddie, his mouth taped, his hands and feet bound, couldn't scream, couldn't even raise a paw to stanch the bleeding. He twisted and turned in silent agony as Lucky snipped a piece here, a piece there.

Finally, Lucky turned to Antonio and handed him the knife. "Saved the best for you, Tony."

But Antonio didn't need Lucky's blade. He pulled Vendicatóre from his belt, unzipped The Mouth's trousers, and, in one quick slice, unmanned him. The man had bled out before they could get back into the Lincoln.

Later, as the dark car swished along the dank Hudson, Lucky and Antonio had had the conversation they always had after one of these events. They had talked about tradition. About how some things never changed. How *vendetta* was a virtue. Vengeance. A tooth for a tooth. An eye for an eye.

A mother for a father.

And if the mother was gone, the daughter would do.

Pomodoro reached out now and fingered the leather

seat that Sam's bottom had warmed the day before. It had been all he could do to keep his hands off her.

He hadn't, actually. He'd touched her flesh several times. There'd been several excuses to touch her, comfort her. He'd squeezed her fingers in his, her flesh so warm as she'd talked about Johanna's death.

The quick and the dead. The hot and the cold. Pomodoro felt a stirring beneath his belt.

He'd watched her mouth when Sam told him about her father, the drunk. He'd wanted to take her bottom lip between his fingers and roll it back and forth. Then he had told her the lie about his own papa. She had believed him when he said that his mother had killed him. But it hadn't been his mother.

It had been *her* mother. Johanna had killed Papa. Had he not been there? Had he not been a witness?

Had he not failed Papa then?

He had told Sam the lie, and she had been so sorry for him. She'd made the cooing noises that women do. She had feelings for him. She was drawn to him. He could sense it in the way she looked at him; he could hear it in her voice. The idea that Johanna's daughter wanted him excited him almost beyond what he could bear.

Now, suddenly, he was overcome with longing to be close to her again. Pomodoro leaned on his horn. *Move* that garbage.

SAM WAS DRIVING BLIND, HER EYES ON THE ROAD, BUT HER mind flying.

Johanna was a blackmailer. A selfish bitch. A taker, just like Sylvia said. Gimme, gimme, gimme. She deserted me. She tormented her friends. She thought only of herself. I hate her guts.

A horn blared, and Sam looked up. A car was almost upon her, nose to nose on this shoestring stretch of Acequia Madre. Sam suddenly realized she'd missed the turnoff a block back and was headed the wrong way.

She rolled down her window. "Sorry, sorry," she called, and began backing down the curving lane.

How could Johanna stoop to blackmail? Why? Did she need the money? No. Okay, so maybe someone made *her do it. Someone was threatening her, had threatened her all these years.* Maybe *threatened me too? Was* that *it? Could that be why Johanna disappeared? And now that same someone is here, forcing her to . . . Right. And she called me here to put me right in the middle of it. To put me in danger too. Hang it up, Sam.*

Johanna was mean. She was crazy. She was perverse.

And that's probably why she died, why someone killed her, because she was blackmailing them. Sylvia could have done it. Or someone else. You have no idea how many people she victimized.

Now Sam was once more on Canyon. She turned right at the top of the road and headed toward Cristo Rey Church and the intersection with Upper Canyon, where, if she made a left, she'd end up at Johanna's house. She slowed, imagining herself walking back through Johanna's door. She'd pick up the first thing that came to hand—a lamp, a black Maria bowl—and dash it to the tile. She'd go crazy, creating greater havoc than the intruder had ever considered. She'd shred books, stomp, smash. She'd chew Johanna's clothes, take in the taste of her mother and spit it out.

Then, scalded by tears, she swerved the car over into Cristo Rey's parking lot. She leaned her head on the steering wheel and sobbed. Why didn't Johanna stay dead? What was the point of this exercise? What was the point of anything? Oh, God, she was so tired, sick of the to-ing and fro-ing and sniffing about. She wanted to go home. She wanted George. She wanted Harry.

"Pomodoro," Deborah said. "Antonio Pomodoro."

"Yeah?" Stuart was sitting at his desk, a desk topped by a slab of blue Apulian marble, which was one of the many treats Stuart had been unable to deny himself. "What about him?"

"Where is he?"

Deborah leaned forward toward Stuart, then grabbed up a letter opener of silver and lapis lazuli and pointed it at his heart. "Don't fuck with me, Stuart. Just tell me where Pomodoro is."

Startled, Stuart shoved back. "Why do you want to know?"

"Because. *Because* is all I'm giving you."

"You've gone over the edge, Deb."

"Oh, yeah?" With that, Deborah whirled and poised the sharp point over "Christina in the Desert." Right over the tip of Christina's pert nose. "Tell me, Stuart."

"Don't! Jesus!"

"Why, Stu? Because if I harm your precious Christina, you can't make nicey-nice with your friend Pomodoro anymore?"

Stuart dropped his head into his hands. "Deb, Deb, you don't know what you're talking about."

"Oh, no? Then fill me in, Stu. And be quick about it." Deborah lowered the blade a quarter-inch closer to the painting. The point of the blade rested in Christina's nostril. Stuart's face crumpled. His mouth trembled.

"From the top, Stu."

So Stuart took Deborah back to that breezy afternoon when he'd walked into Pomodoro's web. . . .

Stuart had been wandering in and out of SoHo galleries when a bronze in the Pomodoro Gallery caught his eye. The next thing Stuart knew, Pomodoro himself had taken his hand in his strong grip and invited him back into his private lair. Pomodoro had flattered Stuart. He knew Stuart's name. He said everyone knew the *big* collectors.

From there it had been a hop, skip, and a jump to Pomodoro's showing him Christina. Stuart's innards had fibrillated. He had to have her, even though half a million, Pomodoro's asking price, was steep, and Stuart's resources were already stretched to the snapping point. He'd promised his money men he'd be good. Then he and Pomodoro had worked out the trade for the Southampton lot. Everything was copacetic until Hurricane Archie struck, and Pomodoro came calling.

He had appeared a couple of weeks earlier, called, out of the blue, inviting Stuart for a drink at Escalara. August, the dog days in New York, his gallery shuttered, friends had been badgering him for years to check out the Santa Fe art scene, the opera, Indian market, *yah-dah, yah-dah, yah-dah.* Then Pomodoro turned on his barstool and said he'd give Stuart a week to come up with what he owed. The look in his eye had puckered Stuart's butt. "And if I can't produce the money?" Pomodoro's answering smile made Stuart realize that the man wasn't just an art dealer. He was a killer shark. And the dampness Stuart felt in his pits, his crotch, Pomodoro sensed. And Pomodoro liked Stuart's fear. "Why don't you tell me about your resources?" he'd crooned.

Stuart had been tempted to pull out his snappy patter and his well-practiced song and dance. But another look in the man's eye and he'd spilled his guts. What he owned. What he owed. He told the man, "What you're asking is impossible. I'm broke."

Pomodoro had thrown an arm around Stuart's shoulder, drawn him close and asked, "Those people who love your guru act, the rich ones who pay the big bucks to work with you one-on-one, don't any of them have naughty little secrets, Stuart?"

Was Pomodoro talking about what Stuart thought he was talking about?

"Persuasion." Pomodoro had rolled the word around in his mouth. "I'd call it persuasion."

It wasn't long after that that Stuart had found himself spewing the confidences of his wealthiest clients. One of them was Sylvia Thissle, who, years ago, had been a very successful florist to the stars. One day Sylvia, with a noseful of toot, had run down and killed an old man crossing Rodeo Drive. She'd panicked and fled L.A., leaving behind her house, the place at Malibu, the stocks and bonds. When she'd had a flat tire near Santa Fe, she'd taken that as a sign. She'd dyed her hair, changed her name, and settled in to make her fortune in real estate. For the past five years, Stuart had been her guru.

Sylvia sounded good, said Pomodoro. Tap her. But Stuart had balked. What was to keep Sylvia from calling his bluff? Stuart was a *known quantity,* a *celebrity,* for chrissakes.

A go-between? Pomodoro suggested.

It was then that Stuart realized that this whole thing was some kind of game to Pomodoro. The man got off on the machinations of fucking with people's lives. He probably tore the wings off flies in his spare time. The man was bad. The man was nuts.

So? So, Stuart thought about it and came up with the name of a possibility. Sylvia had this decorator friend to whom she'd confided her secret past. Now Sylvia was having serious misgivings and wanted to know if Stuart could somehow erase the information from her friend's mind, as if Stuart were some kind of psychic surgeon.

"Tell me about the friend." Pomodoro had rolled a fat cigar in his mouth.

Stuart didn't know much about her. Johanna Hall was her name.

"Johanna? Really? An older woman? Interesting. *Very* interesting. Yes, I like that a lot." Pomodoro had stared at the ember of his cigar and seemed to be lost in thought. "When can I meet her?"

Why did Pomodoro want to do that?

"*Someone* has to set this thing in motion, Stuart."

This thing. Blackmailing Sylvia Thissle and God knows how many others. Stuart, at that point, had had a sick feeling in his stomach. *This thing* could be endless.

The next thing Stuart knew, *Johanna* was doing all the dirty work. *Johanna* was the go-between. *Johanna* was pressuring Sylvia. *Johanna*, at Pomodoro's insistence, had even come up with Jayvee Paris, a pigeon of her own.

How did the man do it? Stuart had asked. Pomodoro had leaned back and laughed long and hard. "Don't worry yourself about it, Stuart. Johanna is perfect. Oh, yes, Johanna's my lifelong dream come true. She's everything I ever hoped for. Better than I could have imagined in a million years. Oh, Stuart if you only knew."

"But now," Stuart said to Deborah, "things have gotten way out of control. Johanna's dead. Suicide, they're saying. But I don't know." Stuart grabbed his sandy curls with both hands and banged his head on his blue marble desk.

"You're saying you think it's possible Pomodoro *murdered* this Johanna Hall?" Fear sat down hard in Deborah's gut. If he'd kill one person, what was to stop him from making it two? Especially if that second person came snooping around, asking questions. Oh, Earl. Where are you?

"I told you, I don't know. But he's getting crazier by the minute. Now all he can talk about is Sam Adams, Johanna's daughter."

Deborah didn't want to hear any more. She wanted to find Earl. Now. She grabbed the front of Stuart's shirt. "Where *is* he, Stuart? Where *is* Pomodoro?"

"He's *staying* at the Eldorado. I just talked with him a little while ago. He said he was going to give Johanna's daughter a sightseeing tour. Like she'd want to do that, her mother barely cold. The way he talks about Sam Adams, I tell you, Deborah, it gives me the creeps. *Jesus*, how did I ever—"

But Deborah was already reaching for her bag.

When Sam pulled into Lo's drive, she was astonished to see Jayvee's old blue Land Cruiser parked there. Then its passenger door popped open and out flew Isabel.

"What are *you* doing here?" Sam asked.

"We came to see Harpo!" the little girl cried. Then, remembering her manners, "And you, Sam!"

"Sam?"

She looked up into Jayvee Paris's amazing blue eyes.

"Right after you left, I realized . . ." He opened a hand. "Listen, could we let Isabel and Harpo play somewhere, and maybe we could talk?"

A few minutes later, they were settled on Lo's patio, untouched glasses of iced tea sweating before them. "Okay, Jayvee. Tell me what's on your mind."

"I lied," he said.

"About what?"

"I broke into Johanna's house and trashed it. I wrote the warning on the mirror. *Go Home!*"

Sam was stunned. She stared off across the valley toward the Jemez, blue and solid on the horizon.

"But that's all."

She laughed bitterly. "That's enough, don't you think?"

"I didn't set the house afire. I didn't kill Johanna."

"Well, there's a lot to be said for that."

Jayvee turned toward her, his face twisted with misery. "Look, I know I was wrong, and I'll do whatever I can to make it up to you. But, put yourself in my . . ." Then he stopped. "How can I ask you that? I can't. You lost Johanna."

"And you were afraid of losing Isabel."

"Yes, I was. So I wanted to scare you off. I wanted you to go away, leave us alone."

"And her scrapbooks?"

Jayvee looked blank.

"You're saying you didn't take them? Big leather volumes? Filled with my pictures and clips?"

"I didn't, Sam. Honest." Then Jayvee laughed. "Not that my word means much to you at this point. But, no, I didn't. I never saw them."

So what did that mean? That someone else had been there before or after Jayvee? *Two* intruders, back-to-back? And *then* the fire setter?"

"Jesus, Jayvee." Sam shook her head and sighed. It

was then that she realized she might be through here. Maybe it was time to stop being so hardheaded, to face the facts. Johanna, who'd deserted her, had also been a blackmailer (and God only knows what else) who'd finally run out of road and taken her own life. As for the myriad of questions she'd left unanswered, well, so be it. Sam was tired of chasing ghosts. "I don't know what to make of any of this. But I do understand your fear. You were trying to protect your child."

"I was," he said, and his voice broke with emotion. "I'm so sorry about Johanna. I don't know why she did what she did, but I'll always love . . ."

Just then, Isabel came running out onto the patio, followed closely by Harpo. "You know what, Jayvee?" she said. "Flora said that Sam went out to Auntie Johanna's mine yesterday, but she didn't go in because there was this coyote! So can we go today? Auntie Johanna said she would take me when she got back from her trip. She said we could have a picnic in the mine."

Sam and Jayvee exchanged looks; then Jayvee said, "Oh, no. I don't think so, sweetie pie. This isn't a good time."

"But when *is* Auntie Johanna coming back?" Isabel insisted. "I want to go now!"

"Isabel. That's enough."

"Wait, Jayvee." Sam laid a hand on his arm. "If you could spare Isabel for a little while, I'd love to spend some time with her."

She left the "before I leave" unspoken, but Jayvee sensed it. He looked from his daughter to Sam, the little girl resembling her enough to be her child. Sam, whose own mother had been his dear friend . . .

"You know"—he smiled—"maybe that *would* be a good idea. If you're *sure* you don't mind being saddled with this hellion."

* * *

From his vantage point two driveways down, Pomodoro watched Jayvee, then Sam pull out of Lo's. A moment later, he was at the door.

"Yes? May I help you?" said Flora.

Pomodoro bowed elegantly from the waist. "I am Count Antonio Pomodoro," he said. "A friend of Samantha Adams. Is she here?"

"No, no," said Flora. "You just missed her. She must have passed you. But you can catch her if you hurry. She said she was going to stop at Alfalfa's to grab a picnic. I told her that I could make sandwiches, but she said no, that I shouldn't go to the trouble. And I said it was no trouble. And then she said . . . Excuse me, please, the phone."

Flora always yelled into the telephone. "Yes? No, she's not. I was just telling Count Pomodoro here that I offered to make her sandwiches, and she said that . . . Who? Harry who? Yes. You're in Los Angeles? Yes. Here tonight? Yes, I will tell her."

She turned back to Pomodoro. "Where was I? Oh, yes. So, Sam said that she and Isabel, the little girl, they would make a picnic, and then they were heading out to Cerillos, to the mine. You know where Alfalfa's is?"

"*Oooo,* LOOK AT THAT!" ISABEL POINTED AT THE VOLCANIC outcropping beside the turnoff to the turquoise mine.

"What do you think it looks like?" Sam smiled down at the little girl buckled into the seat beside her. Harpo was happily perched in Isabel's lap. What a great idea, this little outing.

"The rocks look like a dinosaur!" Isabel chimed. "A brontosaurus!"

"You are really up on your dinosaurs, young lady."

"Jayvee and I saw them on TV. On the *National Geographic.* We saw dinosaur tracks." Isabel walked her fingers down Harpo's spine.

Isabel was irrepressible, joyous, wriggling with life. Minute by minute, she made inroads into Sam's heart. Children did that; they grabbed hold of you, and you, in return, never wanted to let go.

Unless you were Johanna.

Isabel tugged at her. "Is the mine big? Is it deep? Is it dark? Will we have candles?"

"We have the flashlight Jayvee gave us." It lay on the backseat, a heavy nightstick of a torch.

"What about snakes?"

"Definitely not. No snakes allowed."

"Diamonds!" Isabel bounced up and down. Harpo hung on.

Sam smiled. "No diamonds that I know of. No gold, either. But we could always hope."

They were winding down the two-lane, making the long S-curves. The Ortiz Mountains loomed purple in the near distance. Around them was nothing but rolling hills covered with chamiso and mesquite. The sky was a hot blue bowl.

"Did you ever go in this mine before?" Isabel asked.

"Almost. I got just to the door, but I didn't go in. Now I'm glad that I didn't because I get to see it for the very first time with *you*. I was afraid I might not have a chance before I go home."

"You're leaving? When?"

"Pretty soon."

"And you're taking Harpo?"

Sam smiled. "He's my baby, Isabel. Wherever I go, he goes." She was going to have to talk to Jayvee about a puppy for Isabel before she left town. Maybe he'd let her give Isabel one.

"What's that?" Isabel was pointing at the gate to Rancho Maravilloso, which was off to their right.

"*That* is an honest-to-goodness movie ranch where they film cowboy movies. Shoot-em-ups."

"Can we go inside? Can we?" Isabel clapped her hands.

"Umm, I'm not sure. We ought to ask permission." Though there didn't seem to be anything to keep them out, other than a No Trespassing sign, and it was small.

"Oh, pooh," Isabel pouted. "I really want to see it."

"You know what? I met the woman who owns this place. Her name's Deborah, and I bet you she wouldn't mind if we took a quick look around."

* * *

Back in town, Victor Vigil was finishing up a late lunch with his mother, Magdalena, at Tiny's, a Mexican restaurant she'd always liked. Magdalena had come down from Truchas to visit for a few days. She was staying with Eduardo, his brother, the chief of police, which hurt Victor's feelings. Eduardo had always been her favorite.

"That's because Eduardo does not do stupid things," she said.

"*I* don't either," Victor protested, then raised his hand for another beer.

"No," Magdalena said to the waitress. "Victor does not need another *cerveza*. Victor is drunk enough already."

It was true. Victor tucked his chin in embarrassment. Magdalena reached over and raised his head with a touch of a finger. She pinned her gaze on Victor's face. Magdalena Vigil owned huge luminous eyes that everyone in Truchas had always said could see down to the bottom of your soul. "Eduardo tells me you've been up to no good again."

"Eduardo lies."

Magdalena leaned across the table and slapped the face of her thirty-eight-year-old son.

"Mama!" he cried.

She raised a finger in warning. "Do not toy with me, Victor. Eduardo says you've been tormenting this gringa, the daughter of the woman who bought the Canyon Road house from old Mr. Fresquez. In the midst of the daughter's mourning, you are tormenting her. This is terrible, Victor."

Victor opened his mouth, then closed it. He didn't want his mother to slap him again. Not now. Not ever.

"Let me tell you something, Victor, I did not raise you to behave the way you do. Where do you get these ideas, going around talking about the conquistadores as if that were yesterday? As if they had anything to do with you. Now, listen to me. We—your father, may the saints preserve him, and I—sold that property to Mr. Fresquez. That is the end of our concern for that land. If Mr. Fresquez sold it to Johanna Hall, that is none of our business. She didn't do anything wrong. Furthermore, I have been her guest in her house. I was visiting Mrs. Vallejo up the hill, she introduced us, and Mrs. Hall invited us in and we had cake and coffee. Now she is dead and you torment her daughter. You should be ashamed, Victor."

"Yes, Mama." Again Victor's head went down.

"I want you to go and apologize to Mrs. Hall's daughter."

"Okay," he mumbled.

"*Now,* Victor. Go call her and ask her if you can come over right now. This apology should be face-to-face."

Victor nodded and headed for the phone at Tiny's front desk; his cellular phone, like so much else in Victor's life, was in need of repair. He dialed information for Lo Ellen's house.

Antonio Pomodoro lay flat, belly down, on the balcony of Maravilloso's saloon. He had a panoramic view, the movie set having been built on a rise. He'd been watching Sam's car for quite a while, watching it turn off the highway, then disappear, coming into view again out of a long curve. After Lo Ellen's housekeeper had told him where Sam was going, he'd headed out here. At first, he'd thought he'd take her at the mine. But there was no place to hide there, and surprise was part of his plan. The rest of it, he'd play by ear. Though he knew the ending. There was never any doubt in Pomodoro's mind as to this last movement of this scenario.

Shivering with anticipation, he followed Sam now through the crosshairs of the rifle he'd bought last week. He'd also picked up a Browning .380 automatic, but he preferred the Winchester, a beauty with scrolled tooling on the blue steel. A cowboy's rifle.

He watched now as Sam climbed from the car, and then the passenger door opened and out popped the little girl and the dog. He hoped that Johanna was watching this scene from purgatory. He hoped that the sight of both Sam and Isabel within his crosshairs made Johanna twist and writhe.

Now they strolled past the barn, the tack house, the blacksmith's shop, the little girl skipping. "This is the *neatest* place!" Isabel clapped her hands.

"Hello? Hello?" Sam called. "Is anybody here?"

Pomodoro peered through the rifle's sight again, moving the rifle up and down Sam's yellow cotton sweater, short denim skirt, tanned legs.

Come to Papa.

"Look at this, Sam!" Isabel bounced up and down the wooden walkway in front of the bank, then climbed up on a bench and peered in the window. "*Oooo,* it's dark in there."

"Remember what I said, Isabel? None of it is real. They shoot movies here." She peered over the little girl's shoulder. "Think of it like a huge dollhouse. You know what I mean?"

Isabel tugged on Sam's hand. "Look down there? Is that a ghost house?"

"I don't know. We'll go see." Then Sam stopped and pointed straight up at the balcony where Pomodoro crouched. "You see that? That's where the bad guy always hides in the movies. You walk past, and all of a sudden, *pow*!" Sam shot the imaginary gun of her fingers at Isabel, and Isabel clutched her throat and fell headlong into the dirt. "*Aaaaaaargh,* you got me," she said, then went limp. Harpo sniffed the child.

* * *

"Sam Adams is not home," Victor said to his mother, rejoining her at their table in Tiny's.

"So who were you talking to all that time?"

"Flora Verduga, the housekeeper of the woman she's staying with."

"Ah, Flora." Magadalena threw up her hands. "Her mother was a magpie too. So what did Flora say?"

"First she told me about everyone who has already called. Her boyfriend, from the airport in L.A. Deborah Wonder, Stuart Wonder's wife. Then Antonio Pomodoro . . ."

Magdalena made an impatient motion with her hand. Cut to the chase, Victor.

"She said she told them all the same thing she was telling me. Sam has taken the little girl, Isabel Martinez, you remember, Valentina Martinez, from home?"

Magdalena nodded. She knew all about Isabel and Valentina. An odd story, but none of her business.

"And they've gone for a drive out to that old turquoise mine near Cerrillos that Johanna Hall owned."

"Do you know where it is?"

"Sure."

Magdalena stood, brushing the crumbs from her lap. "Then let's get going. I could do with a little drive myself."

"Come on, Harpo!" Isabel stomped her foot, but the little dog wouldn't budge. He sat tight on the saloon steps. He stared upward and growled. "What's wrong with him?" Isabel asked Sam.

Pomodoro held his breath. The dog knew he was up here. He didn't like that. He didn't want it to end like this. Not with a rifle shot; no, the Winchester was just a toy. A play-pretty. A prop in a scenario, but not one he wanted to play out. He didn't want to be rushed, and certainly not by some goddamned dog. There was so much more he wanted to do, *had* to do, to complete his quest.

He hadn't spent his lifetime searching for Johanna, dreaming about *vendetta,* only to have his efforts end prematurely.

At first, in the beginning, when he was young, he'd only dreamed of his moment of triumph, of avenging his father Orlando's death. Later, when he'd had the means, he'd hired agents to search for Johanna, Johanna the murdering bitch. Rome, London, New York, Kansas City—his scouts had searched everywhere. They'd come close a couple of times; he'd almost had her in Boston, but she'd sniffed him and scurried away. But who could keep that up, that level of search? Whose pockets were that deep? Finally, Pomodoro had decided that his need for revenge was like a force of nature. It *would* be satisfied. One day, he would turn a corner, look across a room, and there would be Johanna.

And, sure enough, little more than a week earlier, Stuart had suggested Johanna Hall as the go-between for their blackmail scheme. How about her, Stuart said, Sylvia Thissle's friend and confidante? A decorator. An older woman.

Her given name had made Pomodoro's heart race, but he'd told himself, Don't be stupid. There are millions of Johannas. Besides which, she wouldn't be foolhardy enough to use her own name.

There are no coincidences in Santa Fe.

But then Pomodoro had telephoned this Johanna Hall, set up a meeting, and when he'd walked in, first look, he'd known. He'd almost swooned from the excitement. I'm going die of joy, he'd thought. This can't be happening. Then he'd gathered himself. He'd smiled, taken her hand, and purred, "I've been waiting for this moment most of my life. Do you know who I am?" And he handed her the silver heart he'd carried all those years.

He'd expected her to run, to scream, to try to escape, but she had just sat there with her hands folded neatly in her lap. Finally, she'd said, "So, here you are. I always knew that you'd come, someday."

And then—this was the irony of it, after all those years of burning and searching and longing and substituting little killings and small tortures for the real prey—Pomodoro didn't know what to do next.

He had focused his life on this moment, and now that it was here, he was clueless, bootless, empty-handed.

So he grabbed at the closest thing, the blackmail scheme that had sent him to her in the first place. One of his little amusements. That would do, he told himself, while he figured out the next step.

Then, to his joy, he saw that her role in it—being the bag woman, doing the dirty work—caused her great pain. Especially after he divined whom she was most intimate with in Santa Fe and pointed her toward them. Isabel, Jayvee, Valentina. Those were the ones whose torment hurt *her* the most.

And, oh, how he adored Johanna's anguish. It was nectar to him. He measured it out, savored it drop by drop, delaying the inevitable, and, then, all of a sudden, before he'd meant to—it was an accident, really—he'd killed her.

It wasn't what he wanted. Not then. Not like that.

He had already found her at La Fonda (stupid woman, thinking she could hide) and made her set up the meeting with Jayvee and Sylvia to squeeze them for the money because he knew that would cause her such agony.

What he hadn't known was that Johanna had contacted Samantha and that Samantha had come to town. Sam was in Johanna's room when he called her that last night.

It wasn't until later, after Jayvee and Sylvia had come

and gone, and he was sitting on the sofa across from her that Johanna had told him of her daughter's visit. "But I sent her away. I only got to see her for this little bit." She'd woozily held up her fingers, measuring out half an inch. "You won, Antonio." She'd raised her glass of Scotch then and washed down another handful of pills. Most of them were already gone by the time he arrived.

She'd won, actually, Johanna had. Oh, sure, she was dying, killing herself, and he got to watch, but it wasn't what he would have chosen.

In fact, he'd thought about rushing her to the hospital, having her stomach pumped, and then killing her again, in his own way.

Though what was the point? She *had* been in anguish. Not physical pain, but the torment, the tease, of seeing her beloved daughter for just that tiny instant . . . oh, that had been so very sweet.

Besides, by then, he had Sam.

The realization of that had been like Saint Elmo's fire rolling across the landscape of his mind, a blue ball of electric energy, a crackling voice that said . . .

Not only the sins of the fathers, but the sins of the mothers are also passed along. They move like dark corpuscles through the blood. Like the very wind through the air. They flow like fierce running rivers. They are inescapable. They are visited upon the daughters' bowed heads. The sins of the mothers permeate the flesh and the bone and the sinew of the daughters, and they are guilty, guilty, guilty.

So. There it was. Samantha was responsible for Johanna's sins. Not only dust to dust, but womb to womb, and blood to blood. Mother and daughter were one; they were interchangeable. They owned the same face, the same voice. There was the same fire in their dark eyes, a fire worthy of the battle, a flame to match his own. Johanna's sins lived! Johanna's guilt had quickened! And

Johanna's punishment, her downfall, her slow torturous debasement were still within his grasp.

Right here. Here and now beneath him, only feet away. If only the goddamned little dog would shut his yap.

"What's he barking about?" asked Isabel. "You said he never barks."

"Except when he does," said Sam. "Come on, Harpo, you're making a fool of yourself."

The dog quieted. Sam must have picked him up. Then Pomodoro heard the saloon doors swing. Good, he said to himself, they were inside. They'd look around, then they'd leave, head for the mine, that long dark tunnel, with only one way out.

Hosannas filled his heart.

But wait! What was Sam saying? She was *greeting* someone. He crept as close as he dared to the edge of the balcony to hear Sam say, "What are *you* doing here?"

Victor and Magdalena drove past the state penitentiary, which squatted bleakly back from the road. Magdelena said, "Victor, can you not drive any faster?" A voice had spoken to Magadalena. A voice that said, Hurry. Magdalena knew that it was folly to ignore the spirits.

Victor had heard nothing. "Mama, what is your problem? Forty-five is the speed limit on this road."

"Do not use that tone with your mother, Victor. And what is the point of your being a policeman if you cannot break the rules?"

"Look, I'll apologize to Samantha Adams. But I'm not in a *hurry* to do it."

"Well, you should be. Step on it, Victor."

Sam was saying, "Isabel this is Rosey Bird."

Pomodoro heard the little girl say hello, but missed the woman's reply.

"What do you mean?" Sam said. "I just want to show Isabel the mine."

"It's full of *turquoise,*" Isabel said.

Again, he didn't catch the answer; then Sam said, "We're only going for a little visit. I want to see it before I go." Sam paused, and then she said, "Well, I think that I have to accept the coroner's verdict. I have to go on." Another silence, then Sam said, "Why don't you come along with us, if you feel so strongly about it?"

Damnit! thought Pomodoro. Another woman to deal with? No way. He wanted this thing clean. No distractions. He gripped the Winchester tighter. Then he heard footsteps on the wooden floor below.

"Come on, Isabel," Sam said. "Here, you can take Harpo's leash."

Pomodoro peeked over the edge of the balcony. Only the three of them—Sam, Isabel, and Harpo—were leaving the saloon, headed down the dusty center of the main street, back toward the car. Was this Rosey Bird still inside? Okay, let Sam drive out of the parking lot, away from earshot. Then he could deal with Miss Rosey.

A few minutes later, Sam stood staring at the hasp of the gate to the mine road. That was odd. The balky padlock was missing. Isabel leaned out the car window. "What's the matter?"

Sam opened the gate and drove the car across the cattle guard, down the faint outline of a road, up to the edge of the hill and the mine. "This is it," she announced. "Everybody out."

"Where?" Isabel looked disappointed. "I don't see it."

"Just up there. See that wooden doorway in the side of the hill? That's it."

"I thought a mine was like a cave."

"It is. Come on, let's go see. Here, we can let Harpo off the leash for a minute to do his business. Then I'll carry him in." At the end of the path, she took Isabel's hand. "I bet it's really *something* inside."

Isabel looked doubtful. "You were never *in* the mine?"

"No. I told you, there was a coyote before. Remember what I said about the Fritos?"

Isabel giggled. "Does the coyote *eat* them?"

"No, silly. They're to ward off the bad things. Like you shoo away a werewolf with garlic." Uh-oh. She shouldn't have said that. She didn't want to scare the child.

But Isabel shivered, deliciously. She smiled up at Sam. "Do you really think there's a werewolf here?"

"No, and if there were, Harpo would eat him up." Harpo, however, was off on an adventure of his own, sniffing a plot of what looked like fresh-turned earth. "Come, Harpo," Sam ordered. He whined and pawed at the spot.

"What's he doing?" Isabel asked.

"I don't know. Probably the caretaker buried some garbage. Maybe there's a bone."

"Let's go, Harpo." Isabel snapped her fingers at the dog, but he ignored her.

Sam grabbed him up, and they were on their way. At the mouth of the mine, she said to Isabel, "Now, don't let go of my hand, and be careful where you walk. It's damp in here." Four steps in, she was glad she had Jay-vee's big flashlight. Despite the blinding sun outside, the narrow passageway was pitchdark. Cool and damp and spooky, the tunnel was right out of a horror movie of her childhood.

"This is weird," Isabel whispered.

"Are you scared?"

"No, are you?"

Well, not exactly scared, but she grew a little queasy as they stepped further and further into the blackness. Maybe this *wasn't* such a good idea. She didn't have a clue what was up ahead, though Lo had said the mine was delightful. *Delightful?* What the heck did that mean? Doubts began to poke at Sam. What about that padlock? That fresh-dug plot? Shut up, she told herself. Don't be paranoid.

"How much further, Victor?" Magdalena stared out at the volcanic outcropping. It seemed foreboding to her, a reminder that the earth itself was filled with spirits, good and evil, constantly and eternally in battle with one another.

Victor said, "It's only a couple of miles from here. Just down this road."

"You're sure?"

"Trust me, Mama. I know this whole county like the back of my hand."

"Did you bring your *pistola,* Victor?"

Victor turned and stared at his mother.

Suddenly Sam and Isabel found themselves at the end of the tunnel, stepping into the most amazing room. Roughly fifteen by twenty feet, the space had been carved from cream-colored rock spidered with veins of rust. It was about fifty feet high from top to bottom, with a huge hole of a skylight at the top, through which brilliant sunlight poured.

Johanna's mine wasn't at all what Sam had expected. She'd never imagined this wonderful place. Yes, Lo had said that Johanna had entertained clients here, but she'd pictured guests sitting around in the dark wearing miners' helmets. There was even party equipment here: in a corner stood a pile of little red stools, clusters of votive candles, and a linen tablecloth, long-forgotten, spotty with mildew.

"Where's the mine?" asked Isabel.

"This is it, honey."

"What's that hole in the top?"

"I guess they tunneled both ways, in sideways like we came and from the top too. See here?" Sam pointed at a rust-colored vein of ore. "See that tiny flake of blue-green? I think that's turquoise. Probably the big pieces were mined out a long time ago. I remember, though, my friend Lo said there were pebbles of it around. We'll have to look when we go out. Now, what about our picnic? Are you hungry?" Sam reached in her backpack for the sandwiches and apple juice she'd brought.

"Can we sit on those stools?"

"We most certainly can."

"Can we put the apple juice in that pitcher?"

Isabel had spied a pottery pitcher decorated with green flowers and clover and a little bird painted on a background of white. She picked it up and handed it to Sam.

Sam was stunned. She owned a pitcher exactly like this one. She'd bought it in Assisi on her first trip to Italy because she'd never forgotten her last conversation with her mother. She could hear herself even now, recounting it to George . . .

"Momma's bringing me a green-and-white tea set from Assisi."

"I'm sure she will. And I'm sure it will be lovely. Assisi, you know, Sammie, is the hometown of Saint Francis, the saint who protects all the animals."

She cradled this pitcher. Had Johanna bought it on that long-ago journey and brought it here to Villa Real de la Santa Fe de San Francisco de Asis, the City of the Holy Faith of Saint Francis?

"Can we use it?" Isabel asked once more.

"I don't think so, Isabel. It looks pretty dirty. We don't know how long it's been here."

"Hello?"

The man's voice came from out of nowhere. Harpo

barked. Isabel screamed. Sam dropped the pitcher, and it shattered on the rock floor.

Magdalena said, "You've gone too far."

"How do you know, Mama? You've never been here."

"I know, Victor."

Turn around, said the whispering in Magdalena's ear. *Turn around, Magdalena.* She recognized the voice. It was Rosey Bird, a Pueblo Indian woman, a great seer and healer. Rosey had been dead now for almost five years, but her spirit often spoke to Magdalena. Good friends, they continued to keep in touch.

"Didn't you say there was a gate?" Magdalena asked Victor.

Then Magdalena could see it in her mind. Rosey was pointing at it. "A red gate, *way* back there, Victor. Turn this car around now."

"Antonio! You almost gave me a heart attack! What are you doing here?" Then she commanded Harpo, "Hush."

Pomodoro gave his formal little bow. Today he was all in black, in the style of Jesus Oliva: jeans, western shirt, boots. "I called Lo's house looking for you, and the housekeeper told me you had come here."

Sam frowned. She wasn't happy about being frightened. She didn't like uninvited visitors either. She knelt to pick up the green-and-white shards of the pitcher.

"I really do apologize," he said. "Maybe the surprise I brought you will make up for it." Then he turned to Isabel and extended his hand. "I didn't mean to scare you, Isabel. My name is Antonio Pomodoro."

Isabel eyed him suspiciously, half-hiding behind Sam. "Why did you sneak up on us?"

Pomodoro laughed. "You're very frank, young lady."

"It *is* a good question," Sam countered.

"Dear, dear Samantha, now don't be cross with me. I simply forgot my flashlight in the car, and not knowing what to expect, I crept along, feeling my way. Please tell me that you forgive me." He smiled his charming smile.

Sam thawed. Why was she being so uptight? This was Antonio Pomodoro, her new friend. "I'm sorry," she said. "Maybe I'm over—"

"No need." Pomodoro stopped her, holding up a hand. "Please."

"Come on," Sam invited. "Maybe you'd like to sit with us? We were about to have a little picnic. Weren't we, Isabel? We have plenty of food."

"I'd be delighted." Pomodoro looked questioningly at the red stools, then pulled out three of them and arranged them in a triangle, positioning his stool between Sam and Isabel and the exit.

"So," Sam said, after the juice and cookies were passed, "what was it you wanted to give me?"

Pomodoro reached in a breast pocket and pulled out a silver heart almost as large as Sam's palm. Johanna's locket. He dangled it before her. "Is this what you've been looking for?"

Victor had made a U-turn and was heading back for the mine when his police car coughed and died. The gate was about a mile away, in the blazing sun.

"These jalopies are no damned good," Victor complained, pulling the knob for the hood.

As he opened his door, Magdalena said, "You're out of gas."

"No, I'm not."

"I'm looking at the gauge, Victor. It's sitting on empty. Come on." Magdalena was halfway out the passenger door now. "Hurry up. We'll have to walk."

* * *

Sam reached for the locket, but just before her fingertips touched the old silver, Pomodoro pulled it back. He smiled at her, a very strange smile.

"What?" she said, surprised.

"Who is Rosey Bird?"

Sam shook her head. "I don't know what you mean."

"Tell me who she is," he insisted, still smiling, but his tone had changed. The niceness was gone.

"Rosey's an Indian woman I met," she said. "But why do you want to know? I don't understand." She reached for the locket, and he swung it once more past her fingers, out of reach.

"Where did you meet her?"

"Antonio?" Sam laughed nervously. "I'm not enjoying your Twenty Questions. Give me the locket, please."

"You're not being very nice," Isabel said to Pomodoro. "It's not nice to tease."

Pomodoro looked straight at Isabel, still smiling, his teeth white and strong, and said, "Little girl, why don't you shut your mouth before I shut it for you?"

Was *this* the road, Deborah asked herself, turning right. If she passed the Lone Butte, she'd gone too far; that's what Lo's assistant had said. It had taken her a while to figure out whom to call, but, goddamnit, she was going to find Sam Adams. She was going to warn her about Antonio Pomodoro. And, maybe, fingers crossed, in the process she'd find her dear-heart Earl. She closed her eyes, visualized Saint Hyacintha, and prayed. *Help me here, girlfriend.*

"Hush, Isabel. *Shhhhhh.* Don't cry. I'm sure Antonio didn't mean to hurt your feelings." Sam petted the little girl, while her mind raced. How had she suddenly found herself in a mine shaft with the Big Bad Wolf? What had gone wrong with Antonio? Why was he acting so strange? He was scaring the crap out of her.

But then, she asked herself, what did she really know about this man? She knew that he'd been nice to her. But what was his history? She'd welcomed him into her life, accepted his help, confided in him, all because he was Johanna's friend. Says who?

Says him.

Says this lunatic with Johanna's silver locket dangling from his finger.

Okay. Now what? What was she going to do?

Get the hell out, that's what.

She stood. "I'd like it very much if you'd give me my mother's locket, please," she said to Antonio Pomodoro. "And then, Isabel and I have to be going."

Pomodoro's laughter bounced like a ball from rocky wall to wall.

"Give me your *pistola,*" Magdalena said to Victor. They were at the red gate now. Victor was breathing hard. His color was very bad. "You go on to the movie ranch down there. You'll find water and shade."

"Mama, don't be silly."

"Give me the gun, Victor. And do what I tell you."

Pomodoro swung the locket back and forth on the silver chain just beyond Sam's reach. "Tell me about Rosey Bird," he said. "Tell me, and maybe I'll give you the locket."

Rosey Bird? "Look," Sam said, "I don't know what you're doing, but whatever it is, I'm not enjoying it. So, really, Isabel and I are going to push off." Her heart was racing away from her. She was dizzy with fear. She squeezed Isabel's hand. Don't think, she told herself. Just get the hell out.

"You're not going anywhere." Pomodoro's smile was vicious.

"You're going to stop me?" Sam took a side step. Isabel and Harpo followed.

"Oh, yes. Most definitely." He laughed. It was a terrible sound. "Maybe you should have listened to your friend Rosey back at the ranch when she told you not to come here. But you've always been hardheaded, haven't you, Sam? And stubborn, just like your mother."

Oh, Christ. *Rosey back at the ranch.* What did that mean? Had he been there too? She didn't understand. What the hell? It didn't matter. Right now, first priority, vamoose.

"Come on, Isabel," she said. "Grab Harpo." Isabel gathered the dog into her arms, and then Sam lifted both of them. She'd made three steps when Pomodoro whirled and pushed her hard at the shoulders with both hands. Sam tumbled. Isabel and Harpo fell away from her. "Run!" she screamed at Isabel. "Run!"

"Isabel stay!" Pomodoro shouted over her. "You go, and I shoot Sam. *And* the dog." He pointed a gun at Sam's head as she lay on the floor. The Browning automatic was less romantic than the Winchester, but more efficient in the close range. Close was the operative word here. Proximity was what Pomodoro wanted, what he had now. Intimacy. They were like a little family, snuggled here together in this cave. Finally, he had gathered a family once more.

"Isabel," Sam lamented, "Isabel, why didn't you run?"

"Shut up," Pomodoro snapped, then tossed the silver locket into Sam's face. "Open it and read your bitch of a mother's last will and testament." He cackled then, and the ugly sound ricocheted.

SAM DIDN'T NEED THE TINY KEY SHE WORE ON THE CHAIN around her neck. Pomodoro had pried the silver heart open. Folded tightly inside it was a letter.

My Dearest Sugar, it began. The words were inscribed on sheets of onionskin in a miniature of Johanna's hand. It bore the date of Johanna's death. Sam could hear Johanna's voice as she read. . . .

> *The weather was so lovely that spring, late May and early June of 1962. I had been to Europe several times before, but traveling with a group of friends, with guides and tours, and art lovers in each city entertaining us, well, it was quite something.*
>
> *The one fly in the ointment was your father. Please don't think I'm laying blame for what happened at his door. I never have. And I forbid you to, Sam. His drinking was an illness he was never able to cure, and it was his drinking, for the most part, that made him behave as he did.*
>
> *He behaved very badly on this trip, almost from the beginning.*

Part of it was the wine. You won't remember this, but back in the early sixties Atlanta was still a gastronomic wasteland. And, presented with the opportunity to dine and drink like a king, Rob did. He couldn't handle it, of course.

Much as I tried to shield you from it, I know you suffered from his drinking when you were a little girl. You knew, and I knew you knew, what was going on. The fights. The screaming. Daddy's bad days—his terrible hangovers.

So, there we were in Rome, and not only was there the wine, but there was another woman, a girl really, he'd met in some café. Others in our group had seen them together, and I was quite humiliated. We had a terrible fight, and I stormed out of the hotel in the middle of the night.

I hired a car and drove to Assisi, then down Pompeii, to Naples, and on to Positano on the Amalfi Coast. I was amazed at what a wonderful time I was having on my own. I felt so free. I had married so young. . . .

Sam had been to Positano. She had been drawn as if by a magnet to the beautiful white town tumbling down the hills toward the Tyrrhenian Sea. But once there, she had been overcome with a terrible sense of foreboding and fled.

It was there in Positano that I met Orlando, in a café, just as Rob had met his girlfriend. Sometimes, I think, life is stunning in its banality.

Count Orlando Pomodoro was tall and handsome and possessed buckets of Italian charm.

He also owned an even more vile temper than Rob had at his very worst, but I didn't learn that until it was far too late.

The details of our affair? Once again, banality rules the day. Great food, great wine, great sex in a magnificent hotel overlooking the sea. Orlando was traveling on business, and when he asked me to return with him to Sicily, I said yes. And why not? I was furious with Rob and saw my Italian count as the perfect antidote. Hip-deep in sweet revenge, I thought, I'll have my fun, and then I'll go home. Rob and I will figure it out from there.

Orlando's home, his baronial palazzo in the old part of Palermo, was so mammoth that I didn't realize until the next day that I was staying under the same roof as his wife, his son, his parents, and a host of other relatives. Not nearly worldly enough to deal with that, I began packing.

Orlando caught me halfway out the door. He refused to allow me to leave. I would stay until he said I could go.

He was drunk and as furious with me as I now was with him. When I tried to push my way past him, he knocked me to the floor, then began kicking. I could hear my ribs crack. And then my nose.

Suddenly he was astride me, his hands around my neck, pounding my head on the stone floor. He was trying to kill me. There was no question in my mind.

Then a young boy of about fourteen—Antonio, Orlando's son, I learned later—appeared in the doorway. He watched his father trying to break my skull. He listened to my screams, and he did nothing. Help me, I begged. Please, help me. His father didn't even pause. He was so lost in his rage he didn't realize Antonio was there.

I said to myself, Johanna, you are about to die. Right now. Right here. But then my eye lit on a heavy silver pitcher which had fallen to the floor.

Desperate, knowing that this was my only chance, I inched my fingers until I could grasp it. Then, gathering all my strength, I smashed Orlando with it, aiming blindly, but managing to hit him in the temple.

He collapsed onto my chest. Meanwhile, Antonio stood there silently, frozen as a statue. And then he disappeared.

I lay there for I don't know how long. I was bleeding, in great pain, and afraid that I was dying. I couldn't find the strength to roll Orlando off me, and I was terrified that he was going to regain consciousness before I could.

Finally, it occurred to me that perhaps Orlando was not going to come around. Perhaps he was in a coma. Or perhaps I had killed him.

It hardly seemed possible that this man, almost twice my size, had battered me so viciously, yet I was alive, and he was dead.

Finally, just before dawn, I dragged myself out from under him and crawled from that room. Then—and this was always a blur, I don't know how I did it—I escaped the house, the city. I escaped Sicily and somehow made it back to Rome and a hotel. I must have looked like bloody hell with my broken nose and my swollen face. A doctor was called for me.

The next day, front-page headlines announced that Count Orlando Pomodoro had been brutally murdered, by persons unknown. Thieves, probably, interrupted mid-burglary.

I was stunned. I had actually killed a man. In self-defense, yes, but even so . . . And his son hadn't spoken up with the truth.

What could it mean? And, more important to me at that moment, what was I to do? Call the authorities? Admit that I, a married American woman, had bashed out the brains of my Sicilian lover in the bosom of his family?

I was in a state of panic. I tried to call Rob in Paris, the last stop on our itinerary. Our charter flight was leaving the next day, and I wanted desperately to be on it with him. All I could think of was that I needed someone to shelter me, to protect me, to tell me that this was going to be all right. And, I knew that despite our differences, Rob and I were still mates. I had forgiven him before. He would forgive me. And, most important, he would help *me.*

But the hotel where we were to stay in Paris said that Mr. and Mrs. Adams had already checked out.

I couldn't make any sense of what he'd said. I didn't care. All I knew was that I needed to be with Rob. And then the clerk at my hotel in Rome said that there was someone waiting downstairs to speak with me. An American, I cried, thinking that somehow Rob had come for me. No, the clerk said, an Italian. A young man. He wants to speak to the lady from Atlanta, Georgia, the United States, or perhaps her daughter?

Her daughter? You, my precious?

It was Antonio. I was sure of it. Who else could it be? Even though a young boy, he had connections. He had found me. But how did he know about you? And then I realized, in my struggle with Orlando, the silver heart I wore with your picture had been ripped from my neck.

I raced down the back stairs and fled.

Desperate for your father's sheltering arms, I flew from Rome to Paris, instead of going straight home. I arrived at Orly just in time to check in for our flight to Atlanta. Swaddled with a scarf and sunglasses, I went to the counter with my passport and, because I'd left my ticket with your father, told them a story of our taking separate cabs, the upshot of which was that I wanted to check in without my ticket. But the ticket agent said that Mr. and Mrs. Rob Adams had already checked in.

I'll never know who that woman was. Perhaps Rob was taking his girlfriend to the States, or he had sold my ticket, or had given it to a chambermaid. Whatever, whoever, she was flying under my name. Airport security then was nothing like it is now.

I was so desperate to see him, so afraid, I didn't care about the other woman. I was willing to beg Rob, to humiliate myself, to do whatever it took to go home with him on that plane. But the flight was full. And without a ticket, they wouldn't let me through to the gate. I had him paged, but he didn't answer. So I stood there, helplessly, frantically, watching that plane take off without me.

Then I watched it crash. I watched it burn. I watched Rob and our many Atlanta friends perish in billows of orange flame and black smoke.

I was hysterical. The airport was chaos. People ran and screamed; gendarmes swarmed; ambulances and fire trucks wailed. I felt as if a tornado had picked me up and wouldn't let me go. Finally, I made my way outside and into a taxi. I must have asked the driver to take me to a hotel in a quiet neighborhood, because that's where I was when I awoke the next day.

I stayed there for a week, maybe a little more. Lost in a fog, I slept while my body began to mend itself.

Finally, I limped out and wandered mile after

mile under leafless plane trees through the quiet summer streets. It had grown very hot, was a scorching summer. I tried to make sense of what had happened. Now and again I would stop at a café for a coffee, a cold drink, a cigarette. I couldn't eat. All I thought of was that I had killed a man, and now my husband was dead.

My thoughts were so selfish. One hundred and thirty people were dead. Thousands of their relatives and friends were suffering. But I found grief to be a very particular, a very greedy emotion. It was, for me, a deep slippery well with no handholds. It was all-consuming. It inhabited my guts, my bones, my breath, my heartbeat. That grief—teamed with the shock, the remorse, the guilt I felt about Orlando—paralyzed me.

And there was the fear. Let us not forget the fear. There was no doubt in my mind that the young man who'd come for me, for you, in the Roman hotel had been Antonio. Everywhere I went, I looked over my shoulder for him, or the Italian police. Or, perhaps even worse, other of Orlando's relatives, for I had not only killed a man, I had killed a Sicilian. His relatives, his brothers, his friends—I was convinced they would come after me.

They would come after you.

That was where my terror took me. That was what I thought: I could never go home. I could never see you, my precious Sugar, ever again. That was the worst part, losing you.

And, then, slowly, it dawned on me that I was dead. Officially, if that other woman had flown under my name, I had died in the crash. I found back issues of the newspapers, and, yes, there, in the listings, were our names.

Johanna Hewlett Adams, 30, Atlanta, GA.

Robert Simpson Adams, 36, Atlanta, GA.

What did this mean, to be the walking dead? That I was safe, that you were safe, as long as I never resurfaced. As long as I kept running.

But I so wanted to hear your voice. The last time I had talked with you was from Positano, when I told you I had bought you a tea set in Assisi, which was the truth. I told you I would see you very soon. That was just before I left with Orlando for Palermo.

Sugar, I don't have time or space here (or, I guess, the strength, for I am very tired now, coming to the end) to tell you very much about the years which followed. I left France. I tutored English in a small Belgian town. But eventually I became so homesick for the States that I took the risk of coming back. I knew I had to do it before my passport expired. I flew to Boston. I worked in a department store for several years, then sold antiques in a shop on Beacon Hill. It was there that I met a designer who was willing to take me on as his girl Friday. I loved the work and learned quickly. But never did an hour pass, that I didn't think of you. I had just about convinced myself that I was safe, that I could return home to you and try to explain, when I learned that someone was looking for me. Showing a picture. Asking questions. My most paranoid fears were realized.

Within an hour I was at Logan Airport with one suitcase, headed for Seattle, a destination I picked at random. I stayed there a couple of months and, when it felt safe enough to stick my head out, went to San Francisco. There, I eventually opened my own design business.

From Boston on, I looked over my shoulder

every minute. I knew that Antonio Pomodoro was after me. And in some ways, I thought it would be a relief to let him catch me, kill me, put me out of my misery. Sometimes I told myself that I should let him do that. Perhaps my death would appease him, and he wouldn't harm you. But I couldn't be sure of that.

I'm not sure that my thinking about any of this ever made sense. I just wanted to protect you.

Initially, that was why I hired someone to keep track of you, to make sure you were safe. But then it became a way of feeling that I had some connection to you. I was ecstatic when you decided to go to Stanford, then after you finished school, moved to San Francisco.

For quite a few years, we lived exactly eighteen blocks apart, you and I. I walked those blocks a million times. I strolled past your apartment almost every night. I passed you twice on the street, so thrilled both times I didn't sleep afterwards for weeks.

When you left San Francisco, after your dear Sean was killed, I couldn't stay. But following you to Atlanta was much too risky. Instead, I chose Santa Fe. I'd visited many times and was captivated by the place. Somehow, here, in the high desert, I felt safe. Northern New Mexico was so different from anything I had ever known. It was like a foreign country. Maybe it was that very separation that I needed to feel more at rest.

Then, ten days ago Antonio Pomodoro finally found me. He'd given up the active search long ago, but, nevertheless, here he was. His good luck, my bad.

I bowed my head and waited for him to kill me. But Antonio Pomodoro had much more terrible things in mind. He intended to torture me, to tease out my death. So be it, part of me said. You deserve it, whatever it is. Another part of me wanted me to go ahead and kill myself.

But I didn't have the strength to do it at that first moment. And that was my unforgivable mistake. For what I didn't count on was his involving other people.

He had found me through this terrible blackmail scheme which involved Sylvia Thissle, a realtor. It's a long story that I won't bore you with, but eventually he involved those I loved: Jayvee Paris, Valentina and Isabel Martinez. Isabel, who is six, reminds me so of you. When I first saw her, I thought that I had been given another chance. Pomodoro smelled my love for her, and that was where he struck the hardest. He threatened to harm her if I didn't do as he said.

So I did, for a while, but then I couldn't go on. And, in a moment of pure selfishness, I reached out to you. I endangered you, whom I'd wanted to protect all these years, in order to try to save Isabel. In a moment of insanity I thought that you could help me figure this out. You could save us all.

And, even if you couldn't, I wanted to see you one more time. And you came, sweetheart, didn't you? Without a moment's hesitation, you got on a plane and came to your momma. Those few moments we had together were both heaven and hell for me. When I saw you and heard your voice, the desolation of my life was overwhelming. The unspeakable waste. The loss. And I also realized how foolish I had been in asking you to come here. I have put you in the direct line of Pomodoro's fire.

All I pray now is that you can somehow find it in your heart to forgive me. For everything. Even for the weakness that prevents me from telling you all this in person or even delivering this letter myself. I am so ashamed.

Now I am going to do what I should have done years ago. I am going to say good-bye to you and to this world. Know that I love you. I always have loved you, every moment of every day of every year since you first took breath. Good-bye, my dearest Sugar.

SAM SAT, STUNNED ALMOST INTO UNCONSCIOUSNESS, TEARS streaming down her face. She didn't see Isabel or Harpo. She didn't see Antonio Pomodoro. All she could see was Johanna's face before her. Her crazy wonderful momma. She could hear her laughter, falling like music from her mouth. Now Johanna's brilliant colors, her fierce determination, her life force, whirling insistently as a hummingbird's, all were gone.

Oh, Momma, she mourned. Momma, Momma. Whyfor such tragedy, thick with infidelity, bloodlust, rage, revenge—those ancient human frailties? Why you? Why me? Why us? Why didn't you call me decades ago? Or contact George? If only we'd known, we could have helped you. We could have put an end to all this. You didn't have to kill yourself.

Then Sam sobbed, she wailed, grief tearing from her lungs. Oh, God. Dear God. What senseless waste.

"Sam?" Isabel had snuggled up beside her on the rocky floor, Harpo in her lap. "I'm scared," the little girl whispered.

The cavern whirled back into focus. Pomodoro. Isabel. Harpo. "Oh, honey." Sam drew the small, warm body close. "We're going to be okay. Hold on."

"Shut up! Both of you," Pomodoro snapped. He paced back and forth before them, the Browning automatic in his hand.

Isabel's eyes were shiny with tears. Her little mouth trembled. Harpo looked from Isabel to Sam, from Sam to Isabel, his brow furrowed with worry.

"It's going to be all right, Isabel," Sam said, patting the little girl's dark hair, then the top of Harpo's head. And with that, a fierceness rose up in her breast. Antonio Pomodoro would not prevail. She would protect these small creatures with her last breath.

Pomodoro screamed, "I said, Shut up!"

Sam scanned the cavern, desperate for opportunity. She weighed the relative possibilities for violence within the small red stools, the shards of the green-and-white pitcher. Then she lit on the heavy flashlight Jayvee had loaned her. It lay far to the right behind her, way out of reach. She'd have to distract Pomodoro, somehow, to make a grab for it. "Johanna's gone now," she said softly. "It's over, Antonio. You've had your revenge."

"Shut up!" he screamed once more, spittle flecking his lips. His eyes rolled wildly, and he opened his mouth and began to chant: "Not only the sins of the fathers, but the sins of the mothers are also passed. They move like dark corpuscles through the blood. Like the very wind through the air. They flow like fierce running rivers. They are inescapable. They are visited upon the daughters' bowed heads. The sins of the mothers permeate the flesh and the bone and the sinew of the daughters, and they are guilty, guilty, guilty."

Crazy, crazy, crazy, Sam thought. How had she managed to land here, her back to the wall in a mine with a madman? Sweet Jesus. She scooted a few inches toward escape, toward the flashlight.

"You are responsible," Pomodoro said. "Responsible for your sins. Dust to dust. Womb to womb. Blood to blood. Mother and daughter are the one, the same; you are responsible."

Another inch.

"I see you," Pomodoro crooned.

Sam froze.

"I see your face. Your eyes. They burn with the same fire as your bitch of a mother's. You are worthy of the vendetta. You are worthy of the blood oath."

The ravings of a madman. Two inches closer.

Pomodoro licked his lips. Then, still holding the Browning in his right hand, he dropped his left to his belt buckle.

No. Sam willed him to stop. Not that. She would not allow him to touch her.

Or Isabel.

Her stomach twisted darkly at that last thought. He'd have to kill her first. She would fight him until the last flutter of her heart.

Meanwhile, very slowly, a millimeter at a time, Pomodoro loosened the tongue of his belt. He stared fiercely into Sam's eyes, as if he were trying to mesmerize her. Then he grinned. It was an obscene gesture.

"You don't want to do this, Antonio," she said.

The grin widened, showing white teeth and wet shiny gums. "How do you know what I want to do?"

What to say next? She grabbed wildly at the catalog of words in her brain. Try anything, a voice whispered. "I'm close to you. I can read your mind," she said.

"Really? What am I thinking now?"

"You're thinking that if you do this, the vendetta will continue. Jayvee Paris will come after you and the ones you love."

Pomodoro hesitated, but only a fraction of a moment, before he purred, "And if I don't love anyone?"

"You love your father."

"My father is dead. Your mother made sure of that."

"There's vendetta in hell, Antonio. You don't want your father to suffer for your sins."

"My father is in heaven!"

Our father, who art in heaven. Please help me. Please get me out of here. Sam—the irreligious, the nonbeliever, the heathen—found herself praying. He was right, whoever it was that said there were no atheists in foxholes.

Pomodoro's fingers kept working at his belt.

Can he attack me and hold that gun at the same time? Sam wondered. If he gets close enough, maybe I can knock the gun from his hand.

"You didn't have to come here," he said suddenly. "I tried to stop you."

"Where? Tell me." Keep him talking, yes. She slid closer to the flashlight.

"At Johanna's house."

Ah, yes. Jayvee had not been the sole intruder.

"I came twice," he said slyly, running his tongue across his bottom lip. "The first time I followed in Paris's footsteps. That was when I found the scrapbooks."

"Why did you take them?"

He hissed the answer. "I wanted you."

All the air rushed from Sam's lungs. She could feel Isabel's little fingernails digging into her arm. The little girl was terrified. But Sam had to ask the next question. She couldn't stop herself. "And the second time? What happened the second time you came to the house?"

He smiled. "What do you think?"

"I don't know, Antonio. I haven't a clue. You've been far too clever for me."

His lip curled. "Don't patronize me."

"I'm not. Truly. I never suspected you for a moment. I thought you were my friend."

"Never?"

"Never."

"You liked me, didn't you?"

"Yes, I did."

"Did you want me?" He slipped the tongue of his belt free, then pulled it away from the buckle's retaining pin.

Dear God, she prayed, help me. I don't know what to say. Do I agree with him or not? Which answer is going to push him over the edge?

No, advised a voice in her mind. Say no.

"No," Sam echoed. "I *liked* you, though. I admired you. I believed every word you said. I thought you must have been a great friend to Johanna."

Pomodoro's eyes glittered. "I set the house afire. I came back, that night. I watched you smoking in the living room. Then I waited until you'd gone off to bed and jimmied the back door. I sat in your chair, still warm from your body. I lit one of your cigarettes. I wedged it down beside the cushion."

"Why?"

"Why? I wanted to kill you. I wanted you to fry. I killed your mother, but not the way I wanted. . . ."

He'd killed Johanna.

". . . she slipped away from me. I watched her with the pills and booze, but it wasn't enough."

Isabel whimpered. Sam looked down at the child's big fearful eyes.

"Is Auntie Johanna dead?"

"*Shhhh. Shhhh.* Never mind." Sam smoothed the little girl's hair over her ears as if that could stopper them.

"But when you didn't die in the fire, I knew what I wanted you to do." With that Pomodoro pulled Vendicatóre's double-edged blade from the sheath. Then, with a swift move, he tossed the stubby knife at Sam's feet. "Kill the dog," he said. "Slit his throat."

"No!" Isabel screamed. She was growing hysterical. "No, no, please!"

Sam's blood slowed and ebbed. I'm with you, Isabel. Absolutely not. I'll kill this man with my bare teeth before I'll hurt Harpo. She shook her head, *no,* but as she did, she picked up the blade. Now she was armed. Yes, and what good would it do her, this stub of a knife, if she couldn't get close enough to Pomodoro to use it? He would shoot her long before she was within striking distance.

"Slit his throat!" Pomodoro thundered.

"No! No! No, please, no!" Isabel screamed again.

Pomodoro pulled the trigger. The sound of the blast was deafening, and the bullet pinged and ricocheted around the cavern. A chunk of cream-colored rock splintered and fell to the floor. Isabel screamed once more. Harpo—who hated loud noises, who hid in the tub at the first rumble of thunder—took off running toward the tunnel. Pomodoro pivoted and fired at the dog.

Sam seized the moment of opportunity and lunged. She threw her body at his knees. The knife flew from her grasp. Pomodoro fell beneath her, the two of them tumbling and rolling.

She caught a glimpse of Harpo disappearing into the darkness of the mine shaft. Gone. Safe.

Sam and Pomodoro struggled together, arm in arm like lovers. He was taller and heavier and stronger, but she had the advantage of his using only using one hand as he held on to the gun. She kicked, she climbed, she scrabbled, she jammed her elbow into his throat. Then, with a burst of fury, she made her way atop him. She straddled him and latched onto his shoulders. She grabbed handfuls of his hair and jerked back with all her might.

Pomodoro roared. He was a beast beneath her, a bronco between her legs, a rodeo bull, his privates leashed to make him buck. Pomodoro flailed savagely at her with his free hand. The other still tightly gripped the gun.

He fired again.

"No!" Sam screamed and braced herself for Isabel's cry. But, dear God, it didn't come. He'd missed again. Sam couldn't see the child. She had sunk her teeth now into the side of Pomodoro's neck.

He'd killed her mother. He would kill Isabel.

He fired once more, and again the blast echoed over and over, called and repeated and sang its awful song.

Then, from somewhere way down the tunnel, a woman sang back. "Hold it! Hold it right there!"

Sam went limp. Thank you, God. Thank you for answering my prayers. Anything I can do for you. Just name it. I'm your girl.

Then Pomodoro began rocking hard beneath her, and she was about to lose him. She wasn't heavy enough to hold on. *Help, give me some help here, whoever you are.* She clawed at Pomodoro's scalp, breaking two nails, three, four, down to the nub. Then she laced her fingers through his hair, lifted his head, and smashed it on the rock floor. She pounded his skull with all her force. His nose broke and his scream was a hard, bright sound.

Now the voice heard before commanded again, "Hold it!" Then, like an angel, she appeared in the mouth of the tunnel. An older Hispanic woman Sam had never seen before was pointing a pistol at Pomodoro.

"Shoot him!" Sam yelled.

But Pomodoro bucked again. He twisted, he turned, he was a constantly moving target. Magdalena Vigil couldn't get a clear shot at him. She might shoot Sam. The bullet could ricochet and hit Isabel.

"Shoot! Shoot!" Then Sam rolled and threw all her weight at Pomodoro's right shoulder. His hand smashed against the rock floor. She pounced on his wrist. He slammed his body into hers from behind, shoving her forward. But she'd outmaneuvered him. He'd lost his grip.

The gun skidded away from both of them.

Then, having finally found her way, Deborah Wonder emerged from the mine shaft. She dove for the sliding gun. Pomodoro shook Sam off and dove too, knocking Deborah sideways. Now Magdalena had a clear target. She fired, but Pomodoro rolled. The bullet smacked into the rock, unpeeling a rich vein of blue-green ore.

"I've got it!" Isabel piped. "I've got the gun!" She held it up high for Sam to see.

Pomodoro lunged for Isabel. Just as his hand grazed her shirt, Magdalena fired again.

And again Pomodoro dodged the bullet.

This fucker is *not* invincible, Sam said to herself, as she wound up, reared back, and slammed the side of her foot into his knee. She heard a crack, and he collapsed, howling. Sam grabbed the gun from Isabel's hands. She gripped it in both of hers, squared her stance, and took careful aim. She intended to kill Pomodoro, to kill him dead, not pretend-dead, not fake-dead, but positively dead, deader than twice-dead Johanna, her poor momma, had ever been. She didn't want him rising. No stone-rolling for this son of a bitch.

But before Sam could fire, Magdalena squeezed off another round. She shot Antonio Pomodoro straight through his black heart, and he was gone, long gone, headed south, even before he landed.

Much much later that evening, Sam and Harry sat on Lo's patio holding hands. The yellow lantern of a moon was bright enough to read by.

"I've never seen such a moon," Harry said.

"Oh, yeah, it's real bright here in New Mexico." Sam's voice was rocky. *She* was rocky. Out of gas. She was looking forward to a weeklong nap.

"I really feel sorry for Deborah. Poor woman. To find Earl—and then lose him like that." He squeezed Sam's hand.

"Earl. I never even got to meet him. What did Lavert say?"

"He'll be on the first flight in the morning. The family's still trying to decide whether to bury him here or take him home to the swamps."

"I'd say here. This is the place he chose."

"That the same way you're thinking about your momma?"

"Scattering her ashes here, you mean?" Sam was silent for a long moment. "Probably. Maybe in the Santa Fe River. Or off a ridgetop."

"You could buy one of Jesus's cars. Bury her in that."

"No, Harry. Jesus's cars are art."

"You're absolutely right. You know what I was thinking, when he came by earlier, I saw that pickup of his? My friend Mignon Abernathy—she bought that old Cadillac showroom out on St. Charles—is turning it into a gallery? Jesus's cars as her first show? Is that a natural, or what?"

"Sounds good to me."

"And I talked with George. He'll call again later. Said he can't wait to see you."

"Us. See us."

At that, Harry pulled her closer. "It's all going to be okay, you know. It really is."

Sam leaned her head on his shoulder and nodded. Yes, eventually, somewhere down the road, she'd come to terms with the events of the past few days. There were so many questions that would never be answered. But, nonetheless, someday, she'd finish her grieving for her momma and for their lost years. She'd make some kind of sense of Johanna's sad choices, of the price Johanna had paid for love. For it was love, she realized now, that was at the heart of Johanna's story.

Sam turned Harry's hand over in hers and traced a finger down his long, uninterrupted life line. Then his heart line, straight and strong and true and brave. Brave enough for the both of them. She lifted his palm to her lips and kissed it softly. "It *will* be all right," she said. "I'm glad you're here."

"Where else would I be?"

Then Sam and Harry rocked and talked about the past and rocked and talked about their future, while above them the huge moon rose golden in the star-flung sky.